ABANDON

BOOKS BY MEG CABOT

Abandon

Airhead
Being Nikki
Runaway

Allie Finkle's Rules for Girls series

The Princess Diaries series
The Mediator series
Vanished series
Avalon High series

All-American Girl
Ready or Not
Teen Idol
How to Be Popular
Pants on Fire
Jinx
Nicola and the Viscount
Victoria and the Rogue

Insatiable
Heather Wells series
Queen of Babble series
The Boy Book series

Meg Cabot

Abandon

Point

Library of Congress Cataloging-in-Publication Data

Cabot, Meg.
Abandon / by Meg Cabot. — 1st ed.
p. cm.
Summary: A near-death experience, a horrible incident at school, and a move from Connecticut to Florida have turned seventeen-year-old Pierce's life upside-down, but when she needs him most John Hayden is always there, helping but reminding her of her visit to the Underworld.
ISBN 978-0-545-28410-3 (alk. paper) — ISBN 978-0-545-04064-8 (alk. paper)
[1. Supernatural — Fiction. 2. High schools — Fiction. 3. Schools — Fiction. 4. Family life — Florida — Fiction. 5. Persephone (Greek deity) — Fiction. 6. Hades (Greek deity) — Fiction. 7. Mythology, Greek — Fiction. 8. Near-death experiences — Fiction. 9. Florida — Fiction.]
I. Title.
PZ7.C11165Ab 2011
[Fic] — dc22
2010047447

12 11 10 9 8 7 6 5 4 3 2 1   11 12 13 14 15/0

Printed in the U.S.A.   23
First edition, May 2011

The display type was set in Yolanda Duchess.
The text type was set in Adobe Garamond Pro.
Book design by Elizabeth B. Parisi and Kristina Iulo

ABANDON

Through every city shall he hunt her down,
Until he shall have driven her back to Hell,
There from whence envy first did let her loose.
DANTE ALIGHIERI, *Inferno*, Canto I

Anything can happen in the blink of an eye. Anything at all.
One.

Two.

Three.

Blink.

A girl is laughing with her friends.

Suddenly, a crater splits apart the earth. Through it bursts a man in an ink black chariot forged in the deepest pits of hell, drawn by stallions with hooves of steel and eyes of flame.

Before anyone can shout a warning, before the girl can turn and run, those thundering hooves are upon her.

The girl isn't laughing anymore. Instead, she's screaming.

It's too late. The man has leaned out of his ink black chariot to seize her by the waist and pull her back down into that crater with him.

Life as she once knew it will never be the same.

You don't have to worry about that girl, though. She's just a character from a book. Her name was Persephone, and her being kidnapped by Hades, the god of the dead, and taken to live with him in the Underworld was how the Greeks explained the changing of the seasons. It's what's known as an origin myth.

What happened to me? That's no myth.

A few days ago, if you'd told me some story about a girl who had to go live with a guy in his underground palace for six months out of the year, I'd just have laughed. You think that girl has problems? I'll tell you who has problems: me. Way bigger ones than Persephone.

Especially now, after what happened the other night in the cemetery. What *really* happened, I mean.

The police think they know, of course. So does everyone at school. Everyone on the whole island, it seems, has a theory.

That's the difference between them and me. They all have theories.

I *know*.

So who cares what happened to Persephone? Compared to what happened to me, that's nothing.

Persephone was lucky, actually. Because her mom showed up to bail her out.

No one's coming to rescue me.

So take my advice: whatever you do?

Don't blink.

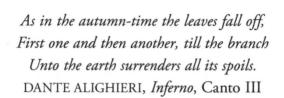

As in the autumn-time the leaves fall off,
First one and then another, till the branch
Unto the earth surrenders all its spoils.
DANTE ALIGHIERI, *Inferno*, Canto III

Once, I died.

No one is really sure how long I was gone. I was flatline for over an hour.

But I was also hypothermic. Which is why — once they warmed me up — the defibrillators, along with a massive dose of epinephrine, brought me back.

That's what the doctors say, anyway. I have a different opinion about why I'm still among the living.

But it's one I've learned not to share with people.

Did you see a light?

That's the first thing everyone wants to know when they find out I died and came back. It's the first thing my seventeen-year-old cousin Alex asked me tonight at Mom's party.

"Did you see a light?"

No sooner were the words out of Alex's mouth than his dad, my uncle Chris, slapped him on the back of the head.

"Ow," Alex said, reaching up to rub his scalp. "What's wrong with asking if she saw a light?"

"It's rude," Uncle Chris said tersely. "You don't ask people who died that."

I took a drink from the soda I was holding. Mom hadn't asked if I wanted a huge *Welcome to Isla Huesos, Pierce* party. But what was I going to say? She was so excited about it. She'd apparently invited everyone she knew back in the old days, including her entire family, none of whom had ever moved — except Mom and her younger brother, Chris — from the two-mile-by-four-mile island off the coast of South Florida on which they'd been born.

Except that Uncle Chris hadn't exactly left Isla Huesos to go to college, get married, and have a kid, the way Mom had.

"But the accident was almost two years ago," Alex said. "She can't still be sensitive about it." He looked at me. "Pierce," he said, his voice sarcastic, "are you still sensitive about the fact that you died and then came back to life *nearly two years ago*?"

I tried to smile. "I'm fine with it," I lied.

"Told you," Alex said to his dad. To me, he said, "So did you or did you not see a light?"

I took a deep breath and quoted something I'd read on the Internet. "Virtually all NDEs will tell you that when they died, they saw something, often some kind of light."

"What's an NDE?" Uncle Chris asked, scratching his head beneath his Isla Huesos Bait and Tackle baseball cap.

"Someone who's had a near-death experience," I explained. I wished I could scratch beneath the white sundress Mom had bought me to wear for the evening. It was too tight in the chest. But I didn't think that would be polite, even if Uncle Chris and Alex were family.

"Oh," Uncle Chris said. "NDE. I get it."

NDEs, I'd read, could suffer from profound personality changes and difficulties readjusting to life after . . . well, death. Pentecostal preachers who'd come back from the dead had ended up joining biker clubs. Leather-clad bikers had gotten up and gone straight to the nearest church to be born again.

I thought I'd done pretty well for myself, all things considered.

Although when I'd glanced through the files my old school had sent over after it was suggested that my parents find an "alternative educational solution" for me — which was their polite way of saying I'd been expelled after "the incident" last spring — I saw that the Westport Academy for Girls may not necessarily have agreed:

Pierce has a tendency to disengage. Sometimes she just drifts off. And when she does choose to pay attention, she tends to hyperfocus, but not generally on the point of the lesson. Wechsler and TOVA testing suggested.

But that particular report had been written during the semester directly following the accident — more than a year before "the incident" — when I'd had a few more important things to worry about than homework. Those jerks even kicked me out of the school play — *Snow White* — in which I'd been cast as the lead.

How had my drama teacher put it? Oh, yeah: I seemed to be identifying a little too much with poor, undead Snow White.

I don't see how I could have helped it at the time, really. Because in addition to having *died*, I'd also been born as rich as a princess, thanks to Dad — he's CEO of one of the world's largest providers of products and services to the oil, gas, and military industries (everyone's heard of his company. It's been in the news a lot, especially lately) — and I also happened to have been born looking like one, thanks to Mom. I inherited her delicate bone structure, thick dark hair, and wide dark eyes. . . .

I also, unfortunately, inherited Mom's princess-tender heart. It's what ended up killing me.

"So was it at the end of a tunnel?" Alex wanted to know. "The light? That's what you always hear people say."

"Your cousin didn't go into the light," his father said, looking worried beneath his baseball cap. "If she had, she wouldn't be here. Quit pestering her."

"It's okay," I said, smiling at Uncle Chris. "I don't mind answering his questions." I did, actually. But hanging around in the backyard with Uncle Chris and Alex was better than being inside with a bunch of people I didn't know. Turning to Alex, I said, "Some people do say they saw a light at the end of a tunnel. None of them knows exactly what it was, but they all have theories."

"Like what?" Alex asked.

Thunder rumbled off in the distance. It wasn't loud. The people inside the house probably couldn't hear it, what with all the laughter and the splashing of the waterfall over in the pool and the music Mom had playing on the indoor/outdoor stereo speakers, not so cleverly designed to look like rocks.

But I heard it. It had followed a burst of lightning . . . not heat lightning, either, even though it was as hot at eight o'clock at night in early September in South Florida as it ever got back in Connecticut in July at high noon. There was a storm out to sea, and it was heading in our direction.

"I don't know," I said. I thought of some more things I'd read. "Some of them think the light is the pathway to a different spiritual dimension, one accessible only to the dead."

Alex grinned. "Cool," he said. "The Pearly Gates."

"Could be," I said, shrugging. "But scientists say the light is actually a hallucination produced by the brain's neurotransmitters firing all at once as they die."

Uncle Chris's eyes looked sad.

"I like Alex's explanation better," he said. "About the Pearly Gates."

I hadn't meant to make Uncle Chris feel bad.

"No one really knows for sure what happens to us when we die," I said quickly.

"Except you," he pointed out.

I felt more uncomfortable than ever in my too-tight white dress. Because what I saw when I died wasn't a light.

It wasn't anything close.

I didn't like lying to Uncle Chris. I knew I shouldn't have been talking about any of this. Especially since Mom had wanted everything to be so perfect tonight . . . not just tonight, but from now on. I really didn't want to disappoint her. She'd gone all out, buying the million-dollar house and flying in the famous friend from New York to decorate it. She enlisted the aid of an environmentally conscious landscaper who planted the backyard with native growth, like ylang-ylang trees and night-blooming jasmine, so the air always smelled a little bit like a magazine ad for one of those celebrity perfumes.

She'd even bought me a "beach cruiser" bicycle complete with a basket and bell — because I still didn't have my driver's license — painted my bedroom a soothing lavender, and enrolled me in the same high school she'd gone to, twenty years earlier.

"You're going to love it here, Pierce," she kept saying. "You'll see. We're going to make a new start. Everything's going to be great. I just know it."

I had good reason to believe everything *wasn't* going to be great.

But I kept it to myself. Mom was just so happy. For the party, she even hired professional caterers to cook and serve the shrimp cocktail, conch fritters, and chicken skewers. She'd released a flotilla of citronella candles in the pool to keep away the mosquitoes, then turned on the waterfall and thrown open every French door in the house.

"There's such a nice breeze," she kept saying, choosing to ignore the giant black storm clouds filling the night sky. . . .

Kind of like the way she was choosing to ignore the fact that she'd moved back to Isla Huesos to further her research on her beloved roseate spoonbills — which look like pink flamingos, except that their beaks are pancaked like spoons — right after the worst environmental disaster in American history had killed off most of them.

Oh, and that her bright, animal-loving daughter had died and come back not quite . . . normal. And because of that, her marriage to Dad had gone down the tubes. Their divorce proceedings started while I was still in the hospital, in fact, when Mom kicked Dad out of the house for "letting me" drown. Dad went to go live in the penthouse apartment he keeps near his company's office building in Manhattan, never imagining that, a year and a half later, he'd still be calling it home.

"It's much better to forgive and forget, Pierce," Dad says every time we speak. "Then you can move on. Your mother needs to learn that."

But really, the term "forgive and forget" doesn't make sense to me. Forgiving does allow us to stop dwelling on an issue, which isn't always healthy (just look at my parents).

But if we forget, we don't learn from our mistakes.

And that can be deadly. Who knows this better than me?

So forgive? Sure, Dad.

But forget?

Even if I wanted to, I can't.

Because there's someone who won't let me.

I don't blame Mom for wanting to come back to the island where she was born and raised, even if it *is* ungodly hot, often battered by hurricanes, and may or may not have clouds of mystery chemicals billowing around it, in the same way I picture the evil that tumbled from the box poor Pandora opened and then let loose on humanity.

But if anyone had mentioned to me before I moved here that the name of the place meant Island of Bones in English — and *why* the Spanish explorers who'd found it had named it that — I probably would never have agreed to go along with Mom's "we're going to make a new start in Isla Huesos" plan.

Especially since it's hard to make a new start in a place where you met the very person who keeps popping up to ruin your life over and over again.

Only I could hardly mention *that* to my mother, either. The fact that I'd ever even been to Isla Huesos once before was supposed to be this big secret (not a *bad* secret. Just a secret between us girls, Mom always said).

That's because Dad can't stand Mom's family, which he feels (not without some justification) is filled with convicts and kooks, not exactly proper role models for his only child. Mom had made me promise never to tell him about the day trip we took to her father's funeral when I was seven.

So I'd promised. What did I know? I'd never told . . .

. . . especially the part about what happened *after* the funeral, in the cemetery. The truth was, I never really thought I *had* to tell anyone, since Grandma knew all about it.

And grandmas never let anything bad happen. Not to their only granddaughters.

So I didn't even know anyone at Mom's party except Mom and Alex and Grandma, all of whom had sat in the same row with me at Grandpa's funeral. That had been a decade earlier, back when Mom's brother was still in jail.

Uncle Chris wasn't adjusting very well to life on the "outside." He didn't seem to know quite what to do, for instance, whenever one of the caterers walked over to refill his champagne flute.

Instead of just saying, "No, thank you," Uncle Chris would cry, "Mountain Dew!" and jerk his glass out of the way, so the champagne would pour all over the pool patio instead.

"I don't drink," Uncle Chris would say sheepishly. "I'm sticking to Mountain Dew."

"I'm so sorry, sir," the caterer would reply, looking with dismay at the growing puddle of Veuve Clicquot at our feet.

I decided I liked Uncle Chris, even if Dad had warned me that he would embark on a dark reign of terror and revenge immediately upon his release from prison.

But all I'd ever seen him do since I'd gotten to Isla Huesos — where he now lived with Grandma, who'd been raising Alex in his absence because Alex's mom had run off when he was just a baby, after Uncle Chris was sent away to prison — was sit on the couch and obsessively watch the Weather Channel, sipping Mountain Dew.

But Alex's dad did kind of scare me in one way: He had the saddest eyes of anyone I had ever seen.

Except maybe one other person.

But I was trying hard not to think about *him*. Just like I tried never to think about when I died.

Some people, however, were making both those things extremely difficult.

"Not everyone who dies and comes back," I said carefully to Uncle Chris, "has the exact same experience —"

It was right as I was saying this that Grandma came teetering down the steps of the back porch on her little high heels. Unlike Uncle Chris and Alex, she'd made an effort to dress up, and had on a filmy beige dress and one of her own hand-knitted silk scarves.

"There you are, Pierce," she said, in a voice that made it sound like she was annoyed. "What are you doing out here? All these people are waiting inside to meet you. Come on, I want you to say hello to Father Michaels —"

"Oh, hey," Alex said, brightening. "I wonder if he knows."

"Knows what?" Grandma asked, looking bewildered.

"What the light was that Pierce saw when she died," Alex said. "I think it was the Pearly Gates. But Pierce says scientists say it's . . . what do they say it is again, Pierce?"

I swallowed. "A hallucination," I said. "Scientists say they've gotten the same results in test subjects who weren't dying, by using drugs and electrodes to their brains. Some of them saw a light, too."

"*That's* what you're standing out here doing?" Grandma asked, looking shocked. "Committing blasphemy?"

After I died and came back, my grades took a downward plunge. That's when my guidance counselor at the Westport Academy for Girls, Mrs. Keeler, recommended that my parents find something outside of academics in which to get me interested. Children who fail to do well in school can often still be successful in life, Mrs. Keeler assured my parents, if they discover something else in which to "engage."

Eventually, I did find an interest outside of academics in which to "engage." One that ended up getting me kicked out of the Westport Academy for Girls and landed me here on Isla Huesos, which some people call paradise.

I'm pretty sure the people who call Isla Huesos paradise never met my grandma.

"No," Alex said with a laugh. "Blasphemy would be saying the light is coming from between the legs of their new mom as they're being born into their next life. Of course, if you were Hindu, that wouldn't be blasphemy at all."

Grandma looked like she'd just bitten into a lemon.

"Well, Alexander Cabrero," she said sharply. "You are not Hindu. And you may also want to remember that I'm the one making the payments on that junk heap you call a car. If you'd like me to keep on doing so, you might want to think about being a little more respectful."

"Sorry, ma'am," Alex murmured, looking down at the champagne puddle on the ground while, beside him, his father did the same, after quickly removing his baseball cap.

Grandma glanced over at me, seeming to force her expression into something a little softer.

"Now, Pierce," she said. "Why don't you come inside and say hello to Father Michaels? You won't remember him, of course, from Grandpa's funeral, because you were too young, but he remembers you and is so happy you'll be joining our little parish."

"You know what?" I said. "I'm not feeling so good." I wasn't making it up either. The heat was starting to feel oppressive. I wished I could undo a few of the buttons in the front of my too-tight dress. "I think I need some air."

"Then come inside," Grandma said, looking bewildered again. "Where it's air-conditioned. Or it would be if your mother hadn't opened all the doors —"

"What did I do now, Mother?" Mom appeared on the back porch and snagged a cocktail shrimp from the tray of a passing caterer. "Oh, Pierce, there you are. I was wondering where you'd disappeared to." Then she saw my face and said, "Honey, are you all right?"

"She says she needs some fresh air," Grandma said, still looking bewildered. "But she's standing outside. What's wrong with her? Did she take her medication today? Are you *sure* Pierce is ready to go back to school, Deb? You know how she is. Maybe she —"

"She's fine, Mother," Mom interrupted. To me, she said, "Pierce —"

I lifted my head. Mom's eyes seemed darker than usual in the porch light. She looked pretty and fresh in her white jeans and loose, silky top. She looked perfect. Everything was perfect. Everything was going to be great.

"I've got to go," I said, trying to keep down the panicky sob I felt rising in my throat.

"Go, then, honey," Mom said, leaning down from the porch to press on my forehead with her hand as if she were feeling for a fever. She smelled like she always did, of her perfume and something Mom-like. Her long dark hair swept my bare shoulder as she kissed me. "It's fine. Just don't forget to turn on your bicycle lights so people can see you."

"What?" Grandma sounded incredulous. "You're just letting her go on a bike ride? But it's the middle of the party. *Her* party."

Mom ignored her.

"Don't make any stops," she said to me. "Stay on your bike."

I turned around without saying another word to Alex and Uncle Chris, who were both staring at me in astonishment, and headed straight for the side yard where my new bike was parked. I didn't look back.

"And, Pierce?" Mom called after me.

My shoulders tensed. What if what Grandma had said made her change her mind?

But all she added was "Don't be too long. A storm is coming."

When I beheld him in the desert vast,
"Have pity on me," unto him I cried,
"Whiche'er you are, or shade or real man!"
DANTE ALIGHIERI, *Inferno*, Canto I

Everyone wants to believe that there's something else — something great — waiting for them on the other side. Paradise. Valhalla. Heaven. Their next — hopefully less horrible — life.

It's just that I've *been* to the other side. So I know what's there. And it's not paradise. At least, not right away.

It's a truth I've had to bear alone, because nothing good has happened to the few people with whom I've shared it.

So sometimes I just have to get out before I say — or do — something I'll regret. Otherwise, something bad will happen.

He will happen.

Mom understood. Not about him, of course — she didn't know about him — but about my needing to get out. That's why she let me go.

Tearing down the hill from our new house, the breeze in my hair instantly cooling me off, all I could think about was Grandma.

"Man? What man?"

That's what Grandma said the other day at her house when I got up off the couch, where I'd been sitting watching the Weather Channel with Uncle Chris, and followed her into the kitchen to ask her about Grandpa's funeral . . . more specifically, what had happened in the cemetery afterwards.

"You know," I said. "The man I told you about. The one with the bird."

We'd never had a chance to speak about it again. Not since the day it happened. Not only was that day supposed to be a secret — just between us girls, Mom and me — Grandma and I had never been in the same room together again, thanks to Dad.

As the years went by, what actually happened that afternoon in the cemetery began to seem more and more like a dream. Maybe it really *had* been just a dream. How could any of it have actually happened? It was impossible.

Then I died.

And I realized that what I'd seen that day in the cemetery not only hadn't been a dream, it had been the singularly most important thing that had ever happened to me in my life. Well, up until my heart stopped.

"Go outside and play for a little while," Grandma had said. "Your mom's busy right now. I'll come get you when we're done."

She and Mom had been in the cemetery sexton's office after the funeral, signing the last of the paperwork for Grandpa's tomb.

Maybe I had been a little fidgety. I think I'd knocked something over on the sexton's desk. I wouldn't be surprised. Like my cousin Alex, who'd also been there, I'd always had a problem paying attention.

Unlike Alex, my problem resulted in being less, not more, heavily supervised. Because I was a girl, and what kind of trouble could a girl get into?

I remember Mom looking up from whatever forms she was helping Grandma to fill out. She'd smiled at me through her tears.

"It's okay, sweetie," she'd said. "Go on outside. Just stay close. It'll be all right."

I had stayed close. Back then, I always listened to my mother.

I found the dove just a dozen yards or so from the cemetery sexton's office. It was limping along the path between the tombs, one wing dragging along behind it, obviously broken. I immediately raced after it, trying to scoop it up, since I knew if I brought it back to my mom, she'd be able to help. She loved birds.

But I just ended up making things worse. The bird panicked and half flew, half leaped into the side of a nearby crypt, crashing against the bricks.

Then it just lay there. As I hurried to its side, I realized with horror that it was dead.

Naturally, I began to weep. I'd already felt pretty sad, considering the fact that I'd just been at the funeral of a grandparent I'd never met, then been kicked out of the cemetery sexton's office for my misbehavior. Now this?

That's when the man had come along the path. To me, a first grader, he'd seemed impossibly tall, almost a giant, even after he knelt down beside me and asked why I was crying.

Looking back, I realize he was only in his teens, hardly a man at all. But as tall as he was, and given that he was dressed all in black, he'd seemed much older to me than his actual years.

"I was t-trying to help," I'd said, nearly incoherent with sobs, as I pointed to the bird. "She was hurt. But then I scared her and made it worse. Now she's dead. It was an ac-ac-accident."

"Of course it was," he said, reaching down to scoop up the limp, fragile body in one hand.

"I don't want to go to hell," I wailed.

"Who said you were going to hell?" he asked, looking bemused.

"That's where murderers go," I informed him tearfully. "My grandma told me."

"Well, you aren't a murderer," he assured me. "And I think you've a bit of time before you have to start worrying about where you're going after you die."

I wasn't supposed to speak to strangers. My parents had drilled this into my head.

But this stranger seemed nice enough. And my mother was only just down the path, inside the office. I was sure I was safe.

"Should we find a coffin for her?" I asked, pointing at the bird. I was bursting with knowledge I'd just learned at the funeral that afternoon. "When we die, we're supposed to get put inside a coffin, and then no one sees us ever again."

"Some of us," the stranger had replied a bit drily. "Not all of us. And yes, I suppose we could put her in a coffin. Or I could make her come alive again. Which would you prefer?"

"You can't make her come alive again," I'd said, so startled by the question, my tears were forgotten. He'd been petting the bird, which was very definitely dead. Its head drooped over the top of his fingers, its neck broken. "No one can do that."

"I can," he said. "If you'd like."

"Yes, please," I'd whispered, and he passed his hand over the bird. A second later, its head popped up, and with a bright-eyed flutter, it took off from his hands, its wings beating strongly as it flew off into the bright blue sky.

I was so thrilled, I'd cried, "Do it again!"

"I can't," he said, climbing to his feet. "She's gone."

I thought about this, then reached out to take his hand and began tugging. "Can you do it to my grandpa? They just put him over there —" I pointed towards a crypt on the far side of the cemetery.

He'd said, not unkindly, "No. I'm sorry."

"But it would make my mom so happy. Grandma, too. *Please?* It'll only take a second —"

"No," he said again, beginning to look alarmed. He knelt down beside me once more. "What's your name?"

"Pierce," I said. "But —"

"Well, Pierce," he said. His eyes, I'd noticed, were the same color as the blades on my ice skates back in Connecticut. "Your grandfather would be proud of you. But it's best just to leave him where he is. It might frighten your mother and grandmother a bit to see him up and walking around after he's already been buried, don't you think?"

I hadn't considered this, but he was probably right.

That's when Grandma came looking for me. The man saw her. He had to have seen her, and she him, since they exchanged polite "good afternoons" before the man turned and, after saying good-bye to me, walked away.

"Pierce," Grandma said when she reached me. "Do you know who that was?"

"No," I said. But I proceeded to tell her everything else about him, and the miraculous thing he'd done.

"And did you like him?" Grandma asked, when I'd come to the end of my breathless narration.

"I don't know," I replied, bewildered by the question. He'd made a dead bird come back to life! But he'd refused to do the same for Grandpa. So it was a problem.

Grandma had smiled for the first time all day.

"You will," she said.

Then she'd taken hold of my hand and walked me back to the car, where Mom and Alex were waiting.

I remembered looking back. There was no sign of the man, just scarlet blossoms from the twisting black branches of a poinciana tree that hung like a canopy above our heads, bursting red as firecrackers against the bright blue sky. . . .

But now, like everyone I'd told about what I'd seen when I died — not a light but a man — Grandma insisted I'd imagined the entire thing.

"Of course there wasn't a man in the cemetery, bringing birds back from the dead," she'd said the other day in her kitchen, shaking her head. "Whoever heard of such a thing? You know, Pierce, I worry about you. Always daydreaming . . . and ever since your accident, I hear you've gotten worse. And don't think you're going to get by on just your looks, either. Your mother has looks *and* brains, and see what happened to her? Pretty is all well and good until Mr. Moneybags decides he's going to let your child drown —"

"Grandma," I said, trying to keep my voice even. "How can you say the man wasn't there when you yourself asked me if I —"

"I really hope this new school works out for you, Pierce," Grandma interrupted. "Because you certainly managed to burn some bridges at your last one, didn't you?" She thrust a tray of sandwiches into my arms. "Now take that in to your uncle before he starves to death. He hasn't had a speck to eat since breakfast."

I had left her house then and there — after delivering the sandwiches, of course — and set off on my bike for home. I felt like I had to before something awful happened. Awful things always seemed to happen when I got mad. Things that weren't my fault. It was better for me to leave before they got worse.

Before *he* showed up.

Now, here I was on my bike again, only this time I was pedaling with no particular destination in mind. I just needed to get away . . . from Grandma. From questions. From the sound of all that party chatter. From the splashing of the waterfall into that pool . . . especially from that pool . . .

Unlike "the incident" last spring at my old school, the accident was my fault. I tripped — on my own scarf — and hit my head, then fell into the deep end of our pool back in Connecticut.

I'd been trying to rescue an injured bird . . . yes, another one.

That bird survived, and without the help of the stranger from the Isla Huesos Cemetery.

I was not so lucky.

The temperature of the water when I hit it was as paralyzing as the blow I'd received to the back of my head. It quickly soaked through my winter coat and boots, making my arms and legs too heavy to lift even to dog-paddle, let alone swim. The heavy canvas pool cover that Dad had forgotten to get fixed collapsed instantly beneath my weight and tangled around me, as constricting as the embrace of a python.

I was too far from the safety ladder or the steps to swim to them, weighted as I was with my clothing and all that canvas pulling me downward. If I had managed to reach the steps, I doubt I'd have had the strength to pull myself up.

I tried my best, though. It's amazing what a fifteen-year-old, even one with a subdural hematoma, can do when she's desperate to stay alive.

Dad had been on a conference call in his study at the time, way at the far end of the house. He'd forgotten that Mom was at the library, working on finishing her dissertation on the mating habits of roseate spoonbills, and that I wasn't over at my best friend Hannah's or the animal shelter, where I volunteered, and that it was the housekeeper's day off.

Just like he'd forgotten to mention to anyone that a couple of the metal rivets that were supposed to hold the pool cover in place had rusted through over the course of the winter.

Not that it would have made much of a difference — at least to me — if Dad had remembered any of these things, or even if he'd been off the phone. I never got a chance to scream for help. Drowning doesn't happen in real life the way it does in the movies. By the time it entered my contused skull that I was in any kind of trouble, the weight from all the water I'd reflexively swallowed from the shock of the cold — it was February in New England — had already caused my body to sink to the bottom of the pool like a stone.

After the initial panic and pain, it was actually quite peaceful down there. All I could hear was my own heartbeat and the sound of the bubbles coming from my throat . . . and both of these were growing fainter, and further apart.

I didn't know at the time that this was because I was dying.

The afternoon sunlight — streaming through the leaves that had blown across the top of the water — made beautiful patterns on the floor of the pool around me. It reminded me of the way the sun had streamed through the stained-glass windows in the church where they'd held my grandfather's funeral. Even though I wasn't supposed to talk about it, I'd never forgotten that day, or how hard my mom and grandmother had sobbed throughout the service. . . .

Nor had I forgotten how tightly Grandma had held my hand as she led me away from the cemetery afterwards, and how red those blossoms from the branches of the poinciana trees had looked against the sky above our heads . . .

. . . red as the tassels on the ends of my scarf floating up and around my face as I lay dying at the bottom of our pool.

Maybe that's why when I saw them again after I rode away from the party — not the tassels, of course, but the poinciana blossoms — I jammed on my bicycle's brakes.

I hadn't realized I'd ridden as far as the cemetery. My feet had taken me there unconsciously.

I knew why, of course. It wasn't the first time it had happened.

I'd ridden through the cemetery more than once since arriving on Isla Huesos — Mom had even included it on the little "orientation" tour she gave me on my arrival. Because all the coffins were in aboveground crypts and vaults, the graveyard had become one of the island's top sightseeing destinations. It turns out if you bury bodies in a place regularly flooded by hurricanes, all the skeletons will pop up out of the ground. Then you'll find your loved ones' remains dangling from trees and fences, or even down at the beach, like something out of a horror movie.

"That's why," Mom had informed me, "Spanish explorers who discovered this island five hundred years ago christened it Isla Huesos — Island of Bones. When they got here, it was covered with human bones, probably from a storm that had washed up an Indian burial ground."

But though I'd ridden through the cemetery several times since my arrival on Isla Huesos, I'd never been able to find the tree I'd seen that day when I was seven. Not until the night of the party.

Which was what made me do it.

"Don't make any stops," Mom had said. "Stay on your bike," she'd said. "A storm is coming."

And now that I was standing in front of the poinciana tree, I could see that the storm coming our way wasn't just the one Mom had referred to.

It was something much, much worse.

Most of the flowers from the tree had fallen to the ground. Dried and withered, they lay around my feet like a red carpet, whispering to one another as the wind picked them up and scattered them farther down the paved path.

The crypt beneath the tree didn't look much different from the way it had the day of my grandfather's funeral. The plaster was still falling off in places, revealing bricks that were as red as the blossoms beneath my feet.

The main difference was that now I could see a name carved in block lettering above the entrance to the vault, a scrolled wrought-iron gate.

No date. Just a name.

HAYDEN.

I hadn't noticed the name when I was seven. I'd had too many other things on my mind. The same way I'd ridden through this cemetery so many times during the past week and never recognized the tree until tonight.

"He wasn't real, Pierce."

It hadn't just been Grandma the other day in her kitchen who'd said it, either, but all those psychiatrists my poor parents dragged me to after my accident, unable to believe the reports they kept receiving from my teachers that their precious daughter wasn't performing at an above-average or even average level.

It's very common for patients who've lost electrical activity in their heart or brain for any interval of time to report having seen some sort of hallucination during the period they were flatline.

But it was vital for my mental health, all those doctors told me, to remember that it had been *only a dream*.

Yes, it had been very realistic. But couldn't I see how there'd been some things I'd read about in books at school, or seen on TV, or maybe seen years earlier — though I never told any of them about what had happened at Grandpa's funeral — in the vision I had during my near-death experience?

This was important to keep in mind, too, as was the fact that while it was happening, I'd been able to control my own actions. This was what was known as lucid dreaming. Had what happened to me been real, I would not have been able to escape my captor.

So I had absolutely nothing to worry about! He wasn't coming back for me. Because he was a figment of my imagination.

I'd sat across from those psychiatrists, and I'd nodded. They were right. Of course they were.

But inside, I'd felt so . . .

. . . *sorry* for them.

Because the walls behind those doctors' desks were filled with so many framed diplomas and degrees — some of them from the very same Ivy League schools my parents now despaired of my ever being able to get into.

And that was what made me saddest of all. Because my parents couldn't see that it didn't matter. All those diplomas, all those degrees.

And those doctors still didn't have the slightest idea what they were talking about.

Because I had proof. I always had. As I stood in front of the crypt beneath the poinciana tree, I undid the first couple buttons of the too-tight dress Mom had suggested I wear to the party, and pressed my fingers against it. I could have pulled it out at any time in any one of those offices and shown it to them and said, "Lucid dreaming? Really? What about this, then, Doctor?"

But I never did. I just kept it where I always did, tucked inside my top.

Because — despite the fact that they didn't believe me — all those doctors had tried so hard to help me. They seemed so nice.

I didn't want anything bad to happen to them.

And I had found out the hard way that bad things happened to people who took too much interest in my necklace.

So after that, I never showed it to anyone. Not even Grandma when she'd said that thing in her kitchen. Not that it would have made a bit of difference to her.

It wasn't until I was standing there in front of the crypt where we'd met that I suddenly realized maybe *I* was the one who was making the bad things happen.

Because I'd come back. Not only come back from the dead, but come back to the place where it had all started.

What was I even doing there? Was I as crazy as everyone back in Connecticut kept saying I was? I was *in a cemetery by myself after dark*. I needed to get out of there. I needed to run. Every hair on my body was standing up, telling me to run.

But of course by then it was too late. Because someone was coming, crushing the dried-up flower petals on the path beneath his feet as he got closer.

Bones. That's what it sounded like as those flowers got trampled. The breaking of tiny bones.

Oh, God. Why had Mom told me that story? Why couldn't I have a normal mother who told normal stories about fairy godmothers and glass slippers, instead of stories about human skeletal remains scattered across beaches?

I didn't even have to turn around to see who it was. I knew. Of course I knew.

The scream I let out when I actually spun around and saw his face was still loud enough to wake the dead.

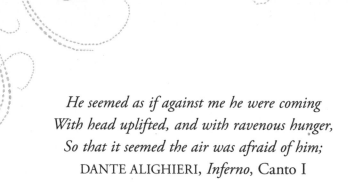

He seemed as if against me he were coming
With head uplifted, and with ravenous hunger,
So that it seemed the air was afraid of him;
DANTE ALIGHIERI, *Inferno*, Canto I

He looked as shocked as I felt. "What are you doing here?"

His voice sounded like the thunder I could hear growing closer every time lightning flashed above the tops of the palm trees, where the towering gray storm clouds were crashing into each other.

I tried to say something, but all that came out was air.

Well, that shouldn't have been too surprising, even if a part of me had known from the moment I'd heard Mom say the words *Isla Huesos* that this moment was coming. I guess I'd even been hoping to get it over with, in a weird way. Why else had my head kept telling my feet to pedal towards the cemetery?

Not my head. My heart. That four-inch cardiac needle they plunged into my chest? It may have gotten my heart started again.

But that doesn't mean it's not still broken.

I tried again, after clearing my throat. I hoped he couldn't see how badly my knees were trembling beneath the skirt of my dress.

"I . . . I'm sorry," I said. "About the screaming. You startled me. I wasn't . . . I didn't . . . My mom and I just moved here." This last part came out in an incoherent rush. "To Isla Huesos. She wants to make a new start here, because of . . . well, you know."

My voice trailed off. I didn't like talking about what had happened back in my old school in Westport.

And what was the point in telling him? He'd been there.

He just stared at me. I was pretty sure from his expression that he wasn't happy to see me. Of course, I'd just screamed in his face. That kind of thing doesn't tend to endear you to people. Especially guys, I'd imagine.

"It's not my fault," I added. My heart was pounding so hard in my chest, I could barely hear the wind anymore, stirring the palm fronds overhead, or the crickets and cicadas between the crypts that rose from the shadows around us. "She wants to save the birds. What was I supposed to say?"

My voice sounded completely unlike my own. Well, no wonder. What girl would be able to speak normally with someone who looked like him glaring down at her? He was so tall — six foot four or five, nearly a foot taller than me — and his biceps and shoulders so wide, he'd easily have made tight end on any college football team in the country. . . . I'd suffered through enough games during "quality time" with my dad to be able to pick out the body type.

Except there wasn't a coach alive who'd actually take him, due to his fairly obvious attitude problem. The black jeans, skintight black T-shirt, black tactical boots, and knuckles crisscrossed with scars — not just his knuckles, either — were dead giveaways he wasn't going to play nicely with anyone. Even his hair, falling carelessly in thick, long brown waves around his face and his neck, seemed to scream *dark*.

Except his eyes. As gray as the clouds overhead, they'd always burned with a bright intensity I'd found difficult to forget . . . and believe me, I'd tried.

Not anymore, though. Now they looked dull, blank as twin bullet holes. You could almost say they were . . . well, dead eyes.

I wondered what had happened to him to cause the change. *I* certainly wasn't to blame. I wasn't that kind of girl.

His voice wasn't dead. It was filled with sarcasm.

"I meant," he said, "what are you doing *here*, now, tonight? In the cemetery. After hours."

I swallowed hard.

Of course. Of course he knew what I was doing on Isla Huesos. He always seemed to know where I was and exactly what I was doing. He'd probably seen my plane touch down. He'd probably watched as I dragged my bags off the luggage carousel, and Mom helped me wheel them to the car. I wondered if he'd been watching when we'd had to struggle so hard to lift them into the back of her hybrid SUV because they were so heavy. Nice of him to come over and offer us some help.

I could practically feel the anger coming off his body in waves.

I knew I'd hurt him once (in my defense, he'd hurt me first. False imprisonment *is* a felony. I'd looked it up).

But given that he'd shown up *twice* since then to save my life — or at least I suppose that's what he thought he was doing — I'd assumed he'd forgiven me.

Yet his eyes weren't showing the slightest flicker of warmth, let alone remorse, for what he'd tried to do to me. So I guess I'd been wrong.

"Look," I said, my voice a little gruff with some anger of my own. He had no right to be so rude. Sure, he'd surprised me, so I'd screamed.

But he'd known this whole time I'd been on the island and he'd never once stopped by to say hello? Not that I wanted him to, since every time he showed up, someone seemed to get hurt. But still.

"I was just in the neighborhood, so I thought I'd come by to make sure everything between us was, you know." I realized I'd really dug myself into a hole with this one. Why hadn't I listened to Mom and just stayed on my bike? "That there were no hard feelings."

He continued to stare at me. "No hard feelings," he echoed.

"Right," I said. This was going even more horribly than I could have imagined. And clearly, I had a reputation for being able to imagine quite a bit. "I'm over what you did to me. And I just wanted to make sure that you understood that what I did to you . . . what happened when I . . . *you know*. Left. That it wasn't personal."

"Oh, I understand," he said. His tone was as cool as his gaze. "You were extremely impersonal about it. You made your decision. Then you acted on it." He shrugged and folded his arms. "Without any regard to the consequences."

Stung at his pointed reminder of my behavior that day — *You were extremely impersonal about it. You made your decision. Then you acted on it* — I felt tears well up.

Oh, God. Now I was going to *cry* in front of him? Mom wanted everything to be perfect? Well, *this* was perfect.

"I was *fifteen*," I said, trying not very effectively to get a grip on myself. I had rehearsed this conversation so many times in my head, I should have had it down cold by now. The problem, of course, was that conversations with him in real life never went the way they did in my head. "Who's ready for that kind of commitment at *fifteen*?"

"Seventeen's better for you?" he asked pointedly.

Horrified, I cried, "What? *No!*"

"Well," he said, "for someone who keeps claiming she's not ready to die, you have an interesting way of showing it."

I stared straight into those dead eyes. "What does *that* mean?"

"Only that most people who place any kind of value on their lives don't go wandering around in cemeteries after dark. But then again, it is *you* we're talking about."

Isla Huesos Cemetery's nineteen acres were completely without security cameras or guards. The cemetery sexton went home promptly at six o'clock, as he'd testily informed me one night after kicking me out (and scolding me for using "a place of public veneration as a thoroughfare") while locking the cemetery gate.

So if he *did* decide to take me back with him to his world — which I was fairly certain he had the power to do — unless there was some drunk who was sleeping it off behind a tomb somewhere who'd heard me scream and gone to call 911, no one was going to come to my rescue.

Good evening. Tonight marks the ten-year anniversary of the mysterious disappearance of seventeen-year-old Pierce Oliviera, who vanished without a trace from the tiny Floridian island of Isla Huesos while taking a seemingly innocent bike ride one hot September night. . . .

"Are you *threatening* me?" I demanded, putting my hands on my hips, trying to appear braver than I actually felt. Because what I felt was utter terror.

I didn't realize he'd been moving closer as he spoke — I'd forgotten he possessed the ability to step as lightly as a cat when he chose to. This time, the dried-out poinciana blossoms hadn't made a sound beneath those steel-toed boots — until he was standing six inches away from me.

The closer he came, the harder my heart began to hammer. Not just because of what I was afraid he might be planning on doing to me, but because I was noticing all those little things about him that were so aggravatingly attractive. Up close, his eyes were as light as mine were dark . . . only mine, I knew, were a *warm* brown, with spots of amber and honey in them — as he himself had once informed me, in a tenderer moment between us.

35

Which isn't exactly a compliment if you think about it, since both amber and honey are sticky, gooey substances that bugs get trapped in.

His eyes were filled with the exact opposite — flecks of steel, one of the hardest metals on earth.

A fact that was hard not to notice, with his face just inches from mine.

"Threatening you?" he echoed, looking down. "With what? What could I possibly do to you? You're not dead. At least, not anymore."

I sucked in my breath, willing my pulse not to pound too loudly, since suddenly it was obvious what was about to happen:

He was going to kiss me . . .

. . . or maybe, I realized, my heart giving a disappointed little flop, not.

I'd mistaken the focus of his attention. It wasn't my lips he'd been staring at, but something farther south . . . the place where my dress had gapped open, thanks to my having undone the buttons in the front. I'd have liked to think he was attracted to my feminine form — and I had reason to believe that he was.

But tonight it was what lay inside that gap, dangling from that gold chain I hadn't removed since the day I died, that had him so interested.

It was supposed to offer its wearer protection from evil. Or at least that's what he'd said when he gave it to me.

But it certainly hadn't done me any good tonight — or any other time, as far as I could tell.

It wasn't until I was standing there in front of him in the cemetery, feeling his soft breath on my cheek, that I realized I'd never even asked if it was all right for me to take it back with me into this world. It hadn't been stealing, exactly, since he'd given it to me.

But I'm pretty sure it had been a gift that came with conditions, and one of the conditions had been that I stay in his world, and . . .

Well, that hadn't happened.

Without any regard to the consequences, he'd said.

My stomach clenched as I quickly folded my arms to hide both the stone and everything else going on beneath the front of my dress.

"You still have it," he breathed.

His voice didn't sound like thunder anymore. It sounded exactly the way it had the day we first met, when he'd been so kind and reassuring.

"Of course I still have it," I said, confused by his surprise.

What did he think, that the minute I'd gotten away from him, I'd thrown it under a steamroller or something?

Then I bit my lip. I suppose he was justified in thinking I might not have wanted to hang on to any reminders of the day I died . . . or of him. I probably *was* a bit of a fool not to have dropped it in the ocean, old-lady-from-*Titanic* style. Any other girl would have. Actually, most girls probably would have sold it, considering how much I'd been told it was worth.

What did it mean that I'd done neither?

Nothing. Certainly not that I had any special feelings for him. I really *would* have to be crazy for that to be true, considering what he'd done to me. Oh, please don't let him think that's why I kept it.

But then, why did the thought of giving it back make me feel . . . well, a little queasy? All I should have been feeling was relief.

Reluctantly, I reached up to pull on the chain. The round, multifaceted diamond — now as gray as the clouds overhead, and about the size of a large grape — fell out from its safe cocoon, managing to find a way to gleam even on a night as stormy as this one. The clouds had yet to overtake the moon.

When he saw what I was doing, it was like seeing someone throw back the storm shutters on a house that had been closed up for hurricane season. All the careful guardedness drained from his expression. Even the life returned to those formerly dead eyes.

He was right to be surprised that I still had it: Who goes around wearing a reminder of the day she *died*? I probably needed to go back to all of those psychiatrists and tell them the whole truth this time.

But what good would it do? It might help *me*. But it certainly wouldn't help them.

"Um," I said hesitantly. *Do it,* my mother's voice warned me inside my head. Except even my mom didn't know where the necklace had come from. Telling her would only make her think I was as crazy as everyone else did. "Do you . . . want it back?"

It nearly killed me to ask it. But the time had come, I told myself. New start.

All this time I'd been hiding it beneath my shirts, I'd been try-ing to protect others.

But if I were truthful with myself, I'd been trying to protect *it*, too. Because I loved it to a ridiculous degree, and had from the moment I'd first laid eyes on it, when he'd given it to me.

But I also didn't want any *consequences*. Not for me. Not for him. Not for anyone.

I pulled the chain over my head, not caring when it tangled in my long hair. I was trying to do this as adroitly and sensitively as possible. Because at the Westport Academy for Girls — which, true, I'd been kicked out of, but so what? — they teach nothing if not adroitness and sensitivity when dealing with others or with diffi-cult issues. That's why my dad had insisted on my going there from kindergarten on up. He'd heard about the school from some of his clients and hoped it would keep me from ending up like him.

So far, things weren't looking promising.

Do it.

I thrust the necklace towards him, knot of hair and all.

"It's all right," I said, silently cursing myself for still hav-ing a shake in my voice. And my fingers. Could he see this, as well as the tears in my eyes, in the moonlight? "You can have it back. I know I should never have taken it. I'm sorry for any . . . consequences this might have caused. But it all happened so fast. Well, you know that. Anyway," I added, with an attempt at some humor to lighten the situation, "at least now you won't have to follow me around anymore."

If I'd been looking for *precisely* the wrong thing to do and say, I'd found it. In an instant, the shutters that had swung open when he saw I still had the necklace came slamming back down over his face and his eyes.

Snatching the pendant out of my hand, he demanded, "*Following* you? Is that what you call it?"

I blinked back at him, stunned by his reaction. So much for adroitness and sensitivity. Also humor.

"I gave you this" — he shook the necklace in my face, his deep voice lashing out at me like the rain I could smell already beating the mangroves offshore — "because, as I thought I made clear, it affords its wearer protection from evil . . . something which, I might add, you seem to need more than most, since every time I see you, you're in some kind of mortal peril or another. But since you obviously don't want me — or it — in your life, here's a thought. Stop coming here. And *don't wear it.*"

On the words *don't wear it*, he turned and threw it — *my beautiful necklace* — as hard as he could. It went sailing through the night sky to land somewhere in the vast darkness of Isla Huesos Cemetery's nineteen acres.

It shouldn't have been like watching him throw my heart away.

But it was.

He governs everywhere, and there he reigns;
There is his city and his lofty throne;
O happy he whom thereto he elects!
DANTE ALIGHIERI, *Inferno*, Canto I

The next time I saw him after that day in the cemetery with Grandma, I was dead.

Of course I said the first thing everyone says when they open their eyes after hitting their head, sucking in a gallon of pool water, and then going flatline.

"Where am I?"

Because I wasn't at the bottom of our pool anymore . . . though I was still wearing the clothes I'd had on when I fell into it. They were damp now, and clung to me like a chilly second skin. I wasn't on a hospital gurney or in an ambulance, either.

Instead, I was in a vast, subterranean cavern that seemed to go on forever, along the shore of a windy lake.

I wasn't alone, though.

"Name?"

A towering man in black, having heard my *Where am I?*, turned towards me, raising the glowing tablet he held in his palm.

I was too dazed to do anything but reply, "Pierce Oliviera."

"You're over there," he said, after inputting my name.

I looked in the direction he was pointing. We were standing, I realized, in a crowd of what looked like thousands of other people — mostly senior citizens, but some my own age, or even younger — all of whom seemed as miserable as I was.

They just weren't necessarily soaked to the skin or dazed from a violent blow to the head.

But they were, like me, being ordered into two lines by huge men dressed all in black. The men looked the way the older girls from school who took the train into New York City to sneak into nightclubs described the bouncers who carded them — muscular, bald, black-leather-clad, and tattooed all over. In other words, super scary.

Unlike my best friend, Hannah, I'd never had the courage to try to sneak, underage, into a club in the city. I didn't have a fake ID. I could barely remember where I put my real one.

So I didn't dare disobey the orders of the man in front of me. The lines snaked towards the lake, into which two docks jutted. One line was extremely long. The other was a bit shorter. He was pointing towards the shorter one.

"Stay in your own line," he growled. It was an order.

I hurried wordlessly to the end of the shorter line, too frightened to utter another sound.

It was only when I found myself standing behind a tiny, sweet-looking old lady that I tapped her on the shoulder and asked, "Excuse me, ma'am?"

She turned around. She had the wrinkliest face I'd ever seen. She had to have been a hundred if she were a day. "Yes, dear? Oh, look at you. You're all wet!"

"I'm all right," I lied. I was shivering so badly, my teeth were chattering a little. "I was wondering. Do you know where we are?"

"Oh, yes, dear," she said with a huge smile. "We're getting on the boat."

I didn't even know how to respond to that. Was this a dream? But if it was, how was I able to wring the water from my scarf and actually feel the drops as they squeezed through my fingers?

"Where is the boat going?" I asked.

"Oh, I don't know," the old lady said, with another sweet smile. "No one will tell us anything. But I do think it must be somewhere wonderful. Because look how badly everyone over there seems to want to get into this line over here."

She pointed at the longer line, a few dozen yards from ours.

It was true. The people in that line, apparently having heard the same thing the old lady had, were almost rioting in an attempt to escape their line and get into ours. Some of the bald, tattooed men in the black leather coats were having to hold them back, like bodyguards at a rock concert trying to contain unruly fans.

"Hey," the guy in line behind me said. He was older than me, but younger than the old lady. Maybe in his twenties. "Can you get any service?" He was holding up his cell phone. "I can't get any service."

I patted my coat pockets. They were empty. Of course I didn't have my phone. This was usually how my nightmares went.

"I'm sorry," I said. "I don't —"

That's when I saw him. The tall man dressed all in black — black boots, black leather gloves, black leather coat — cantering towards the riot on a huge black horse.

I recognized him at once, even though it had been so many years. A rush of relief surged through me. Finally, a familiar face.

Maybe that's why I didn't hesitate — not even when I saw that everyone else had scattered, giving him a wide berth — to duck out of the line and head towards him.

"Oh, dear, I wouldn't if I were you," the old lady called after me.

"It's all right," I said over my shoulder. "I know him!"

"Crazy," I heard the guy behind me mutter (I had no idea at the time how often I'd be hearing this later). "She must be trying to get herself killed."

They hadn't put it together. Neither had I.

Not then.

Not everyone is comfortable around horses, I told myself as I ran towards him across the sand. That's why they, unlike me, were so afraid.

And this wasn't a horse like my best friend Hannah's, Double Dare, whose comfortable placidity — he was starting to balk at even the smallest jumps — might have been one reason Hannah now preferred spending time on the school basketball team, hanging out at the mall in hopes of catching sight of some of her older brother's friends, or even going to nightclubs instead of the stables. Double Dare's name was starting to become a bit of a joke. There was nothing daring about him anymore, really.

This horse, on the other hand, seemed to be daring you just to look at him, let alone to come close.

Which was probably why my doing so spooked him.

All I said was "Hey" in an attempt to get his rider's attention . . . just as he was shouting at everyone in the other line to stay where they were — an order they seemed cowed by the harshness of his tone into obeying.

I had no idea such a brutal tone could come from the sweet man I remembered — the one who'd made a bird come back alive — from my grandfather's funeral. I stood there paralyzed with fright . . .

. . . until the next thing I knew, charcoal black hooves were slashing the air just inches from my head as the horse reared, snorting in outrage.

Then I ducked, afraid for my life, throwing my hands over my face to protect my eyes. A second later, those enormous hooves came exploding down again, spraying bits of sand everywhere, and I was diving for safety.

That's when a noise like the loudest thunderclap I'd ever heard filled the cavern. I wasn't sure if it was a real thunderclap or the sound of the horse's body as it crashed onto the beach, one of its back legs having slipped in the sand beneath it.

A male voice shouted something. When I looked up from where I'd crouched in an effort not to be killed, I realized the shout had come from the rider. He'd cried out the horse's name — Alastor, as near as I could tell — and was kicking his boots from the stirrups as the horse scrambled back to its feet.

It was only then that I realized — with a physical shock that jolted me nearly as much as the horse's violent reaction had — that this was no nightmare. If it had been, I'd have woken by now. I wouldn't be tasting sand in my mouth.

And the man I'd met the day of my grandfather's funeral wouldn't have suddenly been standing over me, staring down at me with silver eyes that held not the slightest hint of recognition . . . or humanity.

It was then that I noticed there was something — other than that awful voice — different about him. No, it wasn't that *he* was different. . . .

I was.

I wasn't seven anymore.

But he was exactly the same as he'd been that day in the cemetery. The dark hair. The flashing eyes. The towering height — only he didn't seem quite as much of a giant as he had then.

How was any of it even possible, when so many years had gone by since the last time I'd seen him?

"Are you all right?" he demanded in a voice that was somehow worse — louder and more authoritative — than the thunder that had torn through the cavern seconds earlier.

"I — I guess," I said, resisting the urge to jump up and run. My heart in my throat, I reached up to take his hand, allowing him to pull me to my feet. His skin felt tantalizingly warm and dry, considering my own was the exact opposite. "Are *you* all right?"

He threw me an incredulous look, the glowing-eyed gaze seeming to rake me.

"Am *I* all right?" he asked. "You could have been trampled. And you're asking if *I'm* all right?"

"Did he roll onto you?" I asked, nervously eyeing his horse, pawing the ground a few yards away, his bridle being held — barely — by one of the guards. The horse had to be at least part Clydesdale. And the rest devil.

His owner did not appear to be the least bit interested in discussing any injuries he might have sustained during the accident I'd caused.

"I'm fine," he snapped. "But you need to learn to follow instructions. Do the words 'stay in your own line' mean nothing to you?" He released my hand to wrap his own around my upper arm instead.

And the next thing I knew, he was dragging me back towards the line. Not the one I'd come from.

The other one.

I tried to say something. I did. But I think the shock of it all was finally beginning to take its toll. All I could do was stare. His eyes were the exact same color as the throwing stars a military client from Japan had given my father. When Dad first opened the box in front of me, the color of the blades had stirred a faint memory.

It wasn't until now I realized what that memory was.

Him.

"Don't ever touch these," Dad had warned. Like I'd even wanted to . . . until he said that.

Then I'd had the strangest compulsion to pull one out from the special drawer in which Dad kept them, and throw it at the trunk of an old tree in our backyard. Dad had to use a pair of pliers to get it out, it was embedded so deeply. After that, he kept the blades locked in his office safe — except when he took them out to try throwing them at the tree himself, to see if he could make them stick the way I had. Which, to his consternation, he could not.

Now, for the first time, I felt as if I knew where that compulsion to touch Dad's throwing stars, despite his warning me not to, had come from.

"Don't bother looking up at me like that," my captor warned me. "It won't work. I've been doing this for a long time. I know all the tricks. And batting those big brown eyes at me won't do a thing, I guarantee."

I blinked. Was he speaking to me? Obviously. I was the only person he was dragging around.

Tricks? What was he talking about?

I'm still not sure how I managed to formulate words, let alone a complete sentence, under that menacing gaze.

But I suppose when you're completely soaked, desperate, terrified, and alone, you realize you've got absolutely nothing else to lose.

"I d-don't know what you're talking about," I stammered. I couldn't keep my voice any steadier than I could my shaking fingers. "I d-don't know any tricks. I didn't mean to upset your horse. And I'm sorry if you got hurt. But I needed to speak to you —"

"It's too late," he said woodenly, looking straight ahead. "And I've heard all the excuses I can take today. Once my decision is made, it's final. I don't make exceptions . . . not even for girls who look like you."

"I understand," I said, even though I had no idea what he was talking about. What decision? And girls who looked like me? I imagined I looked totally pathetic, in my soaking-wet clothes. My hair was probably hanging in rat's tails. Was that what he meant? "But that's not what I wanted to —"

The other line — the rowdy one — was growing closer. I didn't like the look of it one bit. There weren't any sweet old ladies in that line. No one there was trying to get their cell phone to work.

Instead, people were throwing punches and pulling hair, trying to break past the guards to get into the other line.

Things got even worse when, a second later, a horn sounded. A ferry — as big as the one my parents and I had taken to Martha's Vineyard one summer, huge enough to fit hundreds of people and their cars — was chugging through the water towards the dock closest to the line in which I used to be standing.

A ripple of anticipation spread across the cavern. The din grew almost unbearable. Someone from the rowdy line managed to break free, then darted directly across our path, causing me to lose my already unsteady balance. My captor had to throw a protective arm around me to keep me from falling.

"I'll take her place," the man from the line was yelling, "if she's coming over here!"

One of the guards caught him before he got very far and dragged him, screaming, back.

"But it's not fair," he shouted. "Why can't I take her spot?"

The stranger from the cemetery, having watched all this, looked down at me.

"Where did you come from?" he asked suspiciously.

"That's what I've been trying to tell you," I said, my eyes filling with tears. "Don't you remember me?"

He shook his head. But his grip on me had begun to loosen.

"It's *me*," I said. I hated the fact that every time we met, I was crying. Still, maybe it would help jog his memory. "From the cemetery on Isla Huesos, the day of my grandfather's funeral. You made a dead bird come back to life —"

His entire demeanor changed. The hardened glint disappeared from those gray eyes. Suddenly, they were as gentle as they'd seemed the first time I met him.

"That was *you*?" Even his voice had changed. It sounded almost human.

"Yes," I said, smiling despite my tears. I could see I'd gotten through to him at last. Maybe — just maybe — everything was going to be all right after all. "That was me."

"Pierce," he said. I could practically see the memory flooding back. "Your name was . . . Pierce."

I nodded, the tears coming so fast I had to reach up and wipe them away. "Pierce Oliviera."

My name on his lips sounded so nice in that horrible place. The fact anything at all seemed familiar when around me, everything was so awful, was more wonderful than I could describe. I had to restrain myself from throwing my arms around him. After all, I wasn't seven anymore.

And he was no longer the kindly uncle he'd once seemed, doing magic tricks with doves.

Which was why I was keeping my distance.

"I think there's been a mistake," I said when he let go of me to reach into his coat pocket and pull out one of the palm tablets all the guards had. He was looking up my name, I could tell. "That's why I'm so glad I found you. I really don't think I'm supposed to be here. No offense, but this place . . ." — the words tumbled out before I could stop them — "whatever it is, it's *horrible*. Do you run it or something?"

I had the feeling he did, but that didn't stop me from insulting his management skills to his face, a bad habit I'd picked up from my dad, who'd never had any compunction about sending back a steak or a bottle of wine he didn't like.

"Because it could really use some updating," I went on while he was still reading whatever it said on his tablet. "There aren't any signs or anything saying where we are or when the next boat is leaving, and I don't think all of us are going to fit on that one over there, and it's *really* cold in here, and no one can get any cell reception, and" — I took a step nearer to him so the guards wouldn't overhear what I said next, even though I was pretty sure, what with all the loud protesting going on behind us and the clanging of the anchor chain as the boat docked on the other side, I was safe — "those guys organizing the lines? They're very rude."

"I'm sorry," he said. He slipped the tablet back into his pocket, then shrugged off his coat and wrapped it around me, pulling it — and me — close by the collar. "Is this better?"

A little bit shocked that he'd so missed the point of what I was trying to tell him — but undeniably much warmer. His coat weighed a ton and was practically steaming from his body heat — I nodded. He hadn't let go of the collar.

It felt odd to be so near him. He definitely was no kindly uncle. He was, instead, very much a young man close to my own age.

And crackling with male sexuality.

I wondered if I should have just stayed in my line. Everyone in it was filing for the boat, which looked, now that I could see it up close, fairly comfortable.

"I didn't mean just me," I went on more slowly. "*Everyone* here is freaking out. They're wet and cold, too." I pointed towards the line of people who weren't being let onto the ferry that had just docked. "What's going on with them?"

He looked in the direction I'd pointed, then back down at me. He was still holding on to the collar of his coat, keeping it snug around my shoulders.

"You don't need to worry," he said. His expression had hardened again, however, and his eyes gone a stormy gray, as if this was a subject he didn't like discussing. "A boat's coming for them, too."

"Well, they still deserve to be treated better," I said, wincing as another man tried to make a break for the ferry line before a guard used force to subdue him. "It's not their fault —"

He stepped even closer towards me, effectively blocking my view of what was going on in front of the ferry. "Do you want to go someplace else?" he asked. "Someplace away from here? Someplace warm?"

"Oh," I said, feeling a rush of relief. He'd realized there'd been a mistake. He was going to fix it. I was going home. "Yes, *please.*"

And then I blinked. Because that's what human beings do, especially when they've been crying.

But when I opened my eyes again, I wasn't home. I wasn't standing on the shore of the lake anymore, either.

And what I'd been hoping was the end of the nightmare I'd been going through turned out to be just the beginning.

"Thee it behoves to take another road,"
Responded he, when he beheld me weeping,
"If from this savage place thou wouldst escape."
DANTE ALIGHIERI, *Inferno*, Canto I

Instead of home, or standing by the lake, I was in a long, elegantly appointed room.

The horse was gone. The guards were gone. The beach along the lake was gone. All of the people — the people who'd been waiting in the lines — were gone, too.

The wind was still there, though. It caused the long, gauzy white curtains, hanging from the elegant arches along one side of the room, to billow softly.

But the wind was the only thing I recognized. Everything else around me — the white-sheeted bed topped with a dark, heavy canopy on one end of the room; the pair of thronelike chairs at the long banquet table sitting before an enormous hearth at the other; the ornate antique tapestries, all depicting medieval-looking scenes, which hung here and there on the smooth, white marble walls; even the white divan on which I was sitting — I had never seen before in my life.

I was dreaming. I had to be.

Except that everything — the sound of water bubbling in the fountain in the courtyard outside the arches; the softness of the fur rug beneath my suddenly bare feet; the smell of the burning firewood in the hearth — felt so real. As real as everything had felt a split second before.

Most real of all was *him*, sitting beside me on the divan.

"Better now?" he asked.

His voice didn't sound like thunder anymore. Instead, it sounded lush, like the rug into which my feet sank the minute I sprang to them.

Which I did the minute he spoke.

What was going on? I lifted a trembling hand to shove some of my long — now dry — hair from my face, and caught a glimpse of something white. I looked down.

I was no longer wearing his coat, or my wet, chilly clothes. I was in some kind of gown. It wasn't a hospital gown, either. It was closely fitted on top, with a skirt that almost swept the floor. It bore a vague resemblance to what the maidens in the tapestries on the walls were wearing. It would not have looked out of place at the annual cotillion held for the upperclasswomen at the Westport Academy for Girls.

This part I had to be dreaming.

But then, why could I feel my heart pounding so hard in my chest?

He'd risen from the couch when I had. Now he stood looking

down at me with an expression on his face that I could only describe as concerned.

"Isn't this what you wanted?" he asked. "You're warm now, and dry. You did say you wanted to go away from there."

I stared up at him, openmouthed, completely unable to speak.

I was a tenth grader from Connecticut who had just blinked and ended up in some eighteen- or nineteen-year-old guy's bedroom.

Did he not see how this might be disturbing?

"You'll be quite safe here, you know," he assured me.

I used to think I was safe in my own backyard. And look how *that* had turned out.

"I don't understand," I said, when I finally managed to find my voice. Even then, it came out sounding more pathetic than ever. I needed to sit back down. I was pretty sure I was having some kind of stroke or something. "What's going on? Where are we? Who *are* you?"

I guess the fact that I was able to speak at all must have made him think I was fine, because he'd jetted off towards the table.

"John," he said, tossing the name casually over one of those impossibly wide shoulders. "I'm John. Didn't I tell you that last time? I thought I did."

John? His name was *John*?

Maybe I'd hit my head harder than I thought, and I had amnesia or something. Maybe I'd been at a costume party — that would explain the gown — and this guy was one of Hannah's brother's friends, and I'd just forgotten.

Only none of that explained what had happened in the cemetery with Grandma.

John. I'm John.

"How . . . how did you do that?" I asked him in a shaking voice. "One minute we were there, by the lake, and the next —"

"Oh." He shrugged. "A perk of the job, I suppose." He pulled out one of the thronelike chairs. "You must be tired. Won't you sit down? And I'm sure you must be hungry."

It wasn't until he said it that I realized I was. Just looking at the mounds of ripe peaches, crisp apples, and glistening grapes in those gleaming silver bowls — not to mention the cool clear water in those crystal goblets, so cold I could see the condensation dripping from the sides — well, it wasn't easy to stay where I was, especially feeling as wobbly on my feet as I did.

But my dad had warned me about situations like this. Maybe not *this* exactly. But not to accept food — or drinks — from strangers.

Especially young male strangers. Even ones I knew from before.

"Job?" I asked, staying where I was. My mind seemed barely able to grasp what was happening. Because far too much was happening, too quickly. "What job? I don't understand. You still haven't told me where, exactly, I am. And who were all those people?"

"Oh, out there?" Now those gray eyes, when he turned them towards me, weren't stormy looking or filled with steel flecks or anything other than . . . well, regret. That was the only word I could think of to describe it. "I'm sorry about all of that. What

I accused you of before — that was unforgivable of me. I've just never met a girl like you. At least, not in a long time."

"A girl like me?" I echoed. I remembered what he'd said as he dragged me towards the other line . . . the rough-looking one. "What does that mean?"

"Nothing," he said quickly. "I just meant I don't often meet girls of your . . . nature."

"What do you know about my nature?" I asked. My voice was still shaking. I was pretty sure I was becoming hysterical, even though I was no longer wet and it was much warmer in the room than it had been down by the lake. "You barely know me. I was *seven* when we last met. You didn't even recognize me down there until I told who I was, and even then you had to look me up on your little machine. What did it say about me on that —"

"I meant it as a compliment," he insisted, letting go of the chair in which he'd wanted me to sit. He moved towards me, both palms facing out, as if I were a pony he wanted to calm. "And you haven't actually changed as much as you might think. You still have the biggest eyes I've ever seen. They're warm, you know. Like honey."

His own eyes, I couldn't help noticing, were the exact same color as the bowls holding all the fruit.

"*You've* changed," I said. I didn't mean it as a compliment, and he seemed to know it. He had to know it, if only because for every step he took towards me, I took a defensive one back . . . at least until I found myself hitting the divan. Now I had nowhere else to go, and stood looking up at him, my heart fluttering in my throat. What had I gotten myself into? I should never have agreed to let him take me from the beach.

"Actually," he said, standing so close, I could feel the heat from his body. "I haven't changed at all. Neither have you. You're still asking for favors for others. The last time I met you, you wanted me to bring a bird back to life. Then your grandfather. And out there just now, you kept talking about everybody else. *They're* wet and *they're* cold. *They* deserve to be treated better. That's what you said. Was *I* all right? That's what you wanted to know when my horse nearly trampled you. Was *I* all right. Do you know how many times someone's asked me that question since I came here?"

I swallowed. His face was just inches from mine. The smell of wood smoke was very strong. I didn't know if it was coming from him or the fire in the hearth. Maybe both.

"I don't know," I said.

"Never," he said. "And I've been doing this for quite some time. Everyone else always says, '*I'm* wet. *I'm* cold.' No one's ever inquired after *my* health. Not you, though. You care. Not just about birds and horses but about people. And because of that," he said, leaning even more dangerously close, "I'm guessing a lot of people must care about you."

For a moment, I thought he was going to kiss me. I was almost sure he was going to. His mouth was that close to mine, and he'd reached one long, muscular arm out as if he were going to wrap it around me.

I'd heard about people falling in love at first sight. What he'd said about my perception of him having changed was true: He was very striking looking, with that dark hair falling into his face, and the contrast with those very light eyes. He wasn't handsome, necessarily, but he was someone who, if you saw him at the mall or someplace, you wouldn't be able to look away.

At least, I wouldn't be able to.

Except he didn't kiss me. Instead, he turned out to be reaching for something on a shelf just above my head. It was a small wooden box. After he'd pulled it down, he lifted one of my hands and said, "Come sit with me. Just for a moment."

My heart was still hammering from thinking he'd been about to kiss me. Not that I'd wanted him to kiss me. I didn't even want to sit down with him. I just didn't want to seem rude. Especially since he'd started pulling me back towards the table.

What could I do? It would be impolite to refuse to join him. He hadn't tried to do anything to hurt me except yell at me for causing his horse to slip and possibly injure itself, and then get out of the line I was supposed to be in. And he did run this place, whatever it was. I was a guest in it. I had to do what he said.

Still, I said as nicely as I could as I took the chair he'd offered, "Listen, this has been very nice, and I hope everything works out with the job, or, um, whatever it is that you do. Thank you very much for the invitation to" — What time was it, anyway? I had no idea. There were no clocks anywhere, and the light outside the gauzy white curtains was pinkish, just as it had been down by the lake. The entire cavern seemed to be cast in a pink glow. Was it lunchtime? Or dinnertime? I had no idea — "eat with you. I'd love to stay, but —" While I'd been speaking, he'd placed the box he plucked from the shelf down in front of me, then opened the lid.

And there it was.

My voice trailed off as I stared at it. I'm not really a jewelry sort of person.

But this was different.

"Do you like it?" he asked. He seemed almost . . . nervous, in a way. Which, considering what a self-assured — one might even say authoritative — person he was, was unusual. "You don't have to keep it if you feel uncomfortable about it or don't like it."

The stone landed with a soft thump against my sternum.

Because of course I'd nodded in response to his question as to whether or not I liked it. I'd been struck speechless with desire.

And then — naturally — he'd come up to the back of my chair to put the necklace around my neck.

I had never in my life seen anything as beautiful. The stone was the color of a thundercloud . . . smoky gray at the edges, then turning so dark blue in the middle, it was almost black. It was the complete opposite of the shiny white diamond solitaires and bright blue sapphires all the other girls in my school got from Tiffany on their birthdays.

Gray, I could just hear them all saying. Gray is so *Pierce*.

"It suits you," he said shortly, his voice as rough as thunder again. He cleared it. "I thought of it the minute I saw you just now, down there. Only I never thought . . . well, I never thought you'd turn out to be you, or want to come here with me."

I had no idea what he was talking about. Against the white bodice of my gown, the stone was the exact color of the Long Island Sound on a stormy day. It reminded me of the view I saw out my bedroom window back home.

"Do you know anything about colored diamonds?" he asked. I shook my head, still speechless with the beauty of his gift. He nodded and went on, "They come in just about every color you can imagine. Pink, yellow, red, green, black, gray . . . but they're very rare. Any tone of blue, like this one, is the most desirable of all. Men have killed for blue diamonds. Stones like this are buried so deeply in the earth's crust, you see, they're almost impossible to find. There've been only two or three discovered that were anywhere near as large as this one."

He reached from around the back of the chair to lift the heavy stone from where it dangled.

I still wasn't quite sure what had happened to me. But out of everything — hitting my head; struggling in the pool; waking to find myself in a strange world covered by a pink sky made of stone; running into some guy I'd met when I was seven who turned out not only to possess the power to make dead birds come back to life but also to magically transport girls from one place to another — *this* was what finally sent me over the edge: that he'd just casually reached over to invade my personal body space as if he had some kind of right to.

I'm pretty sure he didn't notice my suddenly blazing cheeks.

He went right on talking as if nothing were wrong. It was entirely possible, considering that the only company he was apparently used to keeping was horses, huge tattooed line bouncers, and seven-year-olds, he didn't *know* anything was wrong.

But that didn't make it all right with me.

"I've read that this diamond has special properties," he said. "It's supposed to protect its wearer from evil, possibly even help her detect it. Which is good because true evil often wears the most innocent of guises. Sometimes our closest friends can turn out not to have our best interests at heart. And we never have the remotest suspicion . . . not until it's too late." He was speaking with a bitterness that suggested he'd had personal experience in this area.

"I can't think," he went on, in a different tone entirely — now he sounded slightly amused — "of anyone who needs something like this more than you."

I still had no idea what he was talking about.

All I knew was that the stone, which I'd been watching him hold in those callused fingers as he spoke, had been doing something strange . . . turning from almost black in the middle to the palest of grays, the color of the downy fluff on a tabby kitten's chest.

This was going way too fast for me. I had never even been to a movie with a guy. For all of Hannah's efforts to get her brother's friends to notice her — and dragging me along with her during most of her attempts — none of them ever had.

And now I was in this incredibly sexy guy's room, and he'd given me this necklace, and I didn't even know where my clothes were.

I ducked out from beneath his arm and said, leaping from the chair, "Well, thank you very much, John. But I should probably be going, because I'm sure my mother must be looking for me. She's probably very worried. You know how mothers are. So, if you'll just tell me how to get home from here, I'll go."

A part of me knew it was futile. But I had to try. Maybe there was car service. My dad always said wherever I was, if I called for car service, he would pay, even if it was from New Jersey.

"Then," I finished, "you can get back to whatever it is that . . . you . . . do. . . ."

My voice trailed off as I watched the expression on his face go from mildly amused to grimly serious.

"What?" I said. I did *not* like the look on his face. "What's wrong?"

"I'm sorry," he said. He was frowning now. "Pierce, I thought you knew."

And then I heard his voice reminding me of how I had tripped and hit my head, had fallen in the pool and drowned, and that's why my clothes had been wet, and . . .

Dead. That was the main word I heard. I was dead.

That's where I stopped listening.

I suppose a part of me had known all along. But actually hearing him say the word — *Dead. I was dead* — was the biggest shock of all. Worse than the blow to my head. Worse than choking on the water. Worse than lying at the bottom of that pool, knowing my dad was never going to come in time to save me, and that I'd died because of a bird. A *bird*!

A bird that hadn't been hurt at all but just stunned by the cold or something, because it had flown away as soon as I hit the pool cover. I'd seen it as I drowned.

Dead. I was dead.

So many things made sense now. That's why no one's cell phone had worked. Their cell phones were dead.

Just like we were.

I felt frozen. All of me. Like I was still at the bottom of that pool, in that icy, icy water.

I was only fifteen. Just a few hours ago, I had been talking to Hannah on the phone. We'd been planning on going to the mall to see a movie later. I'd managed to convince her to have her mom drop us by the stables to visit Double Dare first —

Mom! My mom didn't even know where I was. I had to let my mother know where I was.

"I . . ." My tongue and lips seemed to be the only parts of me that weren't frozen. "Thank you," I said to him, interrupting whatever he'd been explaining. Because John was still talking. Who knew what he was saying? He looked nervous again. "Thank you so much for everything. But I have to go now. Good-bye."

I turned away from him and started to walk off in the direction of those gauzy curtains, towards the courtyard. He took a quick step forward, blocking my path.

"I know it's upsetting," he said. "But it doesn't exactly work that way. You see, once you've arrived here, you can't leave."

I shook my head. "But I have to," I said. "I have to let my mom know I'm all right. Except for the being dead part," I added. I wasn't quite sure how she was going to take that news.

"Your mom is fine," he assured me, laying his hands on my bare shoulders and physically steering me back into the room. "I told you, you can't leave. And I think you should sit down again. You've had a shock."

"What do you mean, I can't leave?" I spun back around to face him. Suddenly, I didn't feel vague anymore. "What about all those people down by the lake? They're leaving, aren't they?"

He shrugged. "In a way. To their final destination."

"What's that?" I asked.

"Their just rewards," he said, a little bitterly.

"That's where the boat is taking them?" I asked. "Aren't I supposed to be getting on the boat? The one that's leaving?"

My voice trailed off as I read his expression. It was more serious than I'd ever seen it.

"The one that just left, you mean," he said.

The words seemed to echo around the room. Although they didn't really.

"Wait," I said. "What?"

"The boat is gone," he said. "I asked if you wanted to go someplace else, and you said yes, please. And now the boat is gone. You chose me over the boat, and now this is where you're going to have to stay. Look, you really don't seem well. I think you should sit down. Won't you eat something? What about a drink? Some hot tea?"

Thunder rumbled. But it was inside my head, not outside. Suddenly, I was freezing again, in spite of the blazing fire in the enormous hearth.

"Are you telling me that I have to stay here with you forever because you made me *miss the boat*?" I demanded.

He was so tall, I had to crane my neck to look into his face. What I saw there — the muscle leaping in his lean cheek, the stubborn set of his jaw — made me as frightened as I'd felt back down by the lake.

Even when, despite the determination I could see in his face, I noticed the sadness in those silver eyes . . .

None of that helped the tears I could feel coming, or my racing pulse.

"What about the other boat?" I demanded. My voice sounded shrill even to my own ears. "The one for the people in the other line?"

"You don't want to go where that boat is headed," John said shortly. "Why do you think they all wanted to get on yours?"

I couldn't believe this was happening.

"It's okay," I said, fighting for calm, even though I could feel my heart hammering in my throat. "Because I didn't get on the boat, that means I haven't passed on to my final destination, right? And you can make dead people come back alive. You did it with the bird. So you're going to do it with me. You're just going to make me alive again. You have to, because you messed up, making me miss my boat. So do it. *Now*, John."

His expression remained obstinate, even as his eyes remained sad.

"I can't," he said.

"Can't?" My voice caught on a sob. "Or won't?"

He looked away. "Won't," he said.

Now my heart felt as if it were being constricted back in that pool cover all over again. *"Why not?"*

"Because," he said. But he seemed to have to think about it a while. "It's against the rules."

"Don't you make the rules?" I asked. This was horrible. This was the worst thing that had ever happened to me. Including having died.

"No," he said. I could tell he was trying to keep his temper in check. But he wasn't having any more success with that than I was with my tears. Way off in the distance, thunder was rumbling. This time, it wasn't in my head. "I don't."

"Then who does?" His figure had started to dissolve in front of me. Not because he'd gone anywhere but because of the tears that threatened to spill over from my eyes. I wiped at them furiously.

"I don't know," he said. Now he just sounded tired. "All right? Do you think I like this any more than you do? Don't you think I'd like to leave here to go see *my* mother? But I can't either."

Hearing he longed to see his own mother wasn't exactly helping the situation with my tears. I'd never even considered someone like him might have a mother. But of course he did. Didn't everyone? "Why not?"

"Because of the Furies," he said flatly, as if that explained everything. "Trust me, they make sure that the consequences for breaking the rules around here are much worse than anything you could imagine. And not just for breaking the rules. For anything they feel like —" He broke off and looked at me, then glanced down and shook his head. "Well, just trust me. That's why I gave you the necklace. It will warn you if any Furies are around. That way you'll know if you're doing anything that might put yourself in danger from them, even inadvertently."

When he glanced back up again, his own eyes were bright. Brighter even than Dad's throwing stars. But his voice was gentle. "I promise you, Pierce, in a little while, you'll see, it's not so bad here. You have everything you could possibly want. All the comforts of home . . ."

It was the worst thing he could possibly have said. All the comforts of home . . . except everything — *everything* — I loved.

Now I wasn't frozen anymore. I was melting. The tears started pouring out so thick and fast, everything, including him, disappeared before my eyes.

"I'm sorry." I hid my face in my hands. This was terrible. I was dead, and now I was being tortured as well? "I can't stay here. I *can't*."

"Don't," he said. Now the thunder sounded as if it was right over our heads. *"Don't cry."*

He'd reached out as he said it to lay a hand on my shoulder — to comfort me, I suppose — but I sprang away at his touch, recoiling as if he'd scalded me, and retreated to the hearth, where I collapsed.

Forever? I was going to be trapped here with him forever?

And why? Because of some arbitrary *rule*? Something called a Fury? He had to be joking. I could only imagine what my dad would say if he were here. *Don't you know who I am?* he'd bellow.

Though I felt completely numb inside, I could still sense the heat from the flames against my back. How could I be dead if I could still feel? *How?*

A second later, John was beside me, saying, "Here. Drink this. It will help."

He put a cup of something hot in my hands.

But I couldn't drink.

Then he sat down beside me on the hearth. After a while, I noticed he was speaking again.

"I know it seems bad now, but it gets better, I promise. Soon — not right away, but eventually — you won't even mind. Or at least, you won't mind as much. It's not the same as not minding at all, I know. But at least you won't be alone. That's the important thing. That was the worst part. Being alone for so long."

What was he even *talking* about? I lifted my bruised gaze and let it wander around the room, until it finally came to rest on the bed. It was only then that I noticed how huge it was. Built for two, really.

Oh, God.

Stay away from the pool in the wintertime, Pierce. Even with the cover, it isn't safe.

This was the price I was paying for not listening to my mother.

I never thought it would be *this* high.

It couldn't have been a coincidence that at that very moment, I noticed an open doorway through an arch across the room, just beyond the bed. Through it I could see a long hallway lit by elegant wall sconces. Two stone staircases curled from it. One led up.

The other led down.

I hadn't noticed it before, I was certain, because I hadn't been wearing the necklace. He'd said himself that the diamond protected its wearer from evil.

It was already working.

There was really only one question in my mind: Which staircase would lead me as far away as possible from here?

I was just going to have to make that decision when the time came.

"Well," I said, realizing that if I didn't distract him somehow, I was never going to get a chance to make my escape at all. "I guess you're right. I'm . . . I'm just being silly."

He stared down at me, seeming a little shocked at my abrupt change in attitude. "Really?" he asked. "Do you . . . do you mean that?"

"Of course," I said. Somehow, I even managed a watery grin.

Then I lifted the cup he'd given me as if I was actually going to drink from it.

That's when he did something he'd never done in my company before that moment. Something terrible. Something that showed that, despite what he'd said earlier about knowing my nature so well, he didn't really know me at all.

He smiled.

And then I did something that still causes my heart to twist in my chest whenever I remember it. Something that still haunts my dreams. Something I can't believe I did and, to this day, really wish I hadn't.

Except that I had to. The way that bed was sitting there, and the way *he* was sitting there, and . . . well, what other choice did I have?

It's just that whenever I remember that smile, my heart still breaks a little.

But I was so young, and so scared. I didn't know what else to do.

So I did the first thing I thought of. The thing I'm sure my dad — and even my mom and the Westport Academy for Girls — would have wanted me to do.

I threw that cup of hot tea in his face.

And then I ran.

So did my soul, that still was fleeing onward,
Turn itself back to re-behold the pass
Which never yet a living person left.
DANTE ALIGHIERI, *Inferno*, Canto I

I took the staircase that twisted down, thinking it would lead me back to the lake. I remember — as clearly as if it were yesterday — that with every step, I'd felt as if my heart was going to explode.

That, the psychiatrists assured me later, was the epinephrine.

The next thing I knew, I was looking up at my mom's face. I watched as her expression went from agonized, tormented grief to wild, joyous hope as I responded like a robot to the ER doctor's questions.

Yes, I knew who I was. Yes, I knew who my mother was, and what year it was, and how many fingers the doctor was holding up.

I was alive. I had gotten away from there, wherever it was.

Away from *him*.

Everything after that seemed to happen in a blur. The surgery for the hematoma. My recovery. The doctors. The psychiatrists.

The divorce.

Because of course Dad wasn't the one who saved me, in the end. That was Mom. When she got home from the library and called for me, then looked around and finally found where I'd disappeared to, she was the one who dove to the bottom of the pool and pulled me out. *Her* lips were the ones that turned blue from trying to blow life back into my frozen corpse for the twelve minutes it took the EMTs to get there. It was *her* wet hair that froze, like icicles, to my face.

Dad didn't even realize what was going on until he heard the sirens from the ambulance she had called on her cell. He was still on his conference call.

"But it's a good thing," Dad always says, "that the water in that pool was so cold! Otherwise, you wouldn't be alive today. That's the only way they were able to restart your heart, once they got you warmed up."

He's actually right about that, though. Thanks to the near-freezing temperature of the water, my physical recovery was complete.

It was my psychological "issues" that needed work. Especially when, as she was signing me out of the hospital after my recovery from the surgery, Mom said, "Oh, honey, I've been meaning to ask you. Where did this come from?"

And she dropped a necklace into my lap.

The necklace. The one *he'd* given me.

"Where did you get this?" I asked, clutching it, hoping the horror I felt didn't show on my face.

"They brought it out with your other things while you were being prepped for surgery," she said. "After they revived you. Apparently, you were wearing it under your coat. I almost told them they'd made a mistake and it wasn't yours, because I've never seen it before. *Is* it yours? Did you borrow it from Hannah or something?"

"Uh, no. It . . . was a gift," I said. How was this possible? How could it have crossed over with me? Especially when every single doctor I'd told about what I'd seen while I was dead — my neurologist, the trauma surgeon, even the doctors who had strolled in to check on me over the weekend — had assured me that it had all been just a horrible, terrible dream —

But this meant it hadn't been a dream. This meant that . . .

"Gift?" Mom was distracted by all the forms. Dad usually filled out the forms. But Mom had banished Dad from the hospital. The sight of him upset her so much that, though I didn't know it then, she'd already kicked him out of the house.

"Gift from whom?" Mom had asked, absently flipping the forms in front of her. I'm not sure if it was because I was holding the necklace that I had the wisdom to answer the way I did or if I just knew better than to tell her the truth.

"Just a friend" was all I said at the time as I stared down into the blue-gray depths of that stone. I was too upset to say more than that.

This meant it was real. It was all real. *He* was real.

Thank God I didn't tell Mom the truth. Thank God she was so distracted by the divorce, she never mentioned the necklace again. Thank God I always wore the diamond tucked inside my shirt after that, too confused by what its existence in this world implied about my so-called "lucid dream" to share it with anyone. . . .

Well, except for what I mentioned to Hannah about it when I got back to school. And even that had quickly shown itself to be enough of a mistake that I learned to keep my mouth shut.

But not as bad as the mistake I made a week or two later, when Mom was "unavoidably detained" by Dad's lawyers from picking me up after an outpatient appointment, and I found myself wandering into a jewelry store I'd spied on the same block as my doctor's office while I waited for her. Gazing absently at all the "gray quartz" they happened to have for sale, I must have unconsciously pulled out the diamond and started playing with it, since the man behind the counter noticed it and commented on its beauty.

Blushing furiously, I'd tried to tuck it away, but it was too late. He asked to look at it more closely, saying that he'd never seen such an unusual stone.

What could I do? I let him look but kept the chain around my neck, as always. I'd never removed it since Mom had given it back to me. I don't know why. The stone fascinated me. It never seemed to be any one color or another but was constantly changing. Even as the man behind the counter held it, it was turning from a pale silver to a deep, rain-cloud purple.

The next thing I knew, the guy behind the counter said he just *had* to show it to his boss, who was in the back, having his lunch. He was going to *love* it.

I don't know what I thought was going to happen . . . or why I had such a strong urge to run away.

I should have listened to my instincts. I should have seen what the stone was trying to tell me.

But I didn't.

After the assistant disappeared, the head jeweler came out, wiping his mouth on a napkin. By that time, I could see that my mom had pulled up in her car across the street.

"Actually," I said, a surge of relief rushing through me. Now I had an excuse to leave. "My ride is here. I need to go. Sorry —"

The older jeweler had already seized the end of my pendant by then, though, so I was trapped . . . held suspended across the glass counter by the gold chain.

That's when several things seemed to happen all at once.

Something went cold in the jeweler's gaze when it fastened on the stone. The closer he bent to look at it, the more nervous I got . . . and the darker the diamond seemed to turn at its heart. My own heart began to beat very hard.

And though I couldn't turn my head all the way to look because the jeweler had me almost literally by the neck, I could have sworn I saw, out of the corner of my eye, *him* standing outside the store, looking at us through the window.

"Do you have any idea what this is that you're wearing, young lady?" the jeweler demanded. And then he launched into some kind of bizarre diamond speak. "This is a fancy deep gray blue. If

I'm not wrong, it's probably worth anywhere from fifty to seventy-five million dollars. Maybe more if its provenance can be proven, because it looks uncannily like one I've seen somewhere before."

What could I say? The stone had turned ebony. I tugged gently on the chain, hoping he'd let go.

Except of course he only held on more tightly, keeping me a prisoner in his store.

"I'm sorry," I said. "I really do have to —"

"You shouldn't be walking around the streets wearing this," the jeweler interrupted. "It belongs in a safe-deposit box. By rights I should confiscate it, if only for your own safety. Where did you even get it? Do your parents know you have this?"

It had been only a month since the accident. Everyone at school was already beginning to treat me differently because I'd been acting so weird since coming back from the dead. I'd lost all interest in going to the mall and working with the animal rescue groups I used to love. I'd said that odd thing to Hannah about how I'd always protect her from "the evil" (I'd been referring to my necklace, of course, but she hadn't known that). Soon I would lose the part of Snow White in the school play.

I was already slipping into a glass coffin of my very own.

But somehow I still found a way to assure the jeweler, in a stammering voice, that the necklace was a family heirloom, thank you very much. And that my mother was, in fact, waiting for me in the car outside and that I needed to go meet her right now. Though I was actually more frightened at the idea of walking outside that store and possibly running into *him* than I was at staying inside with the extremely irritable jeweler.

That's when I heard the bells on the shop door tinkle behind me, indicating that someone was coming in.

My heart sank. No. Please, *no*.

"I don't believe you," the jeweler said flatly. "In fact, just so you know, my assistant is on the phone in the back with the police right now. They're on the way. So your mother — if she *is* waiting outside, which I sincerely doubt, since you've clearly stolen this — can come inside and join us, if she cares to, and watch you being arrested for grand theft."

Except that my mother was never given the opportunity to do so. Because John stepped forward.

And the walls of the shop seemed to turn the color of blood before my eyes.

"Excuse me," John said in his deep voice, which sounded completely out of place in such a small, upscale boutique. He *looked* completely out of place in it, already so menacing because of his size but even more so now because of the black leather jacket and jeans he was wearing.

I thought I was going to pass out. What was he doing there? Had he come to take me back because I'd broken the rules? Was that why the stone in my necklace had turned black, to warn me?

The jeweler glanced over at him, annoyed. "My assistant will be with you in a moment, sir," he said.

"No, thank you," John said, as if he were refusing an offer of peanuts on a plane. "Let go of her."

The jeweler's eyes widened slightly. But he didn't let go of me.

"Excuse *me*," the jeweler said, looking indignant. "But are you acquainted with this young lady? Because she —"

That's when John — not looking angry, or annoyed, or anything at all, really — reached across the counter and took hold of the hand the jeweler was using to hold me captive in his shop, as if John were feeling for his pulse.

But John wasn't feeling for the jeweler's pulse. That wasn't what he was doing at all.

The jeweler gave a little gasp. His mouth fell open. Some of the coldness went out of his eyes. Instead, they filled with fear.

I didn't know — then — what John was doing. My mind was still reeling over the fact that he was there at all.

But I recognized, in a way the jeweler clearly hadn't, the dangerous set of his jaw and the determined look in his eyes.

And the anxiety that washed over me had nothing to do anymore with my own safety.

"John," I said. I'd pried the pendant from the older man's clenched fingers and was already backing away from the counter. I couldn't take my gaze from the jeweler's face. It had drained of all color. "Please. Whatever you're doing. Don't. It's all right. Really."

It wasn't all right. It was obvious that it wasn't all right.

But this turned out to be the correct thing to say, since John — after throwing an agitated glance in my direction as if to gauge the truth of my statement — let go of the jeweler's wrist.

As soon as he did this, the old man took another gasping breath and then staggered back, clutching at his heart.

He wasn't the only one. I was clutching at my own heart after the look of stinging reproach John flung me a second later . . . just before the jeweler's assistant appeared in the back doorway and said, "Okay, Mr. Curry, the police are on their way — *oh, my God!*"

Then — coward that I am — I pivoted and ran blindly from the store, the bells on the door tinkling behind me.

But what else was I going to do? Stick around until the cops showed up?

I sprinted straight to my mom's waiting car.

"Pierce," Mom said, lowering her cell phone and looking surprised as I collapsed, shaking all over, into the passenger seat. "There you are. I was just trying to call you. Did you forget your phone again? You weren't picking up. Where were —"

"Drive," I panted. "Just drive."

"What's wrong? Didn't you like that new doctor? Jennifer McNamara's mother said he —"

"It's not that. Let's just go."

The next few hours were agony as I waited for the police — or *him* — to show up at our door. Surely, someone had seen the car I'd jumped into and had written down Mom's license number. What if there'd been security cameras in Mr. Curry's shop?

But the police never came.

Neither did John.

And though I scanned the paper every day, even the obituaries, I never saw a single story pertaining to the jeweler.

I found out why the next time we were in the area. There was a FOR RENT sign in the jewelry store window. When I asked a salesclerk in the dress shop next door about it, she told me that she'd heard Mr. Curry was recovering from a heart attack and had moved . . . possibly to Florida. She thought he said he had grandchildren there.

And thank *God*, because everyone on the block had hated that cranky old man, and now maybe finally they'd get a decent shoe store on the block, and that dress would look *so* cute on me, did I want to try it on?

From what I was able to put together, by the time the police arrived, the jeweler's assistant was too busy giving Mr. Curry CPR to remember the fact that he'd actually called them about some girl who *might* have been in possession of a stolen necklace. . . . Never mind some guy in a leather jacket who'd disappeared as mysteriously as she had.

Maybe that's why I'd never shown my necklace to another person again.

It had been hard not to feel ever since as if . . . well, as if John were watching me. Maybe even protecting me. A little overzealously.

Especially after what happened at school, with Hannah and Mr. Mueller.

What I'd never been able to understand is *why*. Why would he bother? *I'd run away from him.*

And now that he'd just hurled the necklace off into the maze of aboveground crypts that made up the Isla Huesos Cemetery, I knew that wasn't because he'd wanted it back.

I should have gone to look for it. I should have, but I didn't.

Because when he lifted his arm to fling the necklace, I saw — as might be expected of someone who'd been kicked out of the Westport Academy for Girls — that I'd gotten it all wrong.

It wasn't any of my business, of course. Not anymore. He'd just seen to that, by hurling my necklace the equivalent of a football field away. Except that I had decided recently to begin making everyone's business my business. It was part of the "new start" Mom wanted us to have on this island.

And his business had always been my business. He was the one who'd started all of this. *He'd* come up to *me*. The first time, anyway.

So I couldn't go look for my necklace. I had to stay. I had no choice, really.

Which was why that night in the cemetery I stood my ground and asked, "What happened to your arm?"

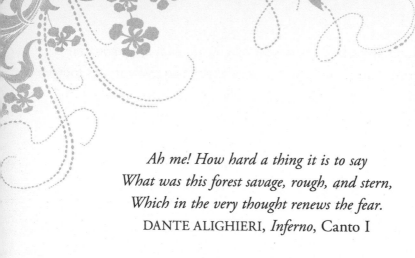

Ah me! How hard a thing it is to say
What was this forest savage, rough, and stern,
Which in the very thought renews the fear.
DANTE ALIGHIERI, *Inferno*, Canto I

He stared down at me as if he suspected I was insane. Well, why would he be any different from anybody else?

"What?" He still seemed pretty mad. A good sign of this was when his chest started to rise and fall as if he'd been running, which it was doing now.

So I should have known better than to do what I did next, which was reach out and run a finger down the scar I'd just spied, snaking up the underside of his arm, then disappearing into his black sleeve.

I should never have said, "That one's new."

But I did anyway.

He jerked his arm away as if my finger were a live wire and I'd just tried to electrocute him.

"Stop that," he said, glaring. "It's nothing."

"It doesn't look like nothing to me," I said worriedly. I'd started to add a few things together in my head and didn't like what I was coming up with. "Is that a consequence?"

His eyes narrowed. I could feel the heat from his body, and smell the scent I remembered so well — a mix of wood smoke and something that reminded me of autumn.

"I am not a bird," he said in a dangerous voice. "I don't require aid, from you or anyone else. Does your mother know where you are right now?"

It was funny that he mentioned my mother. Because it was her voice I was hearing in my head just then, urging me to tell him that thing I hadn't said the last time I'd seen him, that awful day at school . . . that thing he hadn't given me a chance to say. He'd left before I could.

Well, he'd had to. The police were coming. Again.

Not that my mother knew anything about him, except what the psychiatrists (and now, I knew, Grandma) all believed: that he wasn't real.

But if Mom had known what I knew about him, she'd have *wanted* me to say it. I obviously *needed* to say it, now more than ever, because it was clear that my initial assessment of him hadn't been that far off:

He was a wild thing, like that dove I'd found, badly in need of someone's aid, even if he didn't agree.

And though by helping him, I might only be hurting him more, I had to at least *try*.

So I said what I probably should have said to him a long time ago: "I'm sorry."

His eyes narrowed even more. "Pardon me?" he said.

"I'm sorry," I repeated, more loudly this time. "For what I did to you the day I died. If there were . . . consequences. Especially for you."

He didn't respond, except to continue to stare down at me as if *I* were the one with the antisocial personality disorder. Who gives a girl a necklace — especially one with a stone that changed colors like the sky, sometimes gray as a February morning, other times, black as midnight — and then hurls it across a cemetery when she very politely tries to give it back because she suspects he might be enduring *consequences* on her behalf?

But why was *I* the only one apologizing? It would have been nice to hear a "sorry" or two out of him.

Because he *had* been horrible to me the day we'd met.

And, yes, he'd sort of made up for some of it by what he'd done for me at the jewelry store, and later, at school with Mr. Mueller.

But still. I'd lost so much. True, I'd gotten my life back. But what about all the things I *hadn't* gotten back? Like my parents' marriage, and Hannah, for instance. I hadn't been back at school for even a full day after I got out of the hospital before my then best friend, Hannah Chang, dumped me for telling her that — among other things, like hanging out at the mall hoping to catch glimpses of her older brother's friends, and neglecting Double Dare — the "Hold your breath when you go by the graveyard, or evil spirits will possess your soul" thing we used to like to play was stupid, and that I wasn't doing it anymore.

True, at fifteen, we were too old for things like that, anyway.

But I hadn't helped matters by cheerfully informing her, "Don't worry about the evil, Hannah. I can see it now. And I'll protect you from it."

No wonder she called me crazy. It's what *everyone* at school started calling me afterwards.

I guess I can't blame them. Why wouldn't you call someone who says she can see evil — and has the ability to protect people from it — crazy? Especially when she later failed so spectacularly to do so.

I know Hannah only called me crazy because she was worried about me. She must have thought I'd come back from the hospital after my accident acting . . . well, a little mentally unstable.

Hannah told me she was sorry later, and I could tell she really meant it. Friends sometimes drift apart, she said. Like she had with Double Dare. She just didn't have time for horses anymore, she explained. She'd moved on to other things. Like basketball. And boys.

I told her it was fine. By then I was way too deeply dug into my real-life glass coffin to care anymore — about her, about the evil I'd promised to protect her from, or even the fact that everyone thought I was crazy.

It wasn't until the following year that I realized what a mess I'd made of everything.

By then it was too late for Hannah, of course.

I knew I couldn't blame any of *that* on John. It's only in fairy tales that princesses can afford to wait for the handsome prince to save them. In real life, they have to bust out of their own coffins and do the saving themselves.

And in what fairy tale would *John* ever be any sane person's idea of Prince Charming anyway? He was the *opposite* of charming. More like Prince Terrifying.

But then . . . maybe he couldn't help being terrifying.

Any more than I could help being the way I am, or reacting to him the way I had when I was fifteen.

"I'm not just apologizing," I said, wondering why it was that, now that I was older, I *still* couldn't seem to find the right thing to say to him, "because of what you did for me in the jewelry store, or last spring at my old school, either."

This time, instead of tilting his head, he just tilted a single dark eyebrow. This didn't exactly make things easier. His expression was still impossible to read.

"This has nothing to do with that," I said when he remained silent. "Not that I'm not grateful. Because I am. I'm sorry I didn't thank you then. Things just got a little . . . hectic after you left."

Hectic was hardly the word to describe the firestorm John had left in his wake the day he showed up at the Westport Academy for Girls.

"Which," he said, "is why you and your mother are here now. Making a new start."

"Exactly," I said. "So I'm not going to be needing you at my new school. And just so you know, I had that situation back in Westport completely under control before you showed up."

Now both eyebrows rose.

"I did," I insisted. "I didn't need your help. That's what the camera was for —"

His hand shot out, so quickly the gesture was a blur, on the word *camera*. Before I knew it, he'd grabbed my upper arm in a grip that didn't hurt, exactly, but wasn't gentle, either, and I was being dragged towards him.

The shades that had been pulled down over those eyes finally came flying up again — just for a moment.

"What camera?" he demanded.

"The camera," I murmured, beginning to think I probably shouldn't have opened my mouth about this, "that I set up inside my backpack —"

To say he looked shocked would have been an understatement of the grossest proportions.

"Are you telling me that you *planned* it?" he asked. "What happened that day with your teacher. That was on purpose? You *meant* for him to do that to you?"

Maybe he really *wasn't* following me around. Because if he had been, surely he'd have known about this.

"Well," I said, my mouth dry. "Yes." Then, before he had a chance to explode, since I could see he was about to, I added quickly, "It was the only way I could get proof of what Mr. Mueller was really like, because no one believed that he and Hannah had . . ."

My voice trailed off, because when I glanced up into his face, I saw that his mouth was pressed into a flat line . . . like the one my heart had gone into the day I'd fallen into his world.

I knew this wasn't good. This was all very, very bad.

"But I never intended to let it get that far," I said quickly. "I took total responsibility for everything that happened that —"

His grip on my arm tightened.

"How could you have put yourself in such a dangerous situation in the first place?" he demanded. "And for something so *stupid*? Do you have any idea what could have happened to you?"

Well, yes. I did . . . now. Back then, I hadn't had the slightest idea, or I wouldn't have tried it.

But I said, trying to shrug it off, "Really, it wasn't that big a —"

"You shouldn't have been there," he said through gritted teeth. "Any more than you should be here now."

And the next thing I knew, he was physically dragging me away from the crypt.

"The cemetery gates are locked at night," he muttered. Poinciana blossoms exploded beneath those heavy black boots.

I barely heard him. It was true that once, I had somehow managed to escape from him — and from death. But that had been because of those defibrillation paddles and that shot of epinephrine back in the real world . . . or so the doctors insisted. My escape had had nothing to do with anything *I'd* done back in his world, they said. Because his world wasn't real.

Except — as I knew better than anyone — it was.

"How did you even get in here? That fence is seven feet high. With spikes at the top," he was saying under this breath.

I didn't want to say anything to make him angrier . . . like that the fence hadn't really been all that hard to scale once I'd wheeled one of those giant green-lidded Isla Huesos trash cans, which were just sitting around everywhere, up against it.

And that it wasn't my fault the family of Dolores Sanchez, Beloved Wife of Rodrigo, had chosen to place her crypt so close to the fence on the inside of the cemetery, providing me with such an excellent landing pad.

Should I risk setting him off again by pointing out that, even if the police had understood what they'd seen on the tape — which they hadn't — there was obviously no way they could find him to question him? The Westport Police Department didn't know where he lived. I wondered if anyone did, besides me.

I had a few questions for him, though. How had he known to show up that day with Mr. Mueller, right when I needed him most? Was it really because of the necklace, like he'd said, when he'd shaken it in my face? Was that how he'd known the time before, with the jeweler?

But why had he even bothered, since he evidently still hated my guts for what I'd done to him?

Now didn't seem like the best time to bring that, or any of the rest of it, up.

"None of this is my fault, you know," I said, as he pulled me along so fast I was afraid I was going to lose a flip-flop. Although this was hardly foremost among my fears.

"Oh, really?" he said, turning his head to glare at me. "How is none of this your fault?"

"All I did was die," I said. "And then, when presented with an opportunity not to be dead anymore, I took it. It wasn't personal. It had nothing to do with you."

He turned to glare straight ahead. "Right," he said.

"What's that supposed to mean?" I demanded, stung by his tone. "I told you, I was scared. I didn't mean to hurt you. That's why I came here tonight, to apologize. I want to be friends, to help you. I gave you the necklace back. I don't know what more I can do."

"I'll tell you what you can do," he said, stopping abruptly. Now he did reach out to grip both my shoulders. But still not to kiss me. Only so he could wheel me around to glare at me some more. "You can leave me alone."

Tears sprang once more into my eyes. *That's* what he wanted from me? For me to stay away from him?

This had turned into a greater disaster than when I'd died. And I was still breathing, so that was saying something.

"I'd like to," I said. All I could hear besides the deep, disapproving timbre of his voice was the drum of my heartbeat in my ears. *Stupid girl. Stupid girl. Stupid girl*, my heart seemed to be saying. "Except every time I try, you show back up, and act like such a . . . such a . . ."

"Such a what?" he demanded. He seemed to be practically daring me to say it.

Don't, the voice of my mother warned inside my head. *Don't say it.*

"*Jerk.*"

I knew, when the word was coming out of my mouth, it would be neither an adroit nor a sensitive thing to say. Especially since I'd been trying to do the right thing. Because we were going to have to be living on the same island together. And he *had* saved my life, after all, at least that day with Mr. Mueller.

Well, maybe not my life. But he'd saved something, anyway.

But somehow, in apologizing, I'd just ended up making everything worse.

As if that weren't awful enough, after hurling out the word, I lifted a hand to that fresh new scar I'd seen on the inside of his right arm.

I couldn't help it. I'd never been able to stay away from hurt things.

So there it was: my final mistake of the evening.

His mouth twisted into a very unpretty grimace, proving I'd been right about one thing:

He'd never be anyone's handsome prince.

"Well, you don't have to worry about that anymore," he shot out, jerking his arm away as if my touch were poisonous. "Because you won't be seeing me again after tonight."

I realized several things then. The first was that his eyes weren't dead anymore. They were as alive as electric wires, and just as dangerous.

The second realization came to me more slowly, as I looked down at the fingers he'd wrapped around my arm, fingers against which dark drifts of my hair, loosened from my clip, had tumbled.

And that was that his weren't the soft, smooth hands of other people our age, most of whom had known no other labor than texting or moving a video game stick.

John's were hands that had seen work — real, arduous work. The hands of a fighter.

But not just a fighter, I realized, as they gripped me.

His were hands that had killed.

A part of me must have known this all along. But it hadn't really sunk in until tonight.

And by then, of course, it was far, far too late.

Midway upon the journey of our life
I found myself within a forest dark,
For the straightforward pathway had been lost.
DANTE ALIGHIERI, *Inferno*, Canto I

When I got home, Mom said, "Oh, hi, honey. I'm glad you made it back before the storm. It looks like it's about to pour any minute. Did you have a nice ride?"

"Yeah," I said. I turned around and locked the door. I used the dead bolt *and* the lock inside the doorknob.

Then I hit the STAY button on the alarm and entered our code. Our code is our initials, plus the years Mom's alma mater won the NCAA championship. Mom's handling the disappointment that I probably won't be getting into *any* four-year colleges, let alone the one where she and Dad met, pretty well.

"Uh, honey," Mom said, a funny look on her face. "What are you doing?"

"Safety," I said. My heart was still ricocheting off the walls of my chest. As soon as I'd gotten back onto my bike, I'd ridden flat out for home. I hadn't even stopped outside to lock up my bike or turn off its lights, I realized now as I lifted the curtain in one of the foyer windows to peek outside to see if he'd followed me. "Safety first."

"Well, honey," Mom said, pressing the OFF button on the alarm, then putting the code back in. "Some of our guests are still here. So how about we wait to put the alarm on until *after* they leave? Okay?"

I nodded, still peering out the foyer window. I was *not* going back out there to turn off my bike lights. They could blink on and off all night, for all I cared. I'd just buy new lights if they burned out. It would be worth it. If the bike got stolen, so what? I'd just make Dad buy me a new one. This whole thing was his fault, anyway. That's what Mom thinks.

I was never going back outside again.

Not so long as *he* was out there.

"Honey?" Mom asked. "Are you all right?"

"Sure, Mom," I said, letting the curtain drop. "I'm great. Having a nice time at your party?"

"It's your party, honey," she said, smiling. "And I'm having a great time. It's so good to see everyone again. I think even your uncle Chris enjoyed himself —"

"Great, Mom," I interrupted. "Look, I'm really tired. I'm going to go to bed." I was going to pull the covers up over my head and never come out.

"Oh," Mom said, looking disappointed. "Don't you want to say good night to everyone? Your uncle Chris waited especially to see you before he and Grandma and Alex head for home. And

I think Alex wants to make sure you don't have any more questions about starting school tomorrow. I thought that was awfully sweet of him."

Just the reminder that school was starting tomorrow made me want to bite off all my fingernails. But Mom had taken me for a special back-to-school mani-pedi yesterday, so I knew I had to keep them out of my mouth.

"You know what," I said. "I'm really beat. Must be all the last-minute excitement with the party. Just tell Alex thanks, but I'll see him tomorrow morning when he comes to pick me up for school. Good night, Mom."

I rushed up the stairs before she could say anything more.

He'd destroyed the gates to the cemetery.

He'd crushed the lock with a single vicious kick from one of those heavy black boots. Then, when the gates crashed violently open, he'd pushed me through them.

"Get out," he'd warned in his devil-deep voice. "Do you hear me, Pierce? Get out and don't ever come back. It's not safe for you here. Not unless you really do want to end up dead. Forever this time."

A huge bolt of lightning had lit up the clouds right after he said it, and then a crack of thunder, so loud that I thought the sky was splitting in two, had muffled the sound of the gates swinging back into place behind me.

Without looking back, I ran to where I'd left my bike chained, I was so grateful to have escaped.

Now standing in the shower, letting the water pour over me, so hot it was almost scalding, I had to wonder:

Had any of it really even happened? How could it? No one could kick apart a locked metal gate — and the black wrought-iron gates to the Isla Huesos Cemetery were huge, large enough for a hearse to fit through, and thick and strong as jail bars.

No one who lived in *this* world, anyway.

I didn't want to think about it.

I couldn't think about anything else.

Had I really seen him . . . spoken to him . . . touched him . . . been touched *by* him? I looked down at the skin on my bare arms where those killer fingers had been. Incredibly, they'd left no mark, though earlier I could have sworn they'd singed me to the bone.

I didn't even have the necklace anymore to prove to myself that any of it had happened. Now it was lost — *forever this time*, just like he'd said — because I was certainly never setting foot in that cemetery again. Maybe some tourist would find it. It would probably end up for sale online or in a pawnshop somewhere.

Stepping from the shower and wrapping myself in one of the thick, white towels Mom's interior decorator had picked out, I shook my head. It didn't matter anymore. I knew what I'd seen, what I'd felt. I didn't need a piece of jewelry to prove it. Not to myself or to anyone.

Seeing him tonight had only made things worse. My apology for what I'd done to him had obviously gone over like a big fat empty piñata at a five-year-old's birthday party.

On the other hand, I hadn't heard any apologies out of him. So why did I even care? Guys really could be jerks. At least from what I'd observed. Mom certainly thought so. Which was why she packed the two of us up and moved us to Isla Huesos. Because

I wasn't the only thing she loved that she felt Dad had allowed to die through neglect.

"Isla Huesos, Deb? Really?" I'd overheard Dad say to her after dropping me off from one of our last (court-mandated, of course, though I didn't mind) lunches. Neither of them knew I was outside the door, listening. I knew eavesdropping was wrong. But how else was I supposed to figure out what was going on? "You think *that's* what the counselor meant when she said a place better suited to her needs?"

"It can't," Mom said, "be any worse for her than Connecticut has turned out to be."

"You can't peg the teacher on me, Deb," Dad said defensively. "That one was all you. I heard you pushing her to take him up on his tutoring offer —"

"Just drop it," Mom said. Now *she* sounded defensive. "I'm taking her home. End of story."

"Of course you are. Going to save the birds."

"Someone has to," she said tightly.

"It's not going to make any difference, Deb," Dad assured her. "It's going to be a drop in the bucket. I think a more likely reason for your going is that *he's* available again."

Now Mom just sounded mad. "I would think you'd have better things to do right now than look up the marital status of my ex-boyfriends on the Internet."

"I like to keep track of their mating habits," Dad said, "the way you do the roseate spoonbills."

"The spoonbills," Mom snapped, "aren't mating anymore. Most of them are dying. Thanks to *you*."

"Oh, for God's sake, Deborah. You think I did *that* on purpose, too?"

"Like certain other things I could mention," Mom said, "that oil leak wouldn't have happened if you'd been paying attention."

Ouch.

But Dad couldn't deny it, much as I'm sure he would have liked to. It was one of the reasons he was always going on TV. Dad's company was at least partly to blame for the decimation of the local economies of hundreds of communities on or around the Gulf, including Isla Huesos's. Tourists didn't want to vacation in a place where their rented Jet Skis might hit patches of oil. Brides didn't want tar balls in their beachside wedding photos. Sportsmen would no longer charter boats to fish in areas where so much sea life had been deemed inedible owing to the dispersant Dad's company had used with so much careless abandon.

"It's perfectly safe," Dad was always going on news shows to declare. "It's been tested!"

But when one journalist served Dad a plate of shrimp cocktail he claimed had been caught in waters where his company's dispersant had been used, and dared him on air to eat it himself if it was so safe, Dad turned very red and said his doctor told him he wasn't allowed to have shrimp on account of his cholesterol.

Dad didn't have high cholesterol.

I just wondered who the *he* was that Dad had mentioned to Mom. I didn't like to bug her about unnecessary stuff since she seemed to have enough on her mind, what with the spoonbills and the move and Uncle Chris and, of course, me.

Which was why, when I lifted one of the curtains in my bedroom before I got into bed, and thought I saw a man standing by the pool, I didn't say anything to her about it.

By then all the party guests had gone home, and Mom had long since gone to sleep. The storm, meanwhile, had arrived in full force. The power, as it often seemed to in Isla Huesos, so far from the mainland, had gone out.

So much for our crack security system.

Rain was streaming down in sheets. Our little kidney-shaped pool in the backyard was threatening to overflow, and the wind was tossing the palm fronds like pieces of newspaper.

But when a flash of lightning turned the yard from blackness to stark daylight — just for a second — I could have sworn I saw John standing there looking up at me.

That was the only person it could be. Who else could get in?

Dad had agreed to let me live out of state with the provision that Mom send me to a school with a program suited to my "special needs" *and* bought a house in a gated community — he'd known how much this would offend her liberal leanings.

Dolphin Key was the only such community on Isla Huesos. There was a security guard posted twenty-four hours at the entrance, the only way in and out of our street.

The Spanish walls that surrounded our new home were twelve feet high. There was no way anyone could climb them without a ladder.

Walls and security guards couldn't stop someone like John, though.

But why would he bother standing in the rain outside my bedroom window when he'd told me to leave him alone? Not to mention the fact that I'd called him a jerk to his face.

Why had I even bothered apologizing to him for what I'd done? He'd done far worse to me. Why couldn't I hate him, the way I ought to?

Maybe because John was like one of Mom's birds: a wild thing. He couldn't help how he was. I was never going to get through to him. Like Dad had said, what was the point of even trying?

Especially since I'd obviously broken "the rules" John had spoken of so mysteriously, by running away. Surely, I was going to have to be punished for this, most likely by him . . . or maybe those Furies he'd spoken of. You can't escape death. I'd read all about this after my accident. Death *will* come for you, eventually.

When lightning flashed again a few seconds later, though, I saw that the figure was gone. Maybe it had never even been there at all. Maybe it had just been that overactive imagination everyone kept accusing me of having, playing tricks on me.

I let the curtain drop and turned back to bed. This was so stupid. I should have been feeling good. I'd given back the necklace I'd taken under false pretenses, and said all the things I felt like I was supposed to say. I'd literally gotten everything I needed to off my chest. I was making a new start here, just like Mom.

John had even accepted my apology! Maybe a little grouchily, but he had. He was moving on, too, as illustrated by his spiking the necklace a good hundred yards across the cemetery and telling me to stay away from him.

And later, when I went to check on my bike out the bathroom window, and saw that someone had chained it up and switched off the lights, I told myself firmly that it must have been my uncle Chris, or maybe Alex, as they'd left the party. No way had it been John. Why would he do something nice like that for me, when he'd made it only too clear he hated my guts and wanted me to stay away from him?

So why, as I climbed into bed, did I feel *worse* instead of better? I didn't feel any sense of closure or any less a sense of — *dread* was the only word for it. Ever since I'd set foot on this island, that's all I'd felt, this pressure on the back of my neck, like something was going to happen, something bad.

Something bad had already happened! I'd seen *him*. It was over!

So why was I up half the night, unable to sleep? Not because of the thunder, either. It almost seemed as if — but it couldn't possibly be, because it was so stupid — but it was like I missed the familiar weight of that necklace around my neck.

What was wrong with me? Why couldn't I get with Mom's "make a new start" program?

When I thanked Alex the next morning as I climbed into his car, he asked what for.

"My bike," I said. "Didn't you lock it up last night when you left my house? And switch off the lights?"

"Uh," he said. "No. When I left — which I guess was right after you got home, because your mom said you'd gone upstairs. Thanks for saying good night, by the way. Oh, and for taking off like that and leaving me alone with Grandma. That was super sweet — your bike was already chained up and the lights switched off. I thought you'd done it."

"No," I said, feeling cold all of a sudden. Except that the AC in the car Grandma referred to as Alex's junk heap was broken, so we had to drive with the windows down, and it was already over eighty degrees outside. "I didn't."

"Huh," he said. "Well, that's weird. But not the weirdest part." He honked at some tourists who'd wandered out into the middle of the street to take photos of a large banyan tree. "Hello, what do these people think, it's Main Street at Disney? Some of us actually live here, you know." He honked some more.

"What's the weirdest part?" I asked, after the tourists had hurried out of the way and Alex had floored it. I wasn't sure I wanted to hear this.

I wasn't sure I didn't want to hear it, either, though.

"Oh. Only that there were all these dead poinciana petals up and down your front walk. Just lying there. And this was *before* that storm. So they couldn't have been blown there by the wind. I thought that was kind of strange, because there are no poincianas on your street. So how did they get there? . . . Oh, well." He turned up the radio. "Ready for school?"

I swallowed. "No."

I cannot well repeat how there I entered,
So full was I of slumber at the moment
In which I had abandoned the true way.
DANTE ALIGHIERI, *Inferno*, Canto I

Mom signed me up for a nationally recognized (which was the only reason Dad approved. Otherwise, he said, it was boarding school in Switzerland for me) program at Isla Huesos High called New Pathways.

New Pathways was for "troubled" students: boys like Alex, whose dad had just been paroled from jail and whose mom had been pretty much MIA since he was born, and so he'd been forced to live all his life with Grandma, who ran the island's only knitting store, Knuts for Knitting. And yes, it was as bad as it sounded.

New Pathways was also for girls like me, who'd died and then come back with a bit of an attitude.

Really. New Pathways: Whatever you have, it'll cure you (not its official slogan).

"It comes highly recommended," Mom kept telling me all summer. "You'll still go to regular mainstream classes, like everyone else. You'll just get extra supervision during the year by social workers with cognitive behavioral and counseling experience. They *really* know what they're doing, Pierce. I wouldn't have enrolled you if I didn't think they could help."

Uh, I thought, but didn't add, also Isla Huesos High School wouldn't have taken me if I hadn't been enrolled in New Pathways, because of what happened to Mr. Mueller.

But whatever. With boarding school for rich kids with social problems in Switzerland being my only other choice, what was I going to say? Yes to New Pathways!

At least the New Pathways counselors — especially Jade, the one I'd been assigned — had been really nice about making me feel welcome, despite knowing what I'd done (or allegedly done, anyway) to a teacher at my last school. Jade had never seemed scared when she talked to me during our orientation meetings, always making full eye contact and smiling a lot and even offering me strips of red licorice from the jar she kept on her desk. My necklace, I'd noticed, had never turned any color when I'd been in Jade's office. It just stayed a steady, soothing gray . . . the same color as the coat of a retired greyhound.

But when I arrived on my first day at what was the only high school on Isla Huesos, to which hundreds of students were bused from neighboring islands — there are over 1,700 off the coast of Florida, Mom not so helpfully informed me one day while listing the various ways in which Dad's company was slowly destroying their ecosystem — I did not feel soothed. I did not need to glance down at the color of my necklace (which I no longer had anyway) to tell me so, either.

I felt overwhelmed, despite Jade's careful instructions about what to expect. I'd never seen so many kids, particularly so many *guys*, crowded into so many buildings . . . four enormous wings in all, all connected by a central, paved courtyard — the Quad, Jade said it was called — at the center of which were all these shaded picnic tables.

This, Jade had explained, was where we were supposed to have lunch every day. The cafeteria was *outside.*

This made absolutely no sense to me, no matter how many times Jade said it.

Only seniors were allowed to leave campus for lunch. I was a senior, but how was I going to leave campus? I had no driver's license. The State of Connecticut had apparently agreed with my neurologist that it was not a good idea for me to drive.

I'd looked at the written test for the State of Florida online because Jade had encouraged me to, and there were even *more* questions on it than on the one for the State of Connecticut. It was hopeless.

Alex had said on the way to school, "I'll meet you in the Quad for lunch. We'll go grab a burger."

But when lunchtime came, of course I couldn't find him. He hadn't told me where to meet him. This was typical Alex. Also, typical me, unfortunately, to forget to ask.

I selected two caffeinated sodas, a bag of nuts, a bag of chips, and a bag of cookies from the vending machines. Then I hid out in the library to eat them. This seemed like the safest thing to do.

The library was where Jade found me.

"Pierce," she said, pulling out the chair from the study carrel next to me and lowering herself into it. "I've been looking for you."

"I'm here," I said stupidly. Obviously I was there. I took out my earbuds. "How's it going?"

"Good," Jade said. "How's it going with you? Didn't make it to the cafeteria for lunch, I see."

"Not today," I said. "Maybe tomorrow."

What was I supposed to say? I didn't have my necklace to protect me anymore? Not that I believed I needed its protective powers, necessarily.

I just wasn't sure I didn't need them.

"Hey, listen, I get it. It's cool," Jade said. Jade had very dark hair and many black leather cords that she wore around her neck and wrists. A tattoo on her wrist said *Check Yourself Before You Wreck Yourself* in fancy script. "But if you want to talk, maybe about that thing that happened with that teacher at your old school, or about that friend of yours who died . . . anything. You know where to find me."

I did know where to find her. The New Pathways offices were located in D-Wing, which was also where all of my classes happened to be located. Convenient.

And really . . . *anything*, Jade? What about the guy I ran into last night in the cemetery? Can we talk about him? Because I've run into him before, actually during "that thing that happened with that teacher" at my old school. When "that friend" of mine died.

Or at least when I tried to make her death right.

And he put a teacher in the hospital.

"Thanks," I said, not mentioning any of that. "Will do."

Jade gave me a funny look, halfway between a smile and a frown.

"Hey," she said, reaching out to touch my hand. "I mean it. None of what happened at your old school was your fault, you know."

I froze when she touched me. And not just because the librarian was shooting us a disapproving look from across the room, either . . . though I'm pretty sure she didn't appreciate our having a conversation in the quiet zone of her library, let alone my using it as a lunchroom.

"Right," I said. "I know."

Was she kidding?

Jade nodded. "Good," she said. "Just remember that. In the meantime, try to enjoy yourself, okay? I know you've been through a lot, but give yourself a break. It's just high school."

I pasted a smile onto my face. "Sure," I said. Maybe Jade was the one who was crazy, not me. Although she and her fellow New Pathways staff members had taken great pains to remind us all that there's no such thing as "crazy" or "normal." These words aren't *therapeutically beneficial*. "I'll try."

"Okay, well, great talk." Jade got up. "Five minutes till the bell rings. Be sure to stop by to check in with me after school. I got some more of that licorice you like. The red kind. Oh, and there's an assembly in the auditorium at two. Don't miss it. It's gonna be *epic*."

She winked and left. *Epic*, unlike *crazy* or *normal*, is a word the New Pathways staff members love. Especially Jade. *Check yourself before you wreck yourself.*

It was clear that my experience at IHHS was going to be sink or swim.

I already knew what it was like to sink.

I decided I might as well swim.

When I arrived at the auditorium for the assembly, the din was deafening. The two-thousand-seat room was filled with people greeting each other after a long summer apart: girls with long, white-tipped nails — this look was considered totally *over* up north . . . at least according to gossip I'd overheard back at the Westport Academy for Girls, before I was thrown out — screaming and hugging, and tattooed guys in head scarves fist-bumping and high-fiving one another, and some actually greeting one another a bit more aggressively than that. So many students talking at a volume so loud in a room so large, I was tempted to slip my earbuds back in just to keep myself from going crazy. Or whatever the therapeutically beneficial word for crazy is.

But I knew I couldn't. I had promised myself that I would stay engaged this year. If I didn't stay engaged, how would I keep the next girl from dying on my watch?

And okay, I had failed miserably to help the last one.

But you never knew. I had a lot of advantages here on Isla Huesos that I hadn't had back in Connecticut. At least here I wasn't invisible, the way I'd unfortunately made myself for too long back at my old school. I could already tell, because some guy in a white shirt had noticed me and held the auditorium door open for me.

I hadn't quite been able to believe it myself, actually.

"After you," he'd said politely.

I wasn't sure which had startled me more: the fact that he was the first person to have spoken to me all day — besides Jade — or the fact that he was so nonthreateningly gorgeous in a boy-band kind of way: tall, blue eyed, friendly smile at the ready, revealing a set of perfectly straight white teeth, a tan you could tell had come from healthy outdoor living and not from a salon, as had the blond highlights in his sandy-brown hair.

All of this was capped off with a pair of khaki shorts and a white polo that showed off his biceps.

Unbelievable.

Kite sailing, if I had to guess. You didn't get biceps — but also a tan — from regular sailing.

"Thanks," I said, not smiling.

It was right then that the ocean breeze swept my pink class schedule out from the top of my bag.

"Oh, here," he said, letting go of the door. "Let me get that."

"It's okay," I said. I just wanted him to go away. He was like the concept of an outdoor cafeteria: I did not understand.

It was too late, though. He'd already peeled my schedule from where it had plastered itself against a trash can with a sticker on it that said THIS IS FOR CANS AND BOTTLES ONLY.

"So, Pierce Oliviera," he said, looking down at my schedule as he handed it back to me. He let out a laugh. "D-Wing, huh?"

I had no idea what he was talking about. I guess he could tell from my expression, since he was only too happy to explain.

"It's cool, don't worry about it," he said. This seemed strange, coming right on the heels of Jade telling me to give myself a break. At least he hadn't told me to relax. I hate it when people tell me to relax. "New Pathways, right?"

I stared at him. How had he known? Was I wearing a sign or something? I'd dressed so carefully that morning. It was my first day in public school, which meant my first day with no uniform . . . my first day of school wearing *whatever I wanted*. What had I done wrong?

"Everyone in D-Wing is in New Pathways," he explained. "Not that that's a bad thing. New Pathways is great. I've had a lot of friends go through New Pathways. It's a great program. Really grea —"

I leaned over and took the schedule from him, then stuffed it back into my bag. He was making me nervous. The more attractive people were, the more nervous I tended to get around them.

Maybe that was because attractive people also tended to be so engaged, and engaged people freaked me out. How did they keep their clothes so neat? This guy's shirt was *so* white. How had he not spilled anything on it by now? That couldn't be right. The only good thing about not having to wear a uniform anymore — that I could tell — was that at least I could wear black shirts, so the stains wouldn't show.

John never wore white. To me, this was a good thing.

Oh, right, I was never thinking about him again.

"I have rage issues," I informed the guy. Everyone was going to figure it out sometime. Might as well get it out in the open.

"Hey, it's not the worst thing," he said, showing me all those dazzling teeth. "I mean, you're still Pierce Oliviera. That's good, right?"

"Yeah," I said, smiling because he had. Jade had told me when I wasn't sure about how to react to something, I should just mimic the behaviors of the people I saw around me. "I guess."

You're still Pierce Oliviera? What did that even mean? Had that been a smirky "You're related to Zack Oliviera" smile?

Or a "Your mom's brother is the guy who went to jail for so long" smile?

Or a "Aren't you the girl who did that thing to that teacher?" smile?

I couldn't tell. Maybe all three. Maybe none of the above. I wish John hadn't thrown my necklace into the night.

No, I didn't. He was a jerk. I was done with him. I was on a New Pathway.

I pointed at the doors to the auditorium. "Are you —"

"Oh, sure, yeah." The guy leaned over and opened the door again. A deafening blast of sound hit us.

"Thanks," I said, and walked away from him.

Shake it off, I told myself. That was what Jade would call a positive interaction. It had been epic.

Except maybe it hadn't been. Because when I saw the guy in the polo shirt for a second time inside, he looked over at me again and smiled. He'd joined up with a few of his buddies. They all smiled at me, too. Two girls with flat-ironed hair (a miracle to achieve in southern Florida) started giving me the evil eye. They were tapping on the keypads of their cell phones with their white nail tips. I was amazed that they could type and glare at someone at the same time. That was taking multitasking to a whole new level.

"D-Wing," one of them sneered at me. Like this was some huge insult.

What was everyone's obsession with D-Wing around here?

Hoping I wasn't about to have a full-blown panic attack — the throbbing at the back of my neck was stronger than ever — I looked around the auditorium, unable to find Alex anywhere. I did, however, see a girl I recognized from my econ class. She'd been in the New Pathways office last week, having her own orientation sessions with a different counselor. I remembered her because . . . well, she was a little difficult to forget. Also, I'd noticed whenever she'd been around, my necklace turned purple. I didn't know what it meant, but she was sitting on the end of an aisle, and there were tons of empty seats around her.

"Is this seat taken?" I went over to her and asked.

She ignored me. It took me a second or two to realize that she wasn't snubbing me. She was wearing earbuds. I hadn't been able to tell because her giant aurora of dark curly hair, shot here and there with streaks of bright purple, hid them.

She looked up from the screen of her cell phone when I tapped her on the shoulder, then said, "Oh, sorry," and moved her legs for me to get by.

"Thanks," I said, and collapsed into the seat next to hers.

I should have known, of course, that it was going to go like this. Not just after last night — I still wasn't a hundred percent sure any of that had happened, even after Alex's story about the poinciana blossoms. The storm had swept most of them away by the time I got up — but after getting to school and seeing that I was one of the only girls wearing a skirt that wasn't a mini. Mine, in accordance with the IHHS student handbook, which Mom and I had pored over, especially the section marked *Student Dress Code*, was exactly no more than four inches above my knee, just like the handbook specified.

How was I supposed to know that the dress code was in no way enforced — particularly the ban on "bare midriffs and low-riding or sagging pants or slacks" — when I hadn't met any people my own age from Isla Huesos until today? What time I hadn't spent biking around the cemetery in the past week before school started, hoping to catch a glimpse of John, I'd spent hanging out on the couch with Alex and his dad in front of the TV at Grandma's.

And Alex, a typical guy, had answered, "I don't know. Clothes," when Mom and I asked him what girls at IHHS wore to school.

The girl next to me — lip *and* eyebrow piercings — turned back to the screen of her phone as soon as I'd sat down. Some people might have thought it impolite to eavesdrop on what she was doing. Not me. True, to an outsider it might have looked like I was snooping . . . maybe because I myself had no cell phone.

But actually, Tim, the head of the New Pathways program, had taken mine away before school. He said I could have it back at the end of the day. He thought that I'd focus better and "interact more" if I couldn't go online.

I didn't bother arguing. I knew from what had happened at my school last year that everything he was saying was true.

I'd told my best friend, Hannah, the day I'd come back after my accident that I'd protect her from the evil.

But I hadn't. Instead, hurt by the fact that she had called me crazy, still numbed by what I'd seen John do in the jeweler's shop, and worried he'd come back someday and do it to me next time, I'd just lain back inside my glass coffin and waited for my handsome prince to come rescue me.

That's how I hadn't noticed the evil. Not the kind people like to pretend is real, the kind they tell ghost stories and make horror movies about.

But the *real* evil that had been roaming the halls of the Westport Academy for Girls, looking for the sweetest, most innocent victim it could find.

By the time I finally realized there *are* no handsome princes — that it was all up to me . . . that it had *always* been up to me — it was too late.

Hannah was dead.

And unlike me, she was never coming back.

Broke the deep lethargy within my head
A heavy thunder, so that I upstarted,
Like to a person who by force is wakened.
DANTE ALIGHIERI, *Inferno*, Canto IV

In a way, I'm grateful to Mr. Mueller, who started teaching at the Westport Academy for Girls last year, when I was a junior. He gave me the one thing I was beginning to think I'd never have: that interest outside of academics in which to "engage" that Mrs. Keeler recommended my parents find for me after the accident.

Mr. Mueller skyrocketed to instant popularity with both the student body and their parents at the Westport Academy for Girls after being hired as the new basketball coach and taking the team to the state finals.

As if that were not enough, he also began offering free private tutoring sessions after school for his "special" students . . . even those of us who, like me, had been moved to all "alternative" classes, thanks to what had finally been diagnosed as attention deficit hyperactivity disorder, predominantly inattentiveness.

Of course, being the only young, good-looking male instructor at a K–12 girls' school — not to mention an athletic coach — Mr. Mueller probably would have been popular anyway.

But the free tutoring helped.

I seemed to be the only person in the entire school who was suspicious of Mr. Mueller and his motives right from the start. Maybe it was because one of my dad's favorite expressions was "There's no such thing as a free lunch." No one is *that* self-sacrificing, especially when all he's getting out of it is homemade cookies from his students' grateful moms.

It was only when a crumb from one of those cookies fell onto my bare knee as Mr. Mueller was bent over my desk, helping me with a particularly difficult algebra problem during class one day, that I first noticed anything strange about him, aside from his stunningly good looks and apparent overabundance of free time.

"Oops," Mr. Mueller said, pressing the crumb into my knee with his finger. He then lifted his finger to his mouth and sucked the piece of cookie off it. Then he smiled down at me. "Sorry about that!"

Maybe a girl who hadn't died and then ended up getting followed around by a disturbingly large, silver-eyed guy who'd once tried to force her to live with him might have said to herself only *Huh. That guy must really like cookies.*

I, however, felt as if I'd been given an electric shock.

And not in a romantic *Oh, he touched me!* kind of way. Other girls in my class might have been sighing over him, but I definitely did not like Mr. Mueller, nor did I want him touching me.

I did not even want him touching cookie crumbs that might have fallen upon me.

It wasn't until I got home that afternoon that I saw it.

Mr. Mueller just touched Pierce Oliviera's bare knee, then licked his finger. HOT!!!!!!

This was followed by tons of comments on the various social networking sites to which this remark was posted, such as *She's so lucky* and *What did she do to deserve THAT?* and *Who the hell is Pierce Oliviera?*

These remarks actually managed to sink through the thick glass of my coffin. They made me feel uncomfortable, not only because they raised old demons (I had been managing successfully to avoid any trips to the guidance office lately), but because then Mr. Mueller asked — in front of *everyone* — a day or two later, if I'd like to start coming in for some private tutoring sessions.

Things only went downhill from there.

Mr. Mueller just asked Pierce Oliviera if she wants private tutoring! She's so lucky! He's SO hot!!!!

"I don't understand," Mom said. "Mr. Mueller told me at his parent-teacher conference with me that he offered to tutor you because you're behind in so many of your classes, and you said no. Why would you do that?"

"I already have tutors," I said. I did, too. Dad made sure I had tutors for nearly every subject. Not that it helped. You had to care for tutors to make a difference.

"But Mr. Mueller seems so nice," Mom would say.

I should have said something then. *Mom,* I should have said. *Mr. Mueller isn't nice.*

The problem was, she wouldn't have believed me. That the guy gave me the creeps wasn't proof of anything.

Especially since Mom wasn't the only one who thought Mr. Mueller was God's gift to the Westport Academy for Girls. *All* the moms were giving their daughters cards and tins of homemade cookies to present to Mr. Mueller to show how much they appreciated him, and basketball season was long over.

Mr. Mueller would always beam with pleasure when he'd find these on his desk, and say chidingly (but really, you could tell he was delighted), "Girls! You didn't have to do this!"

Until my ex–best friend, Hannah Chang — who'd really filled out over the summer that we hadn't been speaking and who'd become the Westport Academy for Girls basketball team's star player and one of the most enthusiastic attendees of Mr. Mueller's private tutoring sessions — left a note on his desk that actually made him frown.

I know because Hannah was in the study hall I had with Mr. Mueller and sat at the desk in front of mine. I'd watched her write the note, then leave it for him. I'd even watched as Mr. Mueller opened it.

He hadn't beamed with pleasure because of it, though.

Not that I'd thought anything of this. Hannah left notes on Mr. Mueller's desk all the time. They were always elaborately folded and decorated with tiny heart stickers. On my birthday, Hannah had even left *me* a note, on special stationery that had horses all over it. I'd found it when I sat down at my desk.

Happy Birthday, Pierce! Hannah had written in her big loopy cursive. She'd drawn a picture of a dancing cupcake with a candle on top. *Have a great one! Love, Hannah.*

Even as cut off as I'd made myself from the rest of the world back then — *What's the point?* was my attitude. *We're all just going to die and then not be let on the boat* — I couldn't help but be a little touched. Hannah might not have treated her horse, Double Dare, as well as I thought she should have.

But Hannah cared about people. And because she cared, she made people care about her.

Hadn't I heard that somewhere before?

Anyway, in spite of her having called me crazy back in the tenth grade, I still liked Hannah Chang.

Which is why I will always blame myself for what happened to her.

I was having breakfast with my mom the morning after I saw Hannah leave the note for Mr. Mueller. Mom, who was reading the local paper, suddenly gave a little cry, then covered her mouth with her hand.

"Mom?" I looked at her curiously over my herbal tea. My neurologist had warned me not to self-medicate with caffeine, because of my bad dreams and insomnia. Mom joked that if my dad ever stopped self-medicating with caffeine, the world would become a much less dangerous place. "What's the matter?"

"Nothing," she said, lowering the paper. Only it wasn't nothing. Because her face was pale.

"Mom," I said. "What is it? Tell me."

"It's just . . ." It was obvious that the last thing in the world she wanted to do was tell me.

It was also obvious that she knew she had to.

"It's just that it says a girl named Hannah Chang died of a drug overdose last night," Mom said, holding up the paper. "But I'm sure it's not the same Hannah Chang —"

I choked on the sip of tea I'd taken. When I was through coughing, I said, "Let me see that."

Local Girl Dies in Apparent Suicide, the article on the front page of our town paper screamed. Hannah's face, smiling in her school uniform, stared up at me.

Mom hadn't seen Hannah in nearly two years, because of my retreating into my glass coffin since the accident. Hannah had changed a lot during that time.

"It's her," I said, my chest constricting. "It's Hannah."

"She can't have done it on purpose," Mom murmured, stroking my hair as I stared down at the photo. "It says it was sleeping pills. Maybe she took one and then was so sleepy she forgot, and accidentally took some more. I'm sure she didn't mean to kill herself."

I was just as sure that she had. Girls like Hannah Chang didn't *accidentally* take too many sleeping pills.

"Thanks, Mom," I said, giving her a quick hug as I stood up. "But I gotta go or I'll be late."

"Pierce," Mom said, looking at me nervously. "Are you all right? It's okay if you want to stay home today. I know you and Hannah haven't been close since . . . well, the accident. But you two were best friends once . . ."

"It's all right," I said automatically. "I'm fine."

I went to the garage to get on my bike to ride to school. Dad had bought me a BMW convertible for my sixteenth birthday, thinking it would be incentive for me to get my act together and pass the driving test to get my license.

But of course it hadn't worked. I'd taken the written exam forty-two times already online. I'd never passed.

Because I wasn't all right. In so many ways.

Hannah's horse stationery and heart stickers and being star of the basketball team and never forgetting a birthday and pretending evil spirits would possess your soul if you didn't hold your breath when you went by the graveyard — all those things had just been window dressing to disguise the fact that underneath, she wasn't all right, either.

But it had been enough to trick me. So much that I'd missed the fact that the whole time she'd been sitting there in front of me, something had been going on in Hannah's life that was so awful, it had made her swallow a handful of pills and turn herself into a sleeping princess. Permanently.

How could I have been *that* disengaged?

By the time I got to school, everyone knew what had happened to Hannah. They were all talking about her as if *they'd* been her best friend once, and *they'd* sat behind her in study hall. Everyone was speculating about why she'd done it. Their whispers sounded like screams to me, because normally I wore earbuds in the hallway to block out all the noise, which only seemed to increase the buzzing I usually felt in my head.

But that day, I took them out. I had to listen, I told myself. I owed at least that much to Hannah. I had to find out what had happened to her.

All I heard, however, was people asking exactly the same question I was asking myself: How could a girl who seemed as sweet and as happy as Hannah Chang have gone home from school the day before and overdosed?

Where was she now? I wondered. Was she all right? Was she one of the lucky ones who'd been able to get on the right boat, the one that took people to a better place? Or was she still standing, cold and damp, in that other line, waiting for that other boat, on that awful beach?

I didn't know. I realized I might never know.

But there was something I *could* find out:

Why.

That day, for the first time in more than a year, instead of spending my time between classes in the safety of my coffin, ignoring everyone, with my earbuds tucked in, I took them out and joined all the gossipy girls who hung at the vending machines outside the gym.

I put my money in and bought the most caffeinated drink I could find, in spite of my neurologist's warning. I had decided it was time to stop being scared and start being dangerous, like my dad.

I cracked the soda open and downed it while I stood there listening to them speculate about why Hannah had done it.

I drank a second soda more slowly on my way to class — earbuds out — as I tried to remember everything from the last hour I'd seen Hannah alive. Had she seemed upset? Had she seemed sad?

And most important: What had she written on that note to Mr. Mueller, the one she'd left on his desk, the one that had made him frown?

Hearts. I remembered that. The paper she'd used to write the note to Mr. Mueller had been covered with hearts.

And *love*. I thought I'd seen her write the word *love*.

Why. Was that one of the words? *Why* couldn't I have paid more attention to things that actually mattered?

Don't. Had that been one of the words? As in, don't even bother, Pierce. You're as crazy as they all say you are.

When I got to study hall, I could hardly stand to look at her desk, let alone Mr. Mueller's pale, sad face. Trying to engage had left me feeling raw. I hadn't done it in over a year. Now I could see why: Engaging was incredibly taxing. How did people do it all day, every day?

I slid into my seat, careful not to look anywhere but down, in case the sight of Hannah's empty desk unhinged me.

That's how I happened to see a pair of shoes. Mr. Mueller's black loafers, the ones with the tassels on them.

"Pierce," Mr. Mueller said in a low voice. "Can I talk to you? I need to ask you a special favor."

Trying not to think about his shoes — because of course that was a completely ridiculous thing to focus on at a time like this — I lifted my gaze to meet his.

"Yes, Mr. Mueller?" I asked.

"I'm sure you've heard the sad news about Hannah Chang," he said.

"Yes," I said. "I did."

"Well, the administration is really worried about copycat attempts," he said to me in this conversational tone. Like we were the same age. Like we were equals. This was why so many girls adored Mr. Mueller. Because he never "talked down" to us. "Often when one student kills herself, other students get the idea to try it. . . . You've seen how people are putting flowers at her locker."

I'd passed Hannah's locker on my way to class. It was already piled high with bouquets of flowers and cards and stuffed animals. Especially stuffed horses.

"Yes," I said, swallowing hard.

"The school's not planning on doing a memorial service or anything," Mr. Mueller went on. "They've already decided they don't want to glamorize her death. They just want us to proceed like nothing happened."

Like nothing happened. I nodded. I could see that Mr. Mueller had decided not to shave that morning. He was sporting a little goatee. It made him look a bit like that handsome actor who played a doctor on that popular television show. The doctor on that show, I suddenly remembered, also often wore shoes with tassels on them. Why couldn't I stop thinking about tassels?

"So could you do me a favor," he said in his "We're such good friends" voice, "and move up a seat? I can't really leave Hannah's old desk empty like this. It makes it look like we're memorializing her and supporting what she did. And we can't really have that, now, can we?"

I stared at him and the faux goatee he was growing. The next time I went to the city for one of my court-mandated lunches with Dad, I decided, I was going to go through his closet and take every pair of shoes he had with tassels on them and then donate them to the local men's shelter. Even the Pradas. I never wanted to see another pair of men's shoes with tassels on them again.

"Sure, Mr. Mueller," I said, forcing myself to smile. "I'll sit in Hannah's old desk."

Even though she hasn't been dead for twenty-four hours, and it will be like saying she never existed at all.

I got up from my seat and slid into Hannah's. It felt the way I imagined being in someone else's coffin would.

"Thanks," Mr. Mueller said, grinning down at me in a relieved way. "Thanks for being so understanding, Pierce."

It was funny that he said that. Because the moment I slid into Hannah's desk, I *did* understand. I looked down at the diamond nestled inside my blouse and saw that it had turned as black as that time in the jewelry shop.

And suddenly, I remembered the words I'd seen Hannah writing on her note to Mr. Mueller. Just like that.

Maybe it was because I was sitting in her desk. Maybe it was because of all the caffeine. Maybe it was because of the necklace. I don't know.

But suddenly, I understood . . . everything.

Okay, well, maybe not *everything*. But why Mr. Mueller had always repulsed me so much, anyway.

"Of course . . ." I swallowed hard again. "*You* must know why she did it, don't you, Mr. Mueller?"

Mr. Mueller, who'd been on his way back up to his desk, froze. The bell had rung by this time, but everyone was still talking and milling around. No one else heard me, or was even paying attention.

That's the thing, I was starting to notice, now that I'd finally lifted the lid to my coffin and was beginning to look around outside it. People don't really pay attention, do they?

Of course, I was just as guilty of this as everyone else.

"Why she did it?" Mr. Mueller turned around to look at me, his hazel eyes wide. He was smiling, still in a friendly way. "No, I don't. Of course, she was a bit of a . . . troubled girl."

Troubled. *Right.* If he thought Hannah was troubled, he better start running. Now.

Because I was going to make trouble like he'd never imagined in his wildest dreams.

"But she left you a note yesterday," I said, widening my eyes innocently. "I saw it. *I saw you read it.*"

I watched him carefully. Everything depended on how Mr. Mueller would react.

"Oh, that," Mr. Mueller said. He didn't skip a beat. "That was nothing important." He shrugged. "You know Hannah. Always leaving funny notes. I wish I'd known that one was going to be her last. I might have saved it. Instead, I threw it into the recycling bin." He pointed to the blue bin next to his desk. Paper only, the sticker on its side read. I could see from where I sat that the bin was empty. "It's probably on its way to some paper recycling plant in New Jersey by now. Oh, well."

Then he went up to the front of the room to take attendance. When he got to the place where Hannah's name would have been, he skipped right over it, like it had never been there at all.

And no one said a word.

Not even me.

Not then, anyway.

And I, who had my head with horror bound,
Said: "Master, what is this which now I hear?
What folk is this, which seems by pain so vanquished?"
DANTE ALIGHIERI, *Inferno*, Canto III

The girl sitting next to me in the IHHS auditorium was checking the comments on her Facebook page. I saw her flinch, then finally switch off her phone and lean back, muttering something in Spanish. My written Spanish is officially below average, but I know all the swearwords.

"At my old school," I volunteered, even though I knew she hadn't been talking to me, "they wrote that I have a big stick up my butt."

The girl looked at me sharply, as if finally seeing me for the first time. She'd rimmed her expressive dark eyes very expertly with black liner and mascara, and stuck a small silver star at the corner of each lid. I remembered that IHHS had cosmetology classes. Maybe she was enrolled in them.

"What?" she said, looking confused.

"Online." I pointed at her phone. "At my old school. They also called me a skank." I didn't mention the other, worse things they'd called me, after what happened with Mr. Mueller.

She frowned. I couldn't tell if this was a bad or good sign.

"Oh, yeah?" she said. "Well, they call me a skank, too. Because of these." She pointed to her breasts. It was hard to deny they were pretty enormous. The black cotton shirt she wore had ruffles all down the front. This might not have been helping the situation.

"Some people are just stupid," I said, my gaze going involuntarily to the two girls with the straight-ironed hair, who were still standing over by the steps to the stage. They were staring in my direction . . . only now they didn't look contemptuous. They looked stunned.

One, noticing that I'd glanced her way, lifted a white-nail-tipped hand, smiled, and waved. At *me*.

For a second I couldn't figure out why. Then I saw the guy in the white polo shirt walking away from them, and all became clear.

"There's no shortage in stupid around here," the girl next to me was saying sarcastically. "Hey, aren't you in my econ class?"

"Yes. I'm Pierce." I carefully avoided saying my last name. I had a feeling that's what the two girls over by the stage had just found out. That's probably what accounted for their sudden attitude adjustment where I was concerned.

It's a small island, Mom had warned me. *And not everyone is going to be as sophisticated as they were back in Westport. People in Isla Huesos might decide they like you for who Dad is. Or not, considering. It all depends. Just be careful.*

"Kayla Rivera," the girl next to me said, indicating herself. "You're Alex Cabrero's cousin."

It was a statement of fact. So either Alex had been talking about me, or Kayla remembered my name from somewhere else. Had Tim or Jade been urging all the other New Pathways kids to be nice to me? That was the most charitable spin I could put on it. How pathetic, if it were true.

Well, at least she didn't seem to know who my father was. I really hoped when I got my phone back, I wouldn't find all sorts of stuff about me online. I didn't have a Facebook or Twitter page or blog or anything like that. I had enough people following me in real life. Although I guess not anymore.

"Yeah," I said. "Listen. Can I ask you something?"

"Oh, they're real," Kayla said, indicating her breasts. "My mom's insurance covers breast reduction surgery, and I'm getting it, as soon as I turn eighteen. Not for cosmetic reasons, either. I don't care what kind of names they call me. It's just that I'm sick of my knees hitting my nipples whenever I try to pedal a bike. Plus, my back hurts. I'd get it done now, but the doctor says I could still be growing. Can you believe that? These things *could still be growing.*"

"Wow," I said. And I thought *I* had problems. "But not about that, actually. What does it mean when people call you D-Wing?"

Before she could reply, there was a thump on the back of our seats, like someone was kicking them. I spun around fast, sure it was *him.*

But of course it wasn't. It was only my cousin Alex, clambering into the row behind ours.

"Hey," he said to me. "There you are. I was looking all over for you at lunch. Why aren't you answering your phone?"

"Tim took it," I said. "He said I would engage better without it."

Kayla laughed. "Oh, man," she said. "You really *are* new. I can't believe you fell for that one. You never surrender the phone, chickie, no matter what Tim says. *Never.*"

I shrugged. "No one ever calls me, anyway."

This was sad but true. Did John even have a cell phone? Doubtful. How would he pay his bill? In gray diamonds? That would probably go over well with the phone company.

Alex climbed into the seat beside me, then sank into it.

"Thanks," he said. "I guess I don't count as anyone."

"You know what I mean," I said.

He shoved me companionably in the shoulder in response.

"Simmer down, people."

That's what the man — the school principal — said in a tired voice when he climbed up onto the stage and stood there behind the podium, waiting for everyone to take their seats. As he flipped through a bunch of note cards he'd brought with him, checking to make sure they were in order, I heard Alex heave a sigh. I didn't blame him. I looked around, already bored. I needed another soda. I'd only had six since breakfast. This guy had better make his speech snappy.

"So," Alex said to me, "how's your first day been so far?"

"So far?" I shrugged. The girls who'd sneered "D-Wing" to me, I saw, had found seats . . . on either side of the guy in the white polo shirt, who'd held the door open for me. Interesting. "Fine."

"Wow," Alex said. "You lie almost as convincingly as my dad. Really. I'm inspired."

"This place sucks," Kayla said, squirming. "I know the Florida State Department of Education is, like, out of money. But I think there are bedbugs in my seat."

"People." Principal Alvarez's voice boomed into the microphone. "As long as this juvenile behavior continues —"

Someone yelled something unflattering about Principal Alvarez's parentage and then suggested he go do something incestuous with his mother.

That's when the doors to the auditorium were thrown open, and police officers in short-sleeve uniforms — out of deference to the heat — appeared at every exit. They walked into the auditorium and leaned against the walls.

I eyed them nervously. I'd been hoping for something a little more interesting than your typical run-of-the-mill keep-off-drugs convocation.

But having spent a considerable amount of time in the company of the police only a few short months ago — even though I hadn't been the one who'd actually done anything, just the one who'd taken all the blame for it — this was a little much.

The cops seemed to make everyone, not just me, nervous. The auditorium suddenly got very quiet.

"Mr. Flores," the principal said into the microphone, "you may be surprised to know that I can see you perfectly clearly from up here. And you just earned yourself an OSS for the remark about my mother. That's an Out-of-School Suspension, for those of you unfamiliar with the term. Please remove yourself from the school grounds, Mr. Flores, and don't bother returning until Monday."

Everyone in the audience hooted appreciatively at this as a young man in a black head scarf rose and sauntered — not appearing too concerned about his suspension — from the back row of the auditorium. The police officers observed his exit casually from where they stood.

This was a far cry from the Westport Academy for Girls, where the first assembly was always devoted to a loving tribute in song to the school's founder, Miss Emily Gordon Portsmith.

"Hey."

To my surprise, the guy in the white polo shirt had gotten up from his seat. Now he turned to face the entire auditorium. Without so much as wiping the nervous sweat off his hands onto his khaki shorts (probably because he had no nervous sweat), he said in his easygoing voice, "Welcome back, Wreckers."

To my astonishment, everyone shut up to listen to him. I suppose this might have been because of the cops.

But there was something more going on than that. There was an ease, a confidence with which this guy spoke — and I suppose the boy-band good looks didn't hurt, either — that made people seem to just *want* to shut up and listen.

"I know it's been a long summer," he said, looking serious and yet friendly and approachable. "And I'm stoked to be back and to see all of you, too. Well, *some* of you. Right, Andre?" His gaze fell on a guy in the crowd, whom he gave a mock frown. Andre pretended to cower in his seat. Everyone laughed.

"But Mr. Alvarez's got the floor right now," the guy in the white shirt went on. "So let's hear what the man has to say. All right? Peace."

He turned and sat back down to thunderous applause. I clapped, too, not even sure why. Except that everyone else was . . . except, I noticed, my cousin Alex.

"Why aren't you clapping?" I leaned over to whisper.

He shrugged. Like his father, Alex wasn't always super communicative.

"Thank you," Principal Alvarez said as the clapping died down. He clearly wanted to seize control of the situation before anyone else could begin yelling about his mother. "Thank you, Mr. Rector, for that. And for all of you freshmen or transfer students who might be new to IHHS and don't know, that was senior class president Seth Rector, who also happens to be this year's varsity quarterback and treasurer of the Isla Huesos High School Spanish Club —"

Rector? I had definitely heard — or at least seen — that name around the island. Only where?

Oh, right. Since the local economy wasn't doing so well — thanks, in no small part, to Dad's company — every other business in Isla Huesos seemed to have a FOR SALE sign in the window. Rector Realty seemed to be everywhere. Could that be any relation to Seth Rector?

"I just wanted to say welcome to all of you, new *and* returning students, before I hand the microphone over to someone I think you know well. But first, I'd like to discuss an important safety issue with all of you. And that issue is . . . bonfires."

Principal Alvarez looked down at his note cards. Note cards? Really? Snore.

"Why don't we allow bonfires during IHHS football games anymore? Well, let me tell you. Here on Isla Huesos, the average temperature in September is eighty-seven degrees. At temperatures like that, a bonfire can quickly escalate out of control. . . ."

But it wasn't just on realty signs I'd seen the word *Rector*. It had been written somewhere else. . . .

Now I remembered. It had been carved into the high-gloss marble of one of the mausoleums Mom and I had gone past in the cemetery during the bike tour of the island she'd given me.

Unlike all the rest of the crypts in the vicinity, the Rector mausoleum was on its own plot, cordoned off by a little chain fence, and was two stories, with shiny brass nameplates. This family had really gone all out for their dearly departed.

"Someone's got money to burn," I'd remarked, idly wondering why my necklace, tucked inside the front of the V-neck tee I was wearing at the time, had turned such a deep, stormy gray.

"Yes," Mom had replied in a funny voice. "They do."

"What's the matter, Mom?" When I'd looked up from my necklace and over at her, I saw she'd gone as white as the sundress she was wearing. "Do you know these people or something?"

"I used to," she'd said in a distant voice. "A long time ago."

Then she'd seemed to shake herself, put her foot back on the pedal, and smiled at me. "Look at us, spending all this time in a cemetery on such a beautiful day. Let's go get some lemonade."

"And that's why this year," Principal Alvarez droned on, "we'll be taking proactive measures to curb such activity. You should be aware that the Isla Huesos police officers, along with members of Isla Huesos High's nationally recognized, award-winning innovative social services program, New Pathways, will be out in force the coming days — *and* nights — and they plan to be especially vigilant this year —"

That's when the booing erupted. I was so startled by it, still thinking back to that day with Mom in the cemetery, I nearly jumped out of my seat. I had no idea what was going on, really. How had we gone from bonfires to the police — and, for some reason, my New Pathways counselors — being out in force to curb such activity?

But I had never seen such hostility from a crowd. Nothing like this had ever happened at my old school . . . unless you count the scandal that erupted the time I tried to prove my ex–best friend killed herself over an affair with her basketball coach.

"We just don't want to see people get hurt!" Principal Alvarez was shouting into the microphone. "You should know that all of this is for *your* protection! Delinquent behavior, vandalism, and arson will not be tolerated this year and will be prosecuted to the fullest extent of the law. And anyone caught will be held accountable both criminally and by the school system. The charges will range from criminal mischief to battery, not to mention expulsion —"

The boos turned to jeers. People also began to hurl insults, and not just about Principal Alvarez's mother. Slurs about his wife began to fly — though not all in English, so I couldn't quite catch the details.

Alex and Kayla, on the other hand, just looked bored. Well, okay: Kayla looked bored. She was checking her Facebook page again.

Alex looked disgusted.

But then, Alex looked disgusted a lot of the time. Who could blame him? Life hadn't dealt my cousin Alex the fairest of hands. Not only did he have to live with Grandma, but his dad had been in jail for most of his life, and Alex would not even speak about his mom's occasional visits from the mainland, except to say there'd be no more of them now that his father was home because Uncle Chris would not tolerate her (she worked somewhere you can look up online, but only if you are over eighteen).

Check yourself before you wreck yourself.

"Furthermore," Principal Alvarez went on, raising his voice as if by increasing the volume, people were going to become more receptive. I could see that his forehead was becoming shiny. It *was* getting a bit hot in the auditorium. Not just temperature-wise.

"You should know we have contacted all the local hardware stores, asking them not to sell large quantities of wood to juveniles *or their parents* for the next week."

Bedlam. I'd never heard such an explosion. People were standing in their seats. You would have thought he'd taken away their off-campus lunch privileges or something.

The cops who'd been leaning against the walls took steps forward, looking alert. The people who'd stood in their seats sat back down. But they still looked upset.

"What," I turned to ask Alex, uncomprehending, "is going *on*? What are they so mad about? Just because they can't make some stupid bonfire?"

"No," Alex said, shaking his head. His smile was bitter. "It's not about *bonfires* at all. That's not what they're making out of the wood."

I shook my head. "What? I don't get it."

"Don't worry. Neither does he," Alex said, tipping his head in the principal's direction. "It's like New Pathways. They're always doing crap like this. But it never changes anything. Most of the time, it just makes everything worse. Like sticking us all in D-Wing."

"Wait," I said, completely confused now. "What does D-Wing have to do with it?"

Alex looked past me. "She wants to know what D-Wing has to do with it," he said to Kayla with a smirk.

"Ai," Kayla said. She clucked and shook her head. "Chickie."

"What?" I asked, thoroughly confused. "What is it? It's just a building."

"She's so cute," Kayla said to him. "Where did you get her?"

"Mainland," Alex said, in a "Don't you feel sorry for her?" voice.

Principal Alvarez held up both his hands. "People! People, listen. . . . Here . . . here's Chief of Police Santos to explain! Chief . . . they're all yours."

And with that, the principal ran off the stage, obviously eager to let someone else take the blame.

The chief of police, however, took his time getting up to the podium. He, unlike the principal, did not have note cards.

He did, however, have his right hand resting on the butt of the pistol he wore at his hip. Whether or not he did this intentionally, I noticed the booing died down immediately.

And no one yelled a word about his wife. In fact, a respectful — or maybe frightened — hush seemed to fall over the auditorium once again.

Chief Santos *did* look a little scary. A big man, he had a gray mustache, thick gray eyebrows to match, and a very deep, slightly sonorous voice. He took his time not only in getting up to the mike but in choosing his words.

"Thank you, Principal Alvarez," the police chief said, not even bothering to glance at the smaller man. His hawklike gaze was on all of us instead. In fact, it seemed to be targeted directly on *me*.

I felt myself sinking a little lower in my seat. I wanted a soda more than ever.

"Let's not play games," the police chief said, sucking a little on his teeth. "You're not children. And you all know why I'm here." You could have heard a dolphin break the water's surface outside.

I hadn't done anything wrong — not at Isla Huesos High School, anyway. But I felt as if I had.

Wait . . . *was* that it? Had he read my file? Did he know what I'd done back at my old school?

That had to be it. He knew.

Except that I hadn't done anything. Sure, I'd *planned* on doing something.

But I hadn't. It had all been John. Nothing had been proven — not in a court of law, anyway. Criminal charges had never even been filed against me, for lack of evidence.

Civil charges? Well, that's another matter.

"We've already begun to see vandalism in a certain area of town, and it's only the first day of school," Chief Santos went on in his deliberate voice.

Wait. *Vandalism?*

I wanted to laugh. What was wrong with me? Aside from the obvious, of course. Why on earth had I thought, even for a second, that this had anything to do with me?

Jade was right: I needed to give myself a break. It *was* just high school, after all.

"And I think you know what area of town I'm talking about," the chief of police went on.

A subtle shift, I saw, had occurred in the attitude of the police officers standing at the exits. They, like their chief, had their hands resting on the butts of their pistols.

They meant business.

"When your principal came to me," Chief of Police Santos said in a tone that was even more carefully controlled than any he'd used so far, "I told him there was nothing in the world that would give me greater pleasure than to come here and speak to all of you. In fact —"

Here, the chief of police leaned forward against the podium

and stuck his index finger towards all of us, beckoning us to come closer, as if he wanted to tell us a secret.

He, unlike Principal Alvarez, was such a compelling speaker, I actually found myself doing so before I realized how stupid this was. What could the police chief of Isla Huesos have to say to me? He didn't even know me.

And if things went the way I hoped, he never would.

"I'd like each and every one of you to go home after this and tell your parents — many of whom also attended this fine institution — that Police Chief Santos came and spoke to you today about an age-old Isla Huesos tradition I'm sure many of them enjoyed when they went to school here. Here's what I want you to say to them: 'Mom. Dad.'"

His voice rose in both pitch and timbre. Now he wasn't whispering anymore. Now his words rumbled through the auditorium, making the walls shake like thunder.

"'Coffin Night is canceled this year.'"

There was an immediate — and undeniably angry — groan, followed by indignant murmurs. People actually seemed upset that they weren't going to be able to celebrate something called Coffin Night.

What kind of crazy place was this anyway?

"People," the police chief went on, holding up his hands for silence. And he got it. "Maybe you should have thought about this *before* some of you broke into the Isla Huesos Cemetery last night and vandalized it. Not only one of the crypts, but the entrance as well."

I stared at him, hardly daring to breathe.

The cemetery.

Oh, God.

And the gate. That mangled, twisted gate.

"The cemetery is *not* your private playground!" The police chief's voice, which had been a pleasantly pitched drawl, now rose to a thunderous roar, startling even Kayla, who lowered her cell phone and stared at him with widened eyes. "It is a resting place for the dead. Those tombs deserve respect. You will *not* desecrate them for your own childish amusement on my watch. . . . *None* of them! *Am I making myself clear?*"

I felt the pain in the back of my neck begin to throb harder than ever.

"Now that I have your full attention," the chief of police said in a quieter voice, "I want you to know that until further notice, the cemetery gates are going to be kept locked twenty-four hours a day — after they've been repaired, of course — just in case any of you aren't taking me seriously about this. And because there might be one or two of you stupid enough to try to scale that fence" — uh-oh — "several of my officers will be patrolling it at night. Since I'm sure this is going to upset those of you who wish to pay your respects to your loved ones who are buried there, feel free to make an appointment with Cemetery Sexton Richard Smith."

Chief of Police Santos indicated an elderly man, elegantly attired in a linen jacket, bright green bow tie, and straw porkpie hat, who was sitting in a folding chair at the bottom of the stairs to the auditorium stage, a briefcase perched on his knees. At the mention of his name, he stood up, tipped his hat at us, then sat down again.

I recognized him at once as the same man who'd yelled at me so many times for using his cemetery as a public thoroughfare.

"Cemetery Sexton Smith will be happy to unlock the gate and escort any of you who wish to pay respects to loved ones directly to their graves, and wait with you there until you're finished," the chief of police explained.

Cemetery Sexton Richard Smith stood up again and called, in a deep voice for such an old man, "During appropriate visiting hours," before sitting down again.

"During appropriate visiting hours, of course," Chief of Police Santos repeated into the mike.

More unhappy muttering from the crowd — with the exception of Alex, who raised a single eyebrow as if he found the whole thing quite interesting. He began tapping a nervous drumbeat along the back of the seat in front of him with a pen, much to the annoyance of the girl sitting there.

"Would you please *quit* it?" the girl suddenly whipped around to ask.

"Sorry," Alex said, and quit drumming.

"Who's up for Gut Busters after this?" Kayla looked up from her phone to ask.

"I've only got five bucks," Alex said.

"Chickie here can pay," Kayla said. "Isn't her dad supposed to be all kinds of rich? You in, chickie?"

"Sure," I said. "Whatever."

I had no idea what I'd just agreed to. All I could think as I sat there — feeling almost as stunned as if I'd just tripped over my scarf and given myself another subdural hematoma — was that somehow, John had done it again:

Left behind substantive proof that he was real, and committed a criminal act while doing so.

A criminal act that the Isla Huesos police — just like the police back in Connecticut, who'd felt they'd had no other choice because how could they blame a six-foot four-inch shadow, who, though he'd shown up on video, had left no footprints or finger-prints? — were going to blame on me.

Could my day possibly get any worse?

But it turned out my day could get worse. *Lots* worse.

Because when I walked into the New Pathways offices after the assembly to get my phone — Alex and Kayla trailing behind me, bickering over why we even had to stop to pick up my phone since I'd said no one ever called me, anyway — who should I find in there chatting up Tim and Jade and the other counselors but my mom?

But that wasn't the worst part. Not by a long shot. Because sitting quietly in one of the purple vinyl chairs in the waiting area, peering down at an outdated copy of *Time* magazine through a pair of gold-rimmed spectacles, was Cemetery Sexton Richard Smith. His straw hat and the briefcase were both sitting on the chair next to him. On top of the briefcase was a necklace.

My necklace.

"This way there never passeth a good soul;
And hence if Charon does complain of thee,
Well mayst thou know now what his speech imports."
DANTE ALIGHIERI, *Inferno*, Canto III

My heart did a double flip inside my chest as soon as I laid eyes on it. I hadn't realized how much I'd been longing for it until I saw it in someone else's possession.

But it wasn't in just anyone else's possession. My necklace was in the hands of the cemetery sexton. What did that even mean?

I was guessing nothing good.

"Oh, hi, honey!" Mom cried. She managed to restrain herself from flinging her arms around me and giving me a big hug in front of everyone.

But you could tell that's what she wanted to do.

"I hope you don't mind my stopping by," she said. "I know you were supposed to give her a lift home, Alex, but I just couldn't wait. I wanted to see for myself how everything went. I swear, I had worse first-day jitters than you kids!"

*No. I don't think you did, Mom. See, you don't know what hap-
pened to me last night in the cemetery. You slept right through the
storm.*

*And you don't have any idea what that old man sitting in that
vinyl chair over there is about to do. Neither do I, actually.*

*But he can't prove anything. Anyone could have a necklace like
that. Well, maybe not anyone. And maybe not* quite *like that . . .*

*But it doesn't matter. So long as he doesn't do anything to make
me mad.*

"Don't worry, Mom," I said to her, going over and giving her a
little half hug. I hoped she wouldn't be able to feel how hard I was
trembling. "Things went great today."

Lie. And they were clearly about to get much, much worse.

"Oh," Mom said, squeezing me back, "I'm so glad. Not that I
expected things to go any other way," she added in a low voice,
"but I couldn't help feeling a little worried when I drove up and
saw all those police cars outside. . . ."

"Oh, that was nothing," I said, careful to keep my gaze averted
from the cemetery sexton.

"Oh, right," Kayla said with a sarcastic laugh. "Nothing. Just
trying to keep the student body from rising up and killing
Principal Alvarez because he canceled Coffin Night. Again. The
usual."

"Coffin Night?" Mom let out a happy bubble of laughter. If
someone had walked in who didn't know better, they might have
mistaken her for a member of the New Pathways staff, not a mom.
She didn't look all that much different from them, except for
not having any tattoos. The main difference was that Mom was

wearing a navy blue polo with the white Isla Huesos Marine Institute insignia on it. The IHMI is where she'd gotten a job down here. By getting a job, I mean it's where she'd donated a big chunk of the money she got from Dad in the divorce settlement.

Given her credentials, I'm sure the IHMI would have hired Mom anyway. But they wouldn't have been able to pay her a salary, since they were so low on funding. Now — thanks to Mom — they had tons. And the spoonbills — whose population really had been decimated, owing in large part to Dad's company — had a fighting chance . . . not just the spoonbills, either, but a lot of other local marine life.

Sometimes it was kind of a relief to know that not all of my parents' marital problems stemmed from my accident alone.

"Don't tell me Isla Huesos High still has a Coffin Night," Mom was saying, excited as a kid, shaking hands with Kayla, who'd introduced herself. Kayla apparently loved introducing herself to people. I wasn't sure why she was in New Pathways, but shyness was not one of her issues.

"Well, let's just say the administration is doing everything in its power to see to it that it doesn't," Tim said. "But old habits die hard."

I was having a difficult time following the conversation while also keeping an eye on Cemetery Sexton Smith. Did he recognize me from all those times he'd asked me to get off my bike and *show some respect for the deceased*? Surely not.

And even if he did, so what? He didn't know that was *my* necklace or that I'd been in the graveyard last night or that I had anything to do with what had happened to the gate.

Except, of course, there was that clump of hair — the strands I'd pulled from my head while dramatically removing the necklace to give it back to John — still attached to the gold chain. I could see the dark brown tangle now against the lighter brown leather of his briefcase.

Could he demand a DNA sample from me? Not without a warrant.

But even if he could, so what? I'd been in the cemetery lots of times — starting as far back as a decade ago. He couldn't prove I'd been in there last night. And I certainly hadn't done anything to the gate! How could I? I'm just a debutante from the Westport Academy for Girls.

Or at least I would have been if I hadn't been kicked out for assault.

"Speaking of old habits dying hard," Tim said. "Congratulations, Pierce. One day down, no ISSes or OSSes. Keep up the good work." He opened a drawer and pulled out my cell phone, presenting it to me with a flourish.

"Thanks," I said, taking it from his outstretched hand. Director of the New Pathways program, Tim was closer to my mom's age than to Jade's, which meant he didn't tend to use words like *epic* or have any noticeable tattoos. Instead, he said things like ISS — In-School Suspension — and OSS — Out-of-School Suspension — and wore a tie.

"So can we go now?" Alex asked so impatiently that Jade, who'd been leaning against her office door with her jar of red licorice whips cradled in her arms, burst out laughing.

"What's the rush, dude?" she asked, tilting the licorice jar in his direction. "Can't wait to get started on all that homework?"

"We're going to the Queen," Kayla explained, digging her hand into the jar after Jade passed it to her, Alex having shaken his head. "And we want to get there before the teeming hordes."

"Oh," Mom said, with a look I recognized. It was the same look she'd worn when Jade had mentioned Coffin Night, whatever that was . . . Mom's look of dewy-eyed nostalgia for happier days gone by. "Do kids still go to that place across from Higgins Beach after school to get ice cream?"

"Yes," Alex said shortly. "Which is why we have to hurry. I need more than just fat-free licorice to satisfy my three-fifteen sugar fix."

Everyone laughed . . . except Cemetery Sexton Smith, who laid down his magazine, then climbed to his feet.

"I wouldn't joke about fixes if I were you, young man," he said to Alex gravely. "Especially considering how much time your father served in jail, and for what."

The laughter stopped as abruptly as if it had just been swept away by one of last night's forty-mile-an-hour winds.

"I beg your pardon," Mom said tensely, turning towards Cemetery Sexton Smith. "I don't believe we've met. I'm Deborah Cabrero, and this is my daughter, Pierce. Alex is my nephew. Christopher Cabrero — his father — is my brother."

"I know," Cemetery Sexton Smith said. He didn't look uncomfortable at all. He looked like standing around in the New Pathways offices in his linen jacket and bow tie, making trouble, was all he had on his agenda for the day.

Which, considering he worked in a cemetery that now kept its (broken) gate locked 24/7, probably *was* all he had on his agenda for the day.

"It's a shame what happened to your brother. Unnecessary, too. I'd hate to see this one go down the same path." Mr. Smith's dark-eyed gaze settled on Alex, who flushed angrily all the way to his jet-black hairline.

But before Alex had time to respond, Mr. Smith turned to look at my mom over the tops of his gold-rimmed spectacles and said, "Things turned out very differently for you than they did for your brother, didn't they, Deborah? I used to play bocce with your father before he passed. He was very proud of you. What a shame you couldn't seem to visit more often while he was still alive." I didn't miss the reproach in his tone and didn't see how Mom could, either . . . but you never knew with her. A lot of times, her head was off with the spoonbills. "But you're back in Isla Huesos for the time being, I see. I hope you'll be able to show a little more support for Christopher now than you did back then."

Mom's eyes were as wide as quarters. I was pretty sure this time, her head wasn't off with the spoonbills. She'd registered the rebuke about failing to visit Grandpa before he died. *And* the one about failing to support Uncle Chris . . . whatever it had meant.

Even before I looked down, the back of my neck had already begun to throb.

But once I glanced at the cemetery sexton's shoes, I knew it was all over.

Tassels.

"I'm not sure I really understand what you're referring to, Mr. Smith," Mom was saying in a tightly restrained voice. "But thank you for the concern. My brother has been doing very well since his release —"

"Has he?" Cemetery Sexton Smith asked, sounding genuinely pleased to hear it. "Well, that's good. He was quite a popular boy, if I remember, back in high school. He must have nonstop visitors —"

What? That couldn't be right. No one at all had stopped by to see Uncle Chris, at least the times I'd been over at Grandma's for dinner or to hang out with Alex or just to sit on the couch and watch the Weather Channel in silence with his dad. That channel wasn't bad, actually. It had a lot of shows about people almost getting sucked up into tornadoes.

"You two," Grandma would always declare when she'd come in after a long day from Knuts for Knitting. "Like peas in a pod! How can you drink that stuff? It rots your brain, you know. Pierce, does your doctor know how many sodas you drink a day? I don't care if it's diet. I thought you weren't supposed to be having caffeine. That's what your mom says. You get more like your father every day. Christopher, would you kindly stop encouraging her?"

Check yourself before you wreck yourself.

But what the cemetery sexton was saying was undoubtedly true. Uncle Chris, like my mom, *had* apparently been quite popular in high school. When we'd walked into the main building of IHHS — what was now called A-Wing — to deliver my transcripts from Westport Academy and sign me up for my classes this year, Alex had pointed out the trophy case. Uncle Chris's name had been all over it. Mom's, too, for stuff like tennis and swimming. Grandpa had been there for track, and Grandma for being homecoming queen.

The Cabrero family had been all over A-Wing.

All except Alex. And me, of course.

My mom was standing in the New Pathways office in D-Wing, biting her lower lip while staring at the floor . . . though not in the direction of the tassels on Mr. Smith's shoes. Which I couldn't understand. How could she not see them? How could anyone look at anything else? They were *so ugly*.

I glanced at the necklace. I wasn't even wearing it, and it was starting to turn the color of a bruise.

I needed to get out of there, I realized, before something terrible happened.

"Well," Tim was saying in an aggressively cheerful voice, breaking the sudden silence. "Alexander is enrolled in our New Pathways program, and he's doing great. He's a super kid."

"I'm so very pleased to hear that." Richard Smith eyed Alex over the lenses of his gold-rimmed glasses. But while his mouth might have been saying the word *pleased*, his gaze didn't seem it. "I stopped by because I had something of a great deal of importance I wanted to discuss."

He turned away to lean down towards his briefcase, on which my necklace was carefully balanced.

Oh, no. He knew. I don't know how, but he knew. He knew it had been me in the cemetery last night, with the gate. Even though it hadn't. Well, not completely.

He lifted the now purple-gray stone.

I heard my mom catch her breath. She'd recognized it. Of course she had. She'd seen me wearing it a thousand times, throughout the mess following my accident and the divorce, and every day afterwards, though she never asked again where it came from. She seemed to think it was just a piece of costume jewelry to which I'd formed some kind of eccentric attachment.

Now, seeing it in someone else's hands, her gaze flew to meet mine, clearly puzzled.

My blood pumping in my ears, I silently willed her not to say anything. The walls of the New Pathways office had suddenly turned so red, it was as if poinciana blossoms were sprouting from them.

Don't say it, I thought. I wasn't sure if I was saying it to myself or to Mom or to Richard Smith. *Please don't say it. Something terrible is going to happen if you say anything. . . .*

Then the cemetery sexton laid my necklace aside, opened his briefcase, and lifted a stack of papers from inside it.

"I was hoping you all might help me distribute these flyers." He turned around, walked over to us, and handed each of us a pile. "They explain the cemetery's new visitation policy, and I'm quite eager to get them handed out as soon as possible."

Tim, standing next to me, looked down at the pages the cemetery sexton had thrust into his hands. He seemed confused.

He wasn't the only one.

"You could have just given these to the main office," he said. "They usually handle these kinds of things, you know, Richard."

"Oh, yes," Cemetery Sexton Smith said as he bustled around, officiously passing out his piles. "I know. But I've found the staff in D-Wing so much more accommodating."

I stood there staring down at the sheets of paper in my hands. The red that had been oozing down the walls of the New Pathways office was beginning to disappear, my heartbeat — and breathing — to return to normal.

But then I noticed that my flyers were different from everyone else's. On the top page of mine, a note had been scrawled in what appeared to be fountain pen, in flowing cursive.

Make an appointment to see me, the cemetery sexton had written. *You will do this if you don't want trouble.*

Underneath the message, there was a phone number.

Trouble was the *last* thing I wanted.

The problem was, as John had pointed out last night, trouble seemed to follow me no matter where I went.

I stared down at the message, trying to make sense of it — How had he known? How had Richard Smith known it was me? — until I heard a click. When I looked up, the cemetery sexton was just closing his briefcase.

With my necklace locked up inside it.

"Well, good-bye, all," Mr. Smith said, lifting the briefcase and giving us a cheerful wave. "Have a pleasant afternoon."

Then he left the office, whistling a little tune as he walked out — looking me right in the eye as I stared after him through the office's wide glass windows.

It wasn't until later that I realized the song he'd been whistling was "Ring Around the Rosie."

Which doesn't mean anything, really.

Unless you're someone who died once and then came back from the dead. So you've spent a lot of time on the Internet, looking up weird facts about death. Like that some people believe the nursery rhyme "Ring Around the Rosie" is really about the Black Plague, which killed a hundred million people or so during the Middle Ages.

"Huh," Jade said after he was gone. "That is one weird dude." She tilted her candy jar at me. "Licorice?"

I looked down at the red whips. "Uh," I said. "That's okay, but thanks anyway." I'd lost my appetite.

I think Mom must have been feeling the same way. She smiled at me — too brightly — as if to show that everything was fine.

But I could see that she was holding on to the strap of her purse so tightly, her knuckles had gone white. She knew everything was far from fine just as well as I did.

"So!" She looked from Alex to Kayla to me and then back again. "Island Queen! Won't that be fun?"

"Oh, yeah," I said. "It'll be epic."

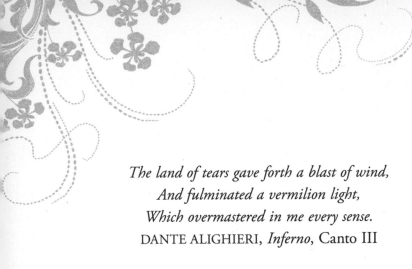

The land of tears gave forth a blast of wind,
And fulminated a vermilion light,
Which overmastered in me every sense.
DANTE ALIGHIERI, *Inferno*, Canto III

I could think of a lot of things I'd rather have been doing than standing in a twenty-person line outside Island Queen — Isla Huesos's down-market version of Dairy Queen — in the burning-hot late afternoon sun.

Sleeping, for one thing. I hadn't gotten a lot of it the night before. And okay, that had been mostly my own fault. But still.

Getting my meeting with Richard Smith over with, for another.

But he hadn't picked up when I'd called him from the girls' room before meeting Alex and Kayla down at the student parking lot — probably because he hadn't gotten home yet. The number he'd left me might not have been a cell. He didn't look like the type who owned a cell phone. Maybe he didn't know what one was.

"Um, hi, uh, Mister Smith," I'd stammered. "This is Pierce Oliviera. We just met in the New Pathways office. You gave me a note asking me to call you?" My palms were still sweating from my encounter with him, even though the school kept the air-conditioning set at what felt like subzero temperatures. "So I'm calling to schedule that appointment you requested," I said.

This was probably the lamest message anyone had ever left in the history of the world. But what was I going to say, *I want the necklace back that I left in the cemetery last night when a crime was committed there*? I wasn't going to leave anything on a recording that might incriminate me. I'd learned that much from what happened back in Westport.

"If you could just call me back," I said, "at your earliest convenience, I'd really appreciate it. The sooner the better, because I'd like to get this resolved today if possible." I left the number, in case he didn't have caller ID, and hung up.

Now there was nothing I could do but kill time until he called back. I'd just have preferred not to have done it standing in a thousand-person line in the broiling-hot sun, waiting to order something called a Gut Burner.

"Buster," Kayla corrected me, when I asked why we couldn't just go someplace else to get them. "Gut Busters. And they only make them here. They're like Blizzards, the ones you can get at Dairy Queen, only better, because they put more stuff in them."

"What kind of stuff?" I asked. I felt testy, and it didn't really have anything to do with the line. What if Mr. Smith asked me straight out where I'd gotten the necklace?

What if? He was *going to* ask me.

"You know," Kayla was saying. "Stuff. I like chocolate chocolate-chip cookie dough. Alex likes Butterfinger bits with M&Ms. What's your stuff of choice, chickie?"

But there was something even worse the cemetery sexton could ask me. And I dreaded having to answer that even more. The memory of how that gate had gotten destroyed — and why — was still too fresh. I wasn't sure I could lie about it yet without giving myself away.

"I'll tell you what you can do," John had said when I asked what more I could do to help him. *"You can leave me alone."*

He'd gone on to say, "I can assure you that you won't have to worry about me showing up and acting like *such a jerk* anymore," just before sending his foot crashing into the Isla Huesos Cemetery gate. The noise had sounded like a sonic boom.

"Chickie. Chickie. *Pierce.*"

I glanced at her. "I'm sorry," I said, blinking. "What?"

Kayla rolled her eyes. "What is *wrong* with your cousin, Alex?"

"She's on medication," Alex muttered. "But she supplements it with high doses of caffeine, even though she's not supposed to."

I glared at him. "Wow," I said. "I can see someone's been listening to Grandma."

He didn't even bother answering. He was looking around at everyone in the line ahead of and behind us, almost as if he were trying to find someone or dreading seeing them. . . .

Only, who?

This wasn't exactly what I'd been expecting when I agreed to come with them to get ice cream after school. I'd just wanted to look like I was normal — like I had friends, like I was one of the crowd — in front of my mother, since that seemed to be the only part of her visit to the New Pathways office that had made her happy, after that whole exchange with the cemetery sexton about Uncle Chris.

What *had* that been about, anyway? I'd never been too clear about what Uncle Chris had gone to prison for. Something about drugs . . . possession with intent to distribute. Nothing violent, anyway. I knew that. I was the only one in the family with that kind of thing on my record. Or at least I would be if Dad's lawyers didn't do what he was paying them to do.

"Have fun," Mom had kept on saying, as she waved good-bye to me back in the New Pathways office.

Please, her eyes seemed to be pleading. *Please, don't mess this up for us, like you did back in Westport.*

So I was trying not to mess this up, like I had back in Westport.

But so far the only fun thing about going to Island Queen was watching my cousin and Kayla fight.

"Well," Kayla was saying to Alex, "it's not like she's Little Miss Innocent."

"Kayla," Alex said, an edge to his voice.

"What?" she demanded. "It's true, isn't it? Everyone's talking about it. It's on Google if you put her name in there."

"Kayla," Alex said. *"Drop it."*

She shot him another indignant look. "It's all going to come out in group this week anyway, Alex, so she might as well just admit it now."

"Uh," I said. "What are we talking about?"

"You," Kayla said. "Did you, or did you not, kill a teacher at your last school?" Alex buried his face in his hands.

"Wow," I said. "Really? Not."

Kayla looked disappointed. "Oh. Everyone says you killed him."

"Well," I said, "I didn't."

"But you hurt him real bad," Kayla said. "Right?"

Before I could reply, one of the girls who'd been giving me dirty looks in the auditorium — I recognized her by her incredibly straight hair — walked by.

"Oh, my God," she said, stopping and coming over to me. "Wait. You're Pierce Oliviera, right?"

I had never seen this girl before in my life except when she'd snubbed me, then had an apparent change of heart, back in the auditorium.

But she came over with a smile as big as if we were long-lost BFFs.

"Uh," I said. "Yes?"

"Oh, my God," she cried again. She actually gave a little jump into the air. "I've been wanting to meet you! I'm Farah. Farah Endicott? Seth Rector's girlfriend. Seth told me he met you today and that you were so cool."

At first I had no idea what she was talking about. Then I remembered the guy who'd helped rescue my runaway class schedule and who'd later calmed everyone down at the assembly. Seth Rector, of Rector Realty. And probably the Rector mausoleum in the cemetery.

Well, one day. He obviously wasn't of it now.

"Oh," I said, not really sure how else to respond. "Hi."

"What are you doing, standing way back here?" Farah asked, looking appalled. Her voice was so loud, everyone in line had stopped looking at me — the girl who'd allegedly killed a teacher at her last school, at least according to Kayla — and was staring at her instead. "This is, like, insane."

"Uh," I said, glancing at Alex and Kayla, whom I couldn't help noticing Farah had completely ignored.

But that seemed to be okay, because they were ignoring her back. Alex was staring stonily out at the water. The beach was only about a hundred yards away, across the parking lot and beyond the three-foot seawall. And Kayla had gotten her cell phone out and was checking her text messages.

"I guess we just got here a little late," I said. "We had to make a stop after school, on our way here."

I didn't mention that the stop had been to the New Pathways office to pick up my cell phone, which I was not allowed to carry in school, due in part to my neurobehavioral developmental disorder.

"Well, come sit with us," Farah said with a great big smile, reaching out and grabbing not my arm but Kayla's . . . a gesture that seemed to surprise not only me but Kayla as well. I saw her tense up and then exchange a quick, astonished glance with my cousin Alex. "We've got tables over on the beach — with umbrellas, so they're in the shade. And Seth is almost to the front of the line. Just tell me what you want, and I'll go add it to our order.

Then we can all go sit out by the water. It's sooooo much nicer over there, you can't even believe it."

"No," Kayla said quickly. "That's okay, Farah. But thanks."

"Yeah," Alex said. "Thanks, but we're good."

I looked from Alex to Kayla and then back again. Something weird was going on.

True, the only thing in the world I wanted to do at that moment was get my stupid Stomach Buster or whatever it was, eat it, then go home and wait for Mr. Smith to call so I could find out what he wanted.

I wasn't exactly looking forward to being accused of yet another crime I did not, in fact, commit.

But since it was going to happen anyway, I wanted to get as much of my waiting over with in air-conditioning, or at least shade.

Even if Kayla and Alex didn't have the exact same problems as mine, it still seemed a bit strange that they preferred standing there sweating for another hour to accepting Farah's invitation.

"But we have a great table," Farah said, looking downcast. Her lips — glossed to a cherry red sheen — puckered. She pointed at an assortment of bright blue metal picnic tables out by the beach, all shaded by huge yellow umbrellas. There were only a few seats left at any of them, and apparently these were reserved for us. "You can't feel it here, but there's a totally nice breeze over there. And I swear, if you tell me what you want, I'll make sure Seth orders it for you. What have you got to lose?"

I glanced at Kayla and my cousin. What *did* they have to lose?

Fear. I could see it in Kayla's exotically made-up eyes. For some reason, she was afraid of Farah.

Or at least of someone who might be at Farah's table.

And Alex? Well, from Alex's dark eyes, I could tell nothing.

I knew Alex had an issue with Seth Rector. I knew the diamond from my necklace had turned a stormy gray when I'd stood in front of the Rector mausoleum that day with Mom in the cemetery, just like I knew it had turned purple when I first saw Kayla in the New Pathways offices.

I didn't know why these things were happening.

And the truth was, I was keeping a few secrets of my own. So who was I to judge Alex or Kayla?

But I also knew, standing in the parking lot of Island Queen after the night I'd had — after the *day* I'd had — I just couldn't do it anymore. The whole point was that I was making a new start: I wasn't going to be the girl who just watched while the people around me got hurt.

So whatever issues Alex and Kayla had with Seth and Farah — or whoever was sitting at her table out there on the beach — I was going to get to the bottom of them. This time, I was going to protect my friends from the evil.

And the only way I knew how to do that was to find out what that evil was.

"I'll have a Coke float," I turned and said to Farah. "That's a large Coke with a scoop of vanilla ice cream in it. And use this" — I thrust a twenty-dollar bill into her white-nail-tipped hand, then jerked my head back towards Alex and Kayla — "to get them one chocolate chocolate-chip cookie dough Gut Buster and one vanilla Butterfinger bits and M&Ms Gut Buster."

Farah's glossy, puckered mouth broke out into a wide smile, revealing a set of perfectly straight white teeth. They were amazing, just like her boyfriend's.

"Fantastic," she said. "I'll meet you guys over at the table."

I noticed that most of the guys around us in line seemed to enjoy the way Farah sashayed — not walked — away, the pleats of her dark green plaid mini swaying behind her (they were definitely more than four inches above her knees).

Most of the guys except my cousin Alex, that is.

"You shouldn't have done that," he spun around to say to me.

"It's okay," I said, shouldering my bag. It was heavy because I'd filled it with all the books I'd need if I were going to do my homework. I don't know why I hadn't left it in the car. I never think things through. Obviously. There was no way I was going to be doing any homework. "You can pay me back la —"

"You think by buying me a Gut Buster," Alex said, his anger hurtling down on me like one of John's thunderclaps, "I'm going to go over and sit with those A-Wingers, and we're all going to learn, despite our apparent outward differences like that they all wear designer labels and drive brand-new cars their daddies bought them for their birthdays, and I wear clothes from the Salvation Army and drive a rusted old junk heap, that we have something in common? Like maybe we can all sing and dance, and then we're each going to get parts starring in Isla Huesos High School's musical, like this is some kind of damned Disney movie? Well, I've got news for you, Pierce. That's not going to happen. And no matter what Grandma says, you're nothing like your dad. You can't just throw money at the problem to make it go away. In fact, you know what you can do with your money, Pierce? You can stick it up your —"

"Whoa," Kayla interrupted, trying to keep the peace. "What is this? I thought we were just here to get ice cream."

"Thank you," I said to her gratefully. I'd never seen Alex so mad.

"Don't thank me yet," Kayla said. "Who orders a Coke float instead of a Gut Buster? That is just crazy."

"Oh." Mom had told me to be careful about inadvertently insulting the locals. I tried to think what Jade would do in my situation. "At least I didn't ask for a *Diet* Coke," I pointed out.

Kayla looked at me and shook her head slowly. "Are you sure she didn't kill that teacher?" This was directed towards Alex.

"It's not a joke," he said. But he wasn't looking at Kayla. He was looking at me. And he wasn't talking about what I'd ordered, either. "Some of us actually live here, you know."

It was what he'd said about the tourists on the way to school that morning.

And it hurt — exactly as he'd intended it to — because I knew it meant that's how he thought of me . . . and Mom, too, probably. Like we were just passing through and didn't care about the locals and their problems.

And it wasn't even like we didn't deserve it. Where had we been the whole time he'd been growing up without a mom *or* a dad, just crazy Grandma?

Of course we seemed like tourists to him. Even Richard Smith, the cemetery sexton, had pointed it out. Mom had never come back to Isla Huesos after I'd been born and Uncle Chris got arrested. I'd never met my grandfather. Not until his funeral. Where I'd met John.

Who, like Alex, just wanted me to leave him alone.

"I'm sorry," I said to Alex, meaning it. "I know they only invited us because they want to play Check Out the New Girl. But who cares? They've got seats in the shade, and we won't have to wait in this line anymore —"

"Maybe *you* want to go sit in the shade with them," Alex said, practically seething with rage. "But the whole world doesn't revolve around you, Pierce. Some of us might have issues with them. *Real* issues. Did you ever think of that?"

"What issues?" I asked. Now we were finally making progress. I'd been wondering this all afternoon. "What did Seth Rector ever do to you, Alex?"

"Just stay out of it, Pierce," he said, scowling. "You don't know what you're getting yourself into, believe me."

"Hey, you guys!" Farah, holding a tray loaded down with tall cups, waved to us from up near the front of the line. "You coming?"

"Uh," I said, waving back. "Yeah! Hold on."

I turned back towards Alex. "I don't know what I'm getting myself into?" I asked him. "Are you kidding me? Do I have to remind you that I died? So whatever's going on with you and Seth Rector, I highly doubt it's worse than that."

Kayla's eyes got very large. "She *died*? Alex, you never told me *that*."

Alex continued to glare down at me for a heartbeat or two. For a second, I thought he might actually tell me the truth. I could see his Adam's apple moving up and down. Sweat was glistening all over his forehead and temples. He seemed to *want* to tell me . . . which would be convenient, since once I knew, I could begin to work on solving the problem. *Some* people might not want my help . . .

But disappointingly all he ended up saying was, "Screw it. You want to hang out with your new A-Wing friends, Pierce? Have fun. Have a blast. I'm out of here."

Then he turned around without another word and headed across the parking lot towards his car.

"Crap," Kayla said, watching him go. She turned to look at me. "All my stuff is still in his car. My books and everything."

"It's okay," I said to her. "Go after him."

Kayla hesitated as she looked past me, towards the table of stunningly attractive A-Wingers, all grabbing at the Gut Busters Farah and Seth had brought to them on trays.

"I don't get it," she said.

I raised my eyebrows. "Get what?"

"Why you'd ditch your own cousin to sit with *them*. They're kind of mean to people who aren't . . . like them."

"I'm trying to make a new start," I explained. "And part of it includes not letting bad things happen to people I love."

"Oh," Kayla said. She didn't look as if she understood. But that was okay. No one did, really. "Well, good luck with that."

Then she called, "Alex, wait up," and took off after him.

I sighed.

Then I picked up my heavy bag and started the long hot walk across the beach, towards the picnic tables.

*And after he had laid his hand on mine
With joyful mien, whence I was comforted,
He led me in among the secret things.*
DANTE ALIGHIERI, *Inferno*, Canto III

Why don't you love me anymore?

That's what I finally remembered Hannah had written in the note she'd left Mr. Mueller on the day she died — the note that no longer existed, thanks to Mr. Mueller having destroyed it.

Why don't you love me anymore?

Hannah may have swallowed the pills that killed her.

And I had failed to be there for her, still too confused and traumatized from everything that had happened to me to remember my promise to protect her from it.

But Mr. Mueller?

He was the one who was truly responsible for Hannah's death. I'd known it in my bones, with the same certainty that I'd known Hannah's mom was keeping her daughter's room preserved as a sort of shrine to her, exactly as it had been the day she died, down to the dirty clothes that had been in Hannah's laundry basket, so her parents could lift the lid of the basket and smell their daughter's scent from time to time, and pretend she was still alive.

For weeks after Hannah's death, I thought of nothing else.

How could I have let it happen?

I'm the one who'd told Hannah evil isn't just in our graveyards.

Evil can be anywhere. In our churches. In our own homes.

In our schools.

And though I'd promised her otherwise, I'd done nothing to protect her from it.

When I overheard my dad say the Changs had no chance of winning their lawsuit against the school and getting Mr. Mueller removed from his position because it was just their word against his — all they had by way of evidence were a few of Hannah's diary entries — I knew what I had to do.

And this time, it wasn't to run like a scared little girl the way I had from John — twice.

Of course things went wrong from the start, though. I didn't expect Mr. Mueller to turn out the overhead lights during the private tutoring session I'd finally agreed to. Because he had a headache, he said, from all the anxiety.

Not, of course, that anyone at the Westport Academy for Girls believed he'd been romantically involved with a student who'd killed herself over him. Anyone but me. The Changs' lawsuit had actually made Mr. Mueller more popular. Frantic about his health as the stress from the trial caused him to grow pale beneath his goatee, many of the moms and daughters started leaving him even *more* baked goods. Some of the girls made up a new cheer to show their support of him. The Mueller Shout-Out, they called it. They performed it at every game and school event.

This was not as bad as the names a lot of them started calling Hannah online: *Slut. Liar. Skank.*

So it wasn't bad enough Hannah had to die. They had to kill her memory, too.

The school didn't even put Mr. Mueller on any kind of administrative leave, either. I guess they couldn't or it would be like they were taking sides or something.

It made me see red. Literally. Every day, I walked down the halls of the Westport Academy for Girls, and most of the time all I saw, everywhere I looked: red. Red as those poinciana blossoms. Red as those tassels on my scarf.

Which might be how I realized I was in way over my head even before the lights in Mr. Mueller's classroom went out that afternoon. My heart was pounding so hard in my chest, I could barely speak, and he hadn't laid a finger on me yet. How was the camera I'd hidden in my backpack — the one with the lens pointing out through a hole I'd cut in the front pocket, the way I'd read online to do — supposed to pick up anything in what was basically semidarkness, thanks to the spring thunderstorm that was rolling in outside?

I hadn't even really thought through what was supposed to happen after I filmed him behaving inappropriately with me. I guess I was going to have to say, *Oh, sorry, I just remembered I have another appointment, Mr. Mueller. I have to go now. See ya!*

How else was I going to get out of there without actually having to do — well, *that* — with him?

I couldn't let that happen. I had to stay in control.

Mr. Mueller kept saying we should give each other neck massages. He knew how tense I had to be from all my problems at home, he said, with my mom and dad's divorce (which had been all over the tristate news because of the amount of money involved and who my dad was). Mr. Mueller said he imagined I had to feel as stressed as he was. But that was all right. We were both adults. We might as well admit we were attracted to each other.

I knew then that I wasn't going to be able to go through with it. Not only was the camera probably not even recording anything due to the lack of adequate lighting, so the whole thing was for nothing — because of course I had to have what the Changs didn't have: evidence — but now that I was alone with him, the idea of Mr. Mueller touching any part of me, even just my neck, made me want to vomit.

The worst part of it all was that no one was going to believe me. Why would they?

I guess that's what got me so mad. So mad that a red tinge began to appear at the periphery of my vision.

Oh, *no*.

When you play back the recording of what happened that day in Mr. Mueller's classroom, you can't see anything much at all because of the lighting issue, except for my white school uniform blouse, and the dark blob of Mr. Mueller's arm coming towards me.

On the tape, you can hear his voice assuring me that every-thing's going to be all right. I just need to relax, he says.

I hate it when people tell me I just need to relax.

Had he told Hannah she just needed to relax? I bet he had.

That's when my vision turned magenta.

"There's no accountability anymore, Pierce," Dad always liked to complain during our fancy lunches. "No one holds anyone accountable for what they do. It's always someone else's fault. Usually people just blame the victim."

Slut. Liar. Skank.

Well, I was holding Mr. Mueller accountable for what had happened to Hannah.

It was as Mr. Mueller was telling me to relax, and reaching his hand towards me — I thought to massage my neck, but I soon found out it was for a different reason — that it happened. You can watch it happen on the tape. There's me, leaning up against the edge of his desk, telling myself I could handle the situation if it got out of hand (once, when we were waiting for Dad to come out of a board meeting, his driver, an ex-cop, taught me how to hit someone in self-defense, should the need ever arise), and there Mr. Mueller is, standing in front of me, lifting his arm. His hand is coming towards my face.

The next second, Mr. Mueller is gone.

I don't mean literally gone. I just mean, on the tape, a black shadow appears, blocking the entire lens for a second or two. It's as if a third person had entered the room. Although no one — no matter how much of an expert in digital film analysis, or how much Dad promised to pay them for their testimony — can say for certain, to me this shadow definitely looks like the figure of a man . . . a very tall man with longish dark hair, maybe eighteen or nineteen years old.

For a few seconds, you can't see anything on the tape. The screen is black. You can just hear sounds. There's a brief scuffle, then a sickening crunching sound, some muffled conversation.

A second later, the shadow is gone.

On the film, I'm exactly where I always was, leaning against the desk. Only now, instead of standing in front of me with his hand out, Mr. Mueller is cowering against the chalkboard, cradling his arm against his chest.

And he's screaming.

That's because every bone in his hand has just been broken.

But especially the bones in the finger that he used to press the cookie crumb into the bare skin of my knee. Those, in particular, were pulverized.

The Westport police say "it's unlikely . . . though not impossible" a girl as small as I am could have inflicted that much damage to a full-grown man.

Unfortunately, Mr. Marzjak, the custodian, swears he saw no one else come in or out of the room until the EMTs arrived a few minutes after he himself called them, upon walking in and finding Mr. Mueller writhing around in so much pain. Mr. Marzjak heard all the screaming. He'd been out in the hallway mopping up. In fact, it was Mr. Mueller's awareness of this fact that caused him to try to cover my mouth with his hand in the first place, fearful that I might start screaming and draw the attention of the custodian.

The police didn't believe Mr. Mueller's story about my assaulting him — which he apparently delivered to them in what they describe in their report as "a highly agitated manner."

They so didn't believe it that they searched the entire school as well as its grounds for "a third party" even before they found the digital camera still running inside my backpack and played back the video.

No one else, however, was found. Because of the rainstorm at the time, anyone who might have jumped from Mr. Mueller's classroom on the first floor would have to have left trace evidence. But the mud beneath the classroom's windows was undisturbed.

Of course no such evidence was found. Why would John bother using windows or doors like a normal person? Why would he bother to say hello? Just *poof.* Crunch. Bye.

Except he hadn't even bothered to say good-bye.

Although he did stop to hurl another one of those wild, reproachful looks at me with his silver eyes just before he disappeared.

"Wait" was what I'd said to him after he appeared from out of nowhere, took a single step forward, seized Mr. Mueller's hand from in front of my face, and twisted it with a force that sent the basketball coach falling to his knees in front of me.

It was not so dark in the room that I couldn't see all the color draining from Mr. Mueller's face. I would have thought he'd passed out for a few seconds, if it hadn't been for the bloodcurdling scream he let out. It was only John's grip on him, holding him half suspended in midair, that kept him from sagging to the floor.

"What?" John already had his other fist cocked, ready to pummel Mr. Mueller into oblivion. He didn't look happy to see me.

I couldn't really blame him, under the circumstances. Every time we met, it seemed, it was because I was in some kind of trouble.

John stood there glowering down at me, his chest heaving up and down exactly like that dove I'd found the day we met, his eyes glazed over with the same kind of confusion and pain. I guess throwing yourself around through alternate dimensions isn't easy.

"Don't," I said, flinging my gaze towards Mr. Mueller's pale face. "Please, John. Just don't."

John stared down at me as if he didn't understand a word I was saying.

I wasn't sure I understood, either. I just knew I couldn't watch anyone else — not even someone I hated as much as Mr. Mueller — die.

I reached out and laid my hand on John's fist.

There were so many things I could have said then. So many things I *should* have said.

But only a single word tumbled out . . . the name I hadn't been able to get out of my head for weeks. The reason I was there, the reason all three of us were there.

"Hannah," I said. There was a world of hurt in those two syllables.

I couldn't bear the thought that she might still be by the side of that lake, waiting in the cold for that boat — that *other* boat. Ever since I'd heard about her death, it had been all I could think about — besides proving Mr. Mueller had been having an affair with her. I had to know if she was all right.

And I knew John would tell me the truth.

As soon as I touched him, I saw some of the wildness leave his expression. His gaze softened, and he seemed to catch his breath. He even shook his head, as if in bemusement, like *Really? That's what this was all about?*

"She's with people who love her," he said.

My shoulders sagged with relief. That's all I'd wanted to hear.

John glanced down at Mr. Mueller, who was still moaning and screaming, then looked back at me.

"Are you —"

He broke off, because the door to the classroom was opening. Mr. Marzjak was coming in, having heard Mr. Mueller's screams.

That's when John disappeared.

And it all happened so fast, I might have thought I'd imagined it . . . if his image hadn't been caught on tape.

Mr. Mueller denies there was anyone else in the room, of course. He says that I just went completely berserk as we were going over SAT study guide questions and attacked him without provocation.

That's the explanation everybody at the Westport Academy for Girls chose to believe. So instead of Hannah Chang, they all started calling *me* a slut, a liar, and a skank online.

This was fine with me, since Mr. Mueller got put on permanent suspension. "The incident," as they all called it, is still under investigation.

And at least no one's doing the Mueller Shout-Out anymore.

But, as Dad's lawyers point out, Mr. Mueller has plenty of incentive to stick to his story. Even if he never teaches again — and he may not, unless he can do it one-handed — he should be able to get a decent settlement out of the civil suit. After all, he got attacked by Zachary Oliviera's half-crazy daughter (or so he claims). Everyone knows people who've died and come back return . . . well, a little *off*.

Still. While no one can agree what exactly went on *during* "the incident," thanks to the poor lighting and Mr. Mueller's moaning, the recording of everything Mr. Mueller said *before* he started screaming has the DA — not to mention the Changs — intrigued.

And then there's *my* statement.

"Why did Mr. Mueller try to put his hand over my mouth?" I asked the police at the scene. I was shaken — anyone would have been. But I had John's words to comfort me. Hannah was with people who loved her. "If he wasn't doing anything wrong, then why was he so worried I might scream?"

"That's a very good question," they said.

After what happened, Mrs. Keeler gently "suggested" that my parents find an "alternative educational solution" for me, a school better able to handle a student with my "issues."

I burst out laughing when she said that, right there in front of my parents.

Issues. Right.

"It's one thing to protect yourself," Dad yelled at me during our very next lunch. "That, I get. Have I ever told you not to defend yourself? No. But did you have to permanently maim him? I spent all that money on that fancy school for girls —

not to mention all that money for shrinks — and what did it get me?"

I shrugged. "A seven-figure civil suit?"

"I even bought you that damned horse," he yelled, ignoring me, "from the Changs, because you said you wanted it so much. And what did you do? You turned around and donated it to some home for mental cases!"

"It's a school for autistic children, Dad," I said calmly, playing with the straw in my soda. "Double Dare will be part of their equine therapy program. He'll make a lot of kids really happy, and he'll get ridden and petted and fawned over every day. It's a tax write-off for you, and the Changs won't have the financial burden of supporting a horse no one rides anymore."

"Not to mention," Dad roared, loud enough to make all the other businessmen in their three-piece suits turn around and stare, "what happened to all my shoes? All the ones with tassels on them are gone! What am I going to have to lock up next time I see you? If it's not my Japanese throwing stars, it's my shoes. Please tell me. I worry about you sometimes, Pierce, I really do. Do you even fully understand the consequences of your actions?"

"I don't know, Dad," I said to him. The truth was, for the first time in a long time, I felt good. Even being yelled at by my dad over Cobb salads in a fancy restaurant in midtown Manhattan.

Sure, I'd been kicked out of school. I couldn't seem to go more than an hour without craving a caffeinated beverage. And a guy I'd met while I was dead had popped by unexpectedly and caused me to be slapped with a seven-figure civil suit.

But I was feeling positive about the future.

"You can't say nothing good's come out of this," I told him.

"One thing," Dad challenged me, holding up a stubby index finger, "name *one* good thing that's come out of this."

I shrugged. "At least," I said, "I finally found an interest outside of academics in which to engage."

Dad didn't think that was so funny.

I guess he was right about one thing:

Sometimes I don't fully understand the consequences of my actions.

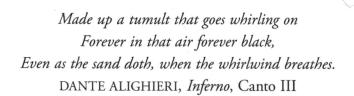

Made up a tumult that goes whirling on
Forever in that air forever black,
Even as the sand doth, when the whirlwind breathes.
DANTE ALIGHIERI, *Inferno*, Canto III

There was no attempt at subtlety.

"Hey, everybody, this is Pierce *Oliviera*," Farah announced meaningfully.

Some guy with a blond crew cut, a complexion the same color pink as an Isla Huesos sunset, and a neck that was as thick as a tractor tire said, looking impressed, "Oh, hey, I heard about you. Isn't your dad that guy that runs that company that keeps the military armed or something? The one who's always yelling on TV?"

"Bryce." Farah rolled her eyes, then smiled at me apologetically. "Please excuse him. He doesn't get off the island much."

"What did I do?" Bryce looked indignant. "I just asked a question. What's wrong with asking if her dad is the guy from TV? He is, isn't he?"

"Yes," I said, taking a seat beside him. "Zack Oliviera is my dad."

That was it. I was *in*.

But not just because of who my father was. There were plenty of other reasons, it turned out.

"Where'd your friends take off to?" Farah asked curiously, looking around for Kayla and Alex.

"Oh, they had to leave," I said airily, hoping if I kept it short and sweet, there'd be fewer questions.

I needn't have bothered. No one cared enough to ask any more about either Kayla or Alex (although Bryce finished off both their Gut Busters, then let out an enormous belch, causing all the girls to squeal in protest and throw their wadded-up straw wrappers at him).

What they wanted to discuss was something else entirely.

"So I've got the four-by-eights," Seth said, smoothing out a sheet of paper he'd pulled from the pocket of his shorts and on which the breeze kept tugging. I squinted down at what the drawing on it depicted, but from where I was sitting, it was impossible to tell what it was. Well, not impossible, exactly.

I just couldn't believe it.

"Where'd you get it?" Bryce demanded. "I thought Alvarez put the hammer down on all wood sales —"

Seth sent him a very sarcastic look. "Dude. Please."

"Oh," Bryce said, burping again. "Right."

"Bryce, really," a girl whose name turned out to be Serena said irritably. "*Must* you?"

"I think I have irritable bowel syndrome," Bryce complained.

"Well, I'm not surprised," she said. "Do you know how many calories are in one of those things? And you just had *three*."

Serena. I made a mental note of the name. When I'd been in the girls' room back at school, making my call to the cemetery sexton, I'd also checked on Kayla's Facebook page. Just out of curiosity.

The person who'd posted the meanest comments on it had called herself SerenaSweetie.

Was this who Kayla was so afraid of, and why she hadn't wanted to accept Farah's invitation?

"I can get access to a circular saw," Seth went on. "It's the assemblage, painting, and storage that's going to be rough. As you probably recall from last year —"

"Right," Farah said, straightening up in her seat. "That's how we caught them. Remember? It was so *obvious*. They were all congregating at Caleb Tarantino's house."

"Oh, right." A girl named Nicole, sitting across from me, brightened. "All the headlights kept waking me up. That's when I called you, remember, Cody? Because they were pulling in and out of his parents' driveway at all hours, and I couldn't sleep, and I was like, 'What's with all the parties at Cal's? And how come we're not invited?'"

"It was a thing of beauty." Cody, another member of the football team — though nowhere near as large as Bryce, and seemingly a bit more cerebral — nodded his head with relish. "They never knew what hit them."

"We were like ninjas," Bryce said. "Ninjas in the night. They learned not to mess with the Rector Wreckers."

Cody and Bryce stood up at the same time, then bumped chests, hard, across the table. Farah and Serena rolled their eyes.

"Yeah," Nicole said, her straw noisily hitting the bottom of her Gut Buster. "Well, I would have appreciated it if you guys had wrecked a little less stuff. Because my house smelled like smoke for months. And construction on the Tarantinos' new garage starts at eight on the dot every morning, and it's *still* going on, and you know how I get if I don't have my full ten hours of beauty sleep."

"So that's what happened to your face," Cody said. "I was wondering."

Everyone snickered as Nicole cried out in feigned outrage, then turned to mock slap him.

I continued to suck on my Coke float. Everyone else might have understood what was going on. But I certainly didn't.

"Okay," Seth said. "So even though we've already established without a modicum of doubt that we're smarter than last year's seniors, and that this year's crop of juniors is nothing but a bunch of sad-ass wusses, we're still going to need to find a secure location."

"Well, guess the cemetery's out," Cody said with a smirk.

Everyone laughed. Everyone but me.

"Obviously," Seth said. "Although don't think I wasn't thinking of that before Santos made his little announcement. Who messed with the gate? Anybody know?"

I froze, the spoonful of what little of my ice cream hadn't melted only halfway to my mouth.

"I heard it was gangs down from Miami," Bryce said.

Everyone scoffed.

"I'm serious," Bryce insisted. "My sister's boyfriend's got a cousin with the Feds, and he says they just made some arrests up in Myrtle Grove. The MGB . . . Murda Grove Boys? Maybe they're using cemeteries as part of their initiation rites. I saw these guys with some *major* rims driving around over by the Wendy's near Searstown Mall last week —"

"Getting back to reality," Seth said, rolling his eyes, "what we need is a place that *isn't* under twenty-four-seven lockdown, but that no one from school can just drive by."

"Like a gated community, you mean," Farah said, sighing wistfully. "If only we knew somebody who lived in Dolphin Key . . ."

I nearly choked on my soda. Was this really happening? Were they actually trying — not very subtly — to get me to let them use *my* house for something that sounded highly illegal and also dangerous?

It seemed likely. Apparently, they didn't think I was very smart. This, I'd ascertained, was because I was in D-Wing. A-Wingers did not hold D-Wingers in high esteem. I'd picked this up through earlier snippets of conversation dropped here and there.

"Yeah, well, what else would you expect? She's so D-Wing," Serena had remarked about another girl, who, it was revealed, had given birth over the summer.

"Well, he obviously should have been put in D-Wing from the start," I heard Cody say about a fellow football player who'd been secreted to "wilderness camp" by his parents due to his out-of-control behavior.

I noticed the warning looks Seth sent across the picnic table and the quickly closed mouths that followed, but it was too late. I got it:

Everyone enrolled in New Pathways was in D-Wing, but not everyone in D-Wing was enrolled in New Pathways. There were only fifty kids in New Pathways. But there were five hundred kids in D-Wing. D-Wing, it turned out, was where the administration sent *all* their "problem" students — all the gangbangers and burnouts, anyone with a drug or disciplinary problem — to keep their bad attitudes from infecting the "normal" kids in the rest of the school.

That was the only reason I could think of, anyway, for why we were all housed in a separate wing from the other students. Even if it seemed almost too weird to be true. Like the fact that these fresh-faced, athletic kids who barely knew me apparently seemed to be asking me to sacrifice my home for their bizarre ritual.

"What," I said, lowering my cup, "are you guys talking about, exactly?"

Farah laughed like I was the most adorable thing she'd ever seen. "Coffin Night, silly!"

"But didn't the chief of police say that Coffin Night was canceled this year?" I asked.

Now everyone at the table started laughing at my ridiculous naïveté.

"The administration cancels it every year," Seth explained patiently, when the laughter died down. "But every year, it happens anyway. It has to. It's Coffin Night. It's tradition."

"Oh," I said, remembering the expression on my mom's face as she'd asked about Coffin Night. It was obviously a big deal around Isla Huesos. "But what *is* the tradition, exactly?"

Cody cough-sneezed the word *D-Wing*, but Seth, after giving him a frown that clearly said *Hey, give the new girl a break*, explained, "Every year, the senior class at Isla Huesos High constructs their own coffin. Then we hide it somewhere on the island. And it's up to the junior class to try to find it."

I waited, expecting to hear more.

But more did not follow. Everyone just looked at me expectantly, as in the background, seagulls swooped around, looking for stray French fries anyone might have dropped. Over on the beach, some shirtless guy tossed a Frisbee to his dog, who missed and then dashed happily out into the water to retrieve it.

"Uh," I said finally. "Okay. But . . . why?"

Seth glanced at everyone else for help. "Why what?" he asked finally.

"Why do they want to find it?" I wasn't trying to be a pain. I honestly didn't get it. "What's inside it?"

Seth smiled as if I'd asked something cute. "What do you mean, what's inside it? Nothing's inside it."

"Well, then why does it matter?" I asked, genuinely bewildered. "Who cares about finding some empty old coffin?"

Seth's smile vanished, and there was some muttering from

down at the other end of the picnic table. I distinctly heard the words *Really?* and *God, she really* is *D-Wing*.

"Hey," Seth said sharply. But to everyone else, not to me. "Cool it." To me, he said, his tone gentle and his perfect smile back in place, "First of all, it's not an *old* coffin. It's a brand-new coffin, like I said, one that we'll be constructing and hand painting, with our class year and all our names on it. Yours, too. And if the juniors find it, they're going to take it out to the middle of the football field during the first game of the season and set it on fire in front of everyone. And film themselves doing it, and then post it online everywhere. Then we'll be totally humiliated. So we don't want that."

I had already put the fire part together, after the incredibly boring speech Principal Alvarez had given, with what Nicole had mentioned about her house smelling of smoke for months after the Rector Wreckers — which I assumed were Seth and his friends — had discovered last year's senior class coffin in her neighbor's garage and apparently had chosen to set it on fire on site.

What I still didn't get was why any of them cared.

"That's why," Farah said, laying a hand on my shoulder, "we were thinking it would be so great if we could hide the coffin at *your* place this year. Just for a little while. Because you live in Dolphin Key. To drive in and out of your neighborhood, people have to have permission from the guard at the front gate, right? You're the only student from IHHS who lives there this year. I know, because my mom's on the booster committee and I checked the database. Dolphin Key's mostly a retirement and snowbird community. It's really exclusive. Most people here on Isla Huesos can't afford to live there. What that means is that no one from IHHS should be able to get in but us, and only when you buzz us in at the gate. You — and the coffin — will be totally safe. What happened at Cal's last year would never happen at your place."

I just stared at her. This was such a joke. None of these people even knew what they were talking about. Safe? I was the least safe person in the world.

Especially right now, with my necklace gone.

Oh, yeah. And the guy who'd given it to me, whom I'd met while I was dead, didn't like me anymore because we were having a huge fight. Or something. Which was fine, because I was making a new start. New Pathways. I needed another soda.

"It's just until we get it painted anyway," Seth added hastily.

"Then we'll move it somewhere else. We can't keep it too long in any one place, in order to avoid detection. After your house, we'll probably move it to an airplane hangar over at the Isla Huesos airport — my dad's got a plane, and those wipes will never make it past FAA security — and then maybe over to the Navy base —"

"My dad's a colonel," Nicole said, batting her eyelashes at me.

"— then maybe up island for a bit," Seth said.

I could see them going on like this all night.

"What happens if they don't find it?" I interrupted. "The juniors, I mean."

"If they don't find it," Serena said, looking at me as if I had asked something extremely stupid, "we bring out the coffin as part of the halftime show during the game and parade it around in front of everyone, while the band and dance team, of which I am captain, perform MC Hammer's 1990 signature hit song, 'U Can't Touch This.'"

"Which you can't. Because the Wreckers rule!" Bryce and Cody did another chest bump.

I stared at them, unable to believe my mom had looked back on Coffin Night with so much sentimentality.

But I tried not to let my true feelings show. I still needed to find out why Alex hated Seth so much. Besides the fact that they all considered everyone in D-Wing such freaks.

Although the term *freak* was subjective. Kind of like *normal* and *crazy*. I, for instance, might consider a freak someone who ran around an island trying to hide a homemade coffin, then paraded it around to a twenty-year-old MC Hammer song during halftime at a sports event.

But that was just me. And it was well known that I was crazy.

And I suspected that when Alex found out Seth Rector wanted to keep the senior class coffin at my house — and he was bound to if I agreed to do it and he noticed so many A-Wingers hanging around my garage — he was probably going to tell me the reason pretty fast.

"I don't know," I said. "I'd have to ask my mom first. You know how it is. . . ."

"Of course," Seth said, his blue-eyed gaze steady. "Totally. We wouldn't want to do anything to upset your mom."

"I'm sure she'll say it's okay," Farah said. "Didn't your mom go to IHHS? I thought I saw her name in the trophy —"

"I have another question," I interrupted. "Why a coffin?"

Farah and Nicole looked at me as if I'd just asked why the sky is blue. "What?"

"Why a coffin?" I asked. "Why build and hide a coffin?"

Now *everyone* was staring. But I didn't see what was so odd about the question.

"Why not a boat?" I persisted. "Aren't we the Isla Huesos High School *Wreckers*? Wreckers are people who used to pillage ships that sank offshore between here and the reef, right? And then they resold whatever they managed to plunder back to the ship's owners, for a profit? So wouldn't it make more sense for us to build and hide a *boat*? Since the school mascot is a pirate-looking guy, not a skeleton?"

In the silence that followed, I could hear the waves as they lapped at the beach behind us. Isla Huesos didn't usually get the kind of big, rolling waves you would typically expect in Florida because the island sat inside a coral reef — the third largest in the world.

But for some reason, I noticed that today, the waves were larger than usual. Maybe they, like me, sensed the unease in the air.

"Hey," Bryce said, raising his eyebrows. "She's right. It *would* make more sense if it was a boat. Why *is* it a coffin?"

"You know what?" Seth lifted his backpack. "I don't know. And I don't care. All I know is that it's always *been* a coffin."

"It's probably for the best," Bryce said thoughtfully. "Because

Boat Night doesn't have the same ring to it as Coffin Night, you know?"

They all laughed.

I didn't know then that I was about to find out why it was a coffin. And if any of them had known what Coffin Night was really about, they definitely wouldn't have been laughing.

The infernal hurricane that never rests
Hurtles the spirits onward in its rapine;
Whirling them round, and smiting, it molests them.
DANTE ALIGHIERI, *Inferno*, Canto V

As I lowered myself out of Seth's black F-150 — a birthday gift from his father, he'd explained casually as he drove me home — I spied Uncle Chris in the driveway, one of our wooden lawn chairs in his arms.

"Who's that?" Farah asked curiously, as she crawled into the front seat I'd just vacated.

"My mom's brother," I said.

Uncle Chris had stopped what he was doing and was just standing there staring at us, his mouth slightly ajar, the big wooden chair in his arms, bright blue and green striped cushions and all.

It's true Seth's truck was quite a sight. No one in my neighborhood back in Connecticut — let alone the Westport Academy for Girls — had driven one quite like it. Seth had jacked up the body so it sat a solid foot or so from the wheels, the rims of which gleamed bright silver. The windows had all been tinted the same color black as the paint job, so you couldn't see who was sitting inside unless the doors were open. Seth had music on — a band that sounded mostly like yelling to me — and the volume was turned up so high, the whole truck seemed to be pulsating.

But I didn't get the feeling that's why Uncle Chris was staring.

"Is that Alex's dad?" Farah asked.

"Yes," I said. Of course she was curious. Who wouldn't be curious about a guy who'd been in jail for nearly the same amount of time she'd been alive? "Thanks for the ride."

"So you have my number," Seth said. "Call me after you find out what your mom says." I guess I must have looked at him a little blankly, since he added, "You know. About the *thing*," throwing me a meaningful look.

"Oh, right," I said, shaking myself. "The *thing*. Sure."

I slammed the door. Intellectually, I knew they'd still be able to see me through the tinted windows.

But psychologically, since I couldn't see them anymore, I felt like they couldn't see me.

And somehow, that felt good.

"Hi, Uncle Chris," I said, walking towards him with my heavy book bag. Behind me, I heard the truck's enormous wheels crunching on some loose bits of gravel in the driveway. The pulse of the music was already getting softer. "What are you doing?"

Alex's dad hadn't moved. He was still watching the truck. "Who was that?" he asked.

"Just some people from school," I said. "They gave me a ride home."

"I thought Alex was going to drive you to and from school," he said.

"Oh, he had some other things to do after school today," I said. It wasn't necessarily a lie. "So I got a ride with some other people. What are you doing with that chair?"

"Moving it into the garage," he said. "They just announced on the Weather Channel that there's a hurricane watch. We're in the cone."

"The what?" I hadn't heard anything about a hurricane. Well, I guess I had, but I hadn't paid any attention because they hadn't said it was coming our way. The sun was going down, but there wasn't a cloud in the sky.

"The cone is what they call the *possible* track of the hurricane, since storms can be very unpredictable," Uncle Chris said. The weather was the interest with which Uncle Chris had chosen to become engaged upon his release from prison. "We'll probably get hit with nothing but feeder bands — those are the thunderstorms that surround the outer eye of a storm. But they really don't know yet with this one. We're in the three-day cone of uncertainty."

I stared at him, shocked that I'd been so wrapped up in my own concerns, I hadn't figured this out for myself, especially considering the waves I'd just seen on the beach, not to mention the violence of last night's storm. Hurricane season lasted from July until November, and it was only September. We were smack in the middle of it.

But in my case, storm season didn't appear to be just literally but figuratively here, too, as I'd realized when I was following Farah and Seth to his truck after we'd finished at Island Queen, and my cell phone had begun to chirp. The number Richard Smith had scrawled on the flyers he'd given me showed up on my screen.

"Hello?" I'd said, answering it with a thumping heart.

"Miss Oliviera?" The gravelly voice sounded familiar.

"Oh, Mr. Smith," I'd said. "Thank you so much for returning my call."

No response.

"Um . . ." Seth and Farah, before climbing into Seth's truck, had decided to have a private moment. Only it wasn't so private, really, since everyone at the Island Queen could see them. They were completely making out against the truck. If this was what I was going to have to look forward to for the next week or so if these people were at my house constantly, building a coffin in my garage, I wasn't sure it was going to be worth it, even for Alex. I, like Uncle Chris, should have chosen the weather as my hobby.

"So, would now be a good time to schedule that appointment you mentioned in your note?" I'd asked.

"Now would be an excellent time," the cemetery sexton had said. "When would you be available, Miss Oliviera?"

"Um," I'd said. I'd glanced back at Seth and Farah. Still kissing. I looked away again. "Now. Now would be very good for me. Would now be convenient for you?"

"Now would *not* be convenient for me," he'd said in his grumpy voice. "But at six o'clock, when my office closes, I should be available. I trust you know where my office is."

"I do," I'd said, ignoring what was obviously a dig at me, since he knew how much time I spent at the cemetery. "I'll be there at six."

"Don't be tardy," he said. "I will leave at six o'clock if you aren't there."

Then he'd hung up on me.

I'd stared down at my phone, my eyes narrowed. *I might look like a honey-eyed schoolgirl on the outside, in my skirt with its regulation four-inch-above-the-knee hem.*

But I'll rip those tassels off your shoes, old man. Just try Googling me.

Okay, well, in my fantasies, that could happen.

"Can't be too careful with these storms," Uncle Chris was going on in my driveway. "Depending on what track they take, they can skirt us or hit us dead-on. Usually nothing to worry about, but we wouldn't want this nice patio furniture to end up in your pool, as much money as your mom spent on it. Seth One."

"Excuse me?" I needed to hustle if I was going to make it to my appointment with Mr. Smith on time. After Island Queen, Seth and Farah had taken me out to Reef Key to give me a tour of their fathers' spec development. I'd had to pretend to find it thrilling, shaking both Mr. Rector's and Mr. Endicott's hands and acting like I cared about the extremely dull things they were saying, which just sounded to me like *blah, blah, blah,* luxury resort atmosphere! *Blah, blah, blah.* Freedom of a private island. *Blah, blah, blah.* Tennis courts! *Blah, blah, blah.* Private seawater swimming lagoons. Along with the eight little words I've gotten used to hearing wherever I go: *Maybe your father would be inter-ested in investing.*

I'd been relieved to escape with my usual "Sure, why don't you give him a call? Here's his card." I always keep one handy now for emergencies. I think Dad likes getting calls from people I give his cards to. He enjoys yelling on the phone as much as he does on TV.

Now Uncle Chris had begun moving towards the open garage door. "Seth One. That's what it said on your friend's license plate."

"Oh," I said. "Yes. His name is Seth. You know, you don't have to do this, Uncle Chris. I think Mom pays for a service to come around and board up whenever there's supposed to be a hurricane —"

"Too early to board up yet. But if you're not using the furni-ture, it never hurts to move it inside. You probably want a truck like that," Uncle Chris said. He stacked the chair on top of several others he'd already placed inside the garage. He didn't appear to be listening to me. "Like Seth One. Don't you?"

"Uh," I said. "No, not really. For one thing, I can't drive. And for another, that kind of thing isn't really my style." That was putting it mildly.

Uncle Chris seemed to look at me — really look at me — for the first time.

"You can't drive?" His expression was perplexed. "Why can't you drive?"

"Well," I said, walking into the garage and setting my book bag down. Why had Alex's dad chosen now, of all times, to suddenly get talkative? "Because I don't really do well on tests, remember?"

I saw his face fill with something I'd never seen in it before: emotion.

"I'll help you pass the test, Piercey," he said.

"Oh," I said, with a laugh. "That's okay, Uncle Chris." He followed as I went back around to the front of the house to unchain my bike. "I'm fine. See? I've got a ride."

"I'll quiz you," he said. "How does that sound? You come over to Grandma's — or if you want, I'll come over here — and I'll quiz you. I'll take you out driving, too, over in the parking lot at Searstown, by the Wendy's. That's where I learned — it wasn't Searstown then, of course, because we didn't have a Sears. But that's all right. I didn't have a chance to teach Alex, but, well, I'll make *sure* you pass the test, Piercey. You just leave it to me."

"That is so sweet of you to offer, Uncle Chris," I said, smiling up at him as I moved my bike away from the porch railing. I wasn't going to have time to change out of my skirt, I realized, which meant I was going to have to ride with one hand holding it to keep it from flying up. But I didn't want to be "tardy." "It's not like other people haven't tried. But I'm pretty horrible at it." I didn't really want to get into the time I'd run into the back of a UPS truck while trying not to hit a squirrel, and how loud my dad had yelled about my destroying the BMW he'd given me. "It's probably better, all things considered, that I don't operate any motor vehicles."

"Don't do that," Uncle Chris said. "Don't ever do that."

I widened my eyes at him. "Excuse me?" I said.

"Don't put yourself down," he said. "I know what happened to you. I heard about it, even though I was away. Your mom kept in touch with me and sent me pictures of you, too. Bet you didn't know that, did you? Well, it's true."

I stared at him. He was right. I hadn't heard this.

"And when I heard about what happened to you — how you weren't doing too good — I told your mom not to worry." He smiled at me, the same sweet smile he always gave me. "'That one's going to be okay,' I told your mom. 'You can see it in her eyes.' Now, Alex? Alex I'm not so sure about. Sad to say about your own son, but . . ." He shrugged. "I worry about him."

I knew exactly what he meant. I worried about Alex, too.

"And it's not just because you're a girl, either, or Deb's daughter." He shook his head. "Deb was never anything like you."

"I know," I said. I tried to keep the bitterness out of my voice. *Check yourself before you wreck yourself.* "They still have all the trophies she won for the school. The trophies *both* of you won. They're on display in A-Wing."

He looked bewildered. "What's A-Wing?"

"It's — never mind." I guess he and Alex really didn't talk much. "They redid the high school since you . . . went away."

"They redid a lot of things since I went away," he said. "But that's not what I meant. Deb's just . . . everything's easy for her. Like winning those trophies. Everyone knew Deb was going to make it off this rock someday. No one thought I would. Except the way I did." He laughed shortly. "Guess it just goes to show, the trophies you win in high school don't necessarily mean much.

So . . ." He looked away, off towards the pinkening clouds of sunset. "Don't ever let them tell you that you're too stupid to do something. I'm not saying it's going to be easy for you, the way it was for your mom. Maybe you're going to have to work for it a little harder than other people, which I know isn't fair. But that doesn't mean you should just give up. Because if you do that, then where will you be?" He looked at me and shrugged.

"Um," I said. "On a bike?"

"Yeah," he said. "On a bike."

Except I was pretty sure the correct answer was *Living with the lady who owns Knuts for Knitting after having just served a sixteen-year prison term.*

Now I was starting to get what Dad meant about Uncle Chris going on a reign of terror and revenge now that he'd gotten out of jail. It was the whole "still waters run deep" thing. There was a lot more going on inside Uncle Chris's head than I'd thought.

"So your mom said for me to tell you she's running late; she had to go back to the office for a meeting," he said.

"Oh," I said. "Actually, I have a meeting, too —"

"Okay," Uncle Chris said. "Well, I'm going to put the furniture in the back away. Unless you need a ride to your meeting or something . . ."

"Oh, no, I'm good, thanks." I steered my bike towards the front gate. Noticing his downcast expression, I added, "But maybe tomorrow you could take me for a driving lesson."

I saw how his face brightened, and I knew I'd said exactly the right thing.

"Great," he said. "It's always so good to see you, Piercey."

If I'd known then how that evening was going to turn out, I might not have just smiled and waved back at him, then opened the gate and ridden off. I might have canceled my meeting with the cemetery sexton and stayed glued by Uncle Chris's side for the rest of the night. To make sure the evil didn't get him. This was supposed to be my new hobby.

But I didn't know then how much the cone of uncertainty had narrowed, or that it was pointing directly at Isla Huesos.

"My son," the courteous Master said to me,
"All those who perish in the wrath of God
Here meet together out of every land."
DANTE ALIGHIERI, *Inferno*, Canto III

The office of the cemetery sexton, as he'd reminded me, closed promptly at six. It was way past that when I tapped on the door.

"You're late," Richard Smith grumbled when he threw it open. "But I wouldn't have expected anything less. Come in."

He stepped aside, allowing me to enter his immaculately neat office. Because the sun had already started sinking past the treetops, he'd turned on a small brass desk lamp, the only thing that seemed in keeping with the historical aspect of the Isla Huesos Cemetery, which a brass plaque by the door outside explained had been established over 150 years earlier, in 1847.

Which I suppose might have surprised most people, considering the fact that the office was housed in a quaint, whitewashed cottage complete with a picket fence, tin roof, front porch, windows with turquoise shutters, and original pine floors.

But inside, it was exactly the way I remembered from ten years earlier, though Richard Smith hadn't been cemetery sexton then: all metal file cabinets and shelves containing badly photocopied applications for internment and construction permits for the sealing and setting of tombs.

That's what cemetery sextons do, though. Supervise the burying of dead people. They're not exactly supposed to be into decorating.

"Well, don't just stand there," Richard Smith said grumpily, closing — and locking — the door behind me. "Sit down."

He indicated one of several faux-leather chairs that sat in front of a large wooden desk. They were a little different from the ones I remembered from my last visit, but not by much. I hadn't gotten to sit in any of them then. Grandma had sent me out before I got a chance. They were comfortable. But I still found myself wanting to fidget.

John had told me not to come back to the cemetery. *It's not safe for you here* had been his exact words. *Not unless you really do want to end up dead. Forever this time.*

Well, I was back in the cemetery. Or at least the office of the cemetery sexton. Was I going to end up dead because of this visit?

I really didn't think that would be fair.

Mr. Smith must have sensed my agitation, since he lowered himself into a creaking office chair behind the desk and got down to business with surprising quickness. Removing my necklace from a top drawer, he laid it upon the dark green desk pad in front of him.

"Recognize this?" he asked, peering at me over the rims of his glasses.

I'd tried to figure out on the ride over how I was going to handle this.

And I'd decided that, as when dealing with the police about Mr. Mueller, denial was probably the safest way to go.

But it was difficult — with the way the dark green leather pad seemed to show off all the necklace's best features, the gleaming gold chain, the stormy gray stone. Did it look paler in the middle than usual, or was this a trick of the light? — not to just grab it and go. What could he do if I did? He couldn't chase me. He was old. Older than the jeweler had been, even. He'd probably have a heart attack on his own, without John's help.

But I couldn't do it. Not to him. I wasn't sure why, exactly. He hadn't been very nice, not to me or to my mom.

Denial. That was the way to go.

"No," I said, tearing my gaze from the necklace and looking him in the eyes. It wasn't the lighting. The stone *did* look white in the middle. Something weird was going on. "I've never seen that before in my life."

"I thought you'd say that," Richard Smith said, smiling. "What's interesting is that I, on the other hand, *have* seen it before."

My heart sank. Oh, great. Not another one. This was exactly what the jeweler had said. How did I get myself into these situations? And with my own two feet? I just seemed to walk — or pedal — into them constantly.

"Never in real life, of course," he went on. "Only in artist renderings. You see, in my spare time, when I'm not in here processing grave site reservation applications or out there trying to keep idiotic teenagers like you from desecrating hundred-year-old tombs, I read. Mostly about death deities . . . those who escort the newly deceased to the afterlife," he added, I suppose because he thought, as one of those "idiotic teenagers," I wouldn't understand the term.

He didn't know, of course, I was an NDE and, as such, highly familiar with all things relating to the dead.

"My partner thinks I'm crazy, too," he said with a shrug. "And I guess I do take my work home with me a bit. But I find our culture's fear of death a bit ridiculous, when death is really only a natural part of the life cycle. I'm not saying life shouldn't be enjoyed to its fullest, because I certainly enjoy mine. But you should see people's reactions at parties when they ask, 'What do you do?' and I tell them. They can't get away from me fast enough."

"Oh?" I said, just to be polite. I knew how the people at the parties must have felt. Also, not to be mean, but I thought his partner might be onto something with the crazy thing. Although I was hardly one to be casting stones.

"So you see," Richard Smith said, "that's why, when I stumbled across this" — he patted the necklace — "in my cemetery this morning, I not only knew exactly what it was, but I also knew it hadn't been dropped by some tourist who just happened to be passing through our little graveyard to take a few pictures on her way back to one of the cruise ships. And when I found these attached to it" — he smoothed across the desk pad some strands of my long, dark hair, which had clearly been gently extracted from the knotted tangle that had been caught in the chain — "I thought, who have I seen in the cemetery lately with hair like this, who might possibly have gotten her hands on such a singular item? It certainly couldn't be that young lady I see in here almost daily, who not only refuses to abide by my simple request not to use the paths as a public thoroughfare but who also habitually wears a long gold chain around her neck. Could it?"

I realized I had underestimated him back in the New Pathways office. The bow tie and tassels were just window dressing.

This guy was good. Really good.

"I've never seen that necklace before in my life," I said. That was my story — for now — and I was sticking to it.

He smiled some more and went on as if I hadn't spoken.

"I thought a young lady who whips through this place with no regard for pedestrians, almost as if she were in training for the Tour de France, might say that the night after a terrible act of vandalism was committed here. So, naturally, I went to the area where the vandalism occurred. And look what I happened to find lying by the gate."

He held up another long, dark hair. First he laid it down alongside the ones he'd extracted from the necklace. "Same color. Same length." Then he held it up in the air and closed one eye, as if measuring it against the hair tumbling from the top of my head down past my shoulders. "A good match, I would say."

There was no way to know, of course, if he'd really found it by the gate. There was no way to tell if any of it was true or if he was just putting all of this on for show, to get me to crack and trick me into admitting I'd been in the cemetery last night.

But suddenly, I felt weak. Like I was going to faint or something.

Please, don't mess this up for us, Mom had asked me. Not in words but with her eyes. I was messing this up. I was messing this up big-time.

Why? I asked myself. Why wasn't I seeing red, when I most needed to? What was wrong with me? This guy wasn't *that* good. He was just what Dad would have called a kook.

Maybe that was why. He *was* just a kook. I didn't get the sense that he wanted to hurt me.

So what *did* he want?

"That . . . doesn't prove anything," I managed to murmur.

"No," he agreed, sweeping all the hair back into his desk drawer and locking it away. Evidence for later, I thought bleakly. "It doesn't. I only mention it because I was so surprised to see you, of all people — Carlos Cabrero's granddaughter — involved with something so . . . messy. I would think you'd want to stay *out* of trouble, at least for your uncle's sake."

Oh, God. Not Uncle Chris. He really *was* good.

"I do," I said, my eyes filling with tears. "I *do* want to stay out of trouble." That's what John had given me the necklace for.

And now look at what had happened. Why had he thrown it away?

It's not safe for you here.

"Well," Richard Smith said, looking a little taken aback, perhaps because of my tears. "You've certainly got an interesting way of showing it. Now, tell me. Who gave you this necklace?"

I looked down at the stone. It wasn't the lighting. It wasn't my imagination. The diamond wasn't gray anymore. It was white. *White.*

The opposite of what it had become outside his office windows, where it was now almost as dark as night. Thunder rumbled. It was distant, but it was there. Maybe it was the feeder bands Uncle Chris had mentioned we were supposed to get. They seemed to have come on awfully quickly, though, considering we were supposed to have been only under a watch.

I shook my head.

"I can't tell you," I said. It was hard to talk with the tears prickling my nose. "I'm sorry. I'd like to. But you seem like a nice man. And . . ." I couldn't help thinking about what had happened to the jeweler. I didn't think John would be coming back — ever. But I didn't know for sure. "I just can't."

Mr. Smith frowned, obviously frustrated with me.

"Miss Oliviera," he said. "Are you aware that this diamond is stolen? Not just stolen but *cursed?*"

I sucked in my breath, but I shouldn't have been surprised. It was so like John to have given me a cursed, stolen diamond.

"It's quite famous, actually, in certain circles," he went on. "Well, mine, anyway. Allegedly, it was mined by Hades, the Greek death deity, to give to Persephone, his consort, in order to protect her from the Furies. . . ."

I felt goose bumps break out all over my entire body. Cemetery Sexton Smith, of course, was seated too far away to notice.

The Furies. John had mentioned them.

"As a death deity, Hades was, of course, disliked by the spirits of a good many souls who weren't satisfied with where they ended up after they passed through the Underworld," Mr. Smith went on, oblivious to my discomfort. "The Furies — this is what the spirits who disliked him so much were called. There's some scholarly dispute over it, of course, but I believe this version. The Furies could be quite tricky in their efforts at retaliation. So Hades needed to make sure his consort had a way to protect herself, or supposedly — Are you all right, Miss Oliviera?"

I thought I was going to throw up my Coke float. I couldn't stop thinking about all those people I'd seen in line for the other boat . . . the one John had told me I didn't want to be on. Had they all turned into Furies?

Something told me they had.

"No," I said. Outside, lightning flashed so abruptly, it made me jump. "I need to go. I'm on my bike, actually. I need to go before it starts raining. So —"

"Don't worry. I'll give you a lift." Mr. Smith reached for a large book that was sitting on a shelf behind him. "Personally, I've never been a fan of the Hades/Persephone myth. So much drama, with him kidnapping the poor girl in that distasteful manner and forcing her to live with him down in the Underworld against her will, and then Persephone's mother having to intervene. . . . I never enjoy stories where the mother gets too involved. Let the kids work it out for themselves, I always say. But I digress. That's what they call this diamond, you know. The Persephone Diamond. Ah, here it is."

He held up the illustration to show me. "Marie Antoinette, in all her glory, wearing your diamond. Her husband, King Louis the Sixteenth, gave it to her. I have no idea how he got his hands on it. Furies allegedly have the power to possess any human they wish to — that is, any human who has a weak enough character for the Furies to bend to their will — so perhaps a Fury possessed the king, or the queen, or whomever gave the necklace to them, hoping to cause mischief. Bad luck for them both, however it happened. This portrait was the only time Marie Antoinette had a chance to wear the stone before the peasants rose up against both her and her husband and had them executed for treason and crimes against the state. They *have* mentioned the French Revolution to you in school, haven't they, Miss Oliviera?"

I stared at the picture, a reproduction of a portrait of Marie Antoinette, the doomed queen of France. Amazingly, she was wearing a gown that resembled the sort of toga in which Persephone, the reluctant bride of Hades, was always depicted on the sides of ancient vases. There were even grape leaves woven through the queen's enormous powdered wig. Well, grape leaves made of gold, but whatever.

And at her neck — that slender neck that would soon be sliced in two by Madame Guillotine — hung my diamond, but on a dark green velvet choker instead of a gold chain.

John had told me men had died for the diamond he'd given me. Not just men, it turned out.

Had he known? Had he known its bloody "provenance," as the jeweler had called it?

Of course he had. He *had* to have known.

And he'd given it to me anyway. He'd said it was supposed to *protect* me. . . .

A lot of good it had done Marie Antoinette.

I was shivering uncontrollably by now. I'd left my cardigan back at the house. I wished I'd thrown it in my bike basket.

But how was I to know? How was I to know I'd be hearing about . . . well, *this*?

The cemetery sexton still didn't appear to notice my discomfort, though. He was quite cheerfully telling his morbid story.

"The diamond disappeared," he said, closing the book, "along with most of the rest of the queen's jewelry, after her arrest. Until, quite randomly, it showed up again, a little more than fifty years later, on the cargo list of a merchant ship that was docked here in Isla Huesos, of all places, on October eleventh of 1846. And that's the last time it — or anyone on that ship — was seen again. It, like every ship that was in port that day, was sunk by what was likely a Category Five hurricane that appeared from nowhere, drowning over a thousand people, destroying every boat and building on the island — including the hospital, so there was nowhere to treat the wounded, and the lighthouse, so there was no way to signal for help. It also," he added, "washed every coffin that was buried here in this cemetery out to sea. So there was nowhere to bury the newly dead, either." He shook his head. "Must have been quite a mess, what with the mosquitoes and the cholera."

I think I made some kind of choking noise that Richard Smith mistook for disbelief, since he hastened to assure me, "Oh, yes. That's why we keep the coffins in crypts now, you know. Of course, they ought to have known better, even then, considering what the Spaniards found three hundred years earlier when *they* got here, but . . ." He gave an elaborate shrug. "Some people choose to turn a blind eye to history."

I didn't feel like fainting anymore. Or cold. Now I just felt . . . nothing.

"Interesting fact about that hurricane," the cemetery sexton went on. "It was the deadliest in recorded Isla Huesos history. A more superstitious man than I might say it was almost as if someone didn't want this diamond — with its bad juju, as my partner would call it — making it off that ship. Because it never did, you know. It sank down to the bottom with the rest of the ship's cargo, never to be seen again . . . though the company that owned the ship hired wreckers to salvage for it, and they looked for months, even years, in water that was only ten feet deep. Never found a trace of it. Is that where you got it?" His gaze, over the rims of his glasses, sharpened. "From a wrecker? Because it's not called wrecking today, Miss Oliviera, or treasure hunting, or whatever the person who gave this to you might have told you. It's called violation of submerged archaeological sites and destruction of underwater cultural heritage, and it, like desecrating someone's tomb, is illegal."

I shook my head, shocked. What was he even talking about?

"No," I said, my heart beginning to thump more loudly than the thunder outside. "No, of course not. It was nothing like that —"

I thought of it the minute I saw you, John had said when he'd given the necklace to me. *Only I never thought . . . well, I never thought you'd turn out to be you, or want to come here with me.*

Is that how he'd gotten it? By causing that horrible hurricane that had killed so many people and sunk so many ships, then collecting their bounty from the bottom of the sea?

But that was impossible.

Then again . . . none of what I'd seen him do was possible.

"Whoever gave it to you," Mr. Smith grumbled, picking up the necklace and examining it more closely in the light, "had it reset since Marie Antoinette's time. And in a fashion I can only call — and that's if I wanted to be charitable — whimsical."

"I told you," I said. "I don't —"

"Oh, right," he said, looking towards the ceiling. "You don't know anything about it. Well, this setting is highly unique. Do you see how each prong forms a little curlicue design across the top of the diamond? Quite beautiful. And unusual. Do you know what these five prongs represent?" He didn't even wait for my reply. "Rivers," he said. "Five in all. Now, can you think of a place that has five rivers? Go on. Guess."

"I don't know. I'm terrible at geography." And every subject, really, that didn't have to do with avenging the death of Hannah Chang. "Look, I really have to —"

"It's quite simple." He picked up a pencil and pointed with it to the first prong. "Sorrow." He pointed to the second. "Lamentation." He pointed to the third. "Fire." The fourth. "Oblivion." The fifth. "And hate."

Thunder cracked. Now the storm was so close, it seemed to be right above our heads.

"The five rivers of the Underworld," Richard Smith said, sounding thrilled with himself. He ticked them off on his fingers. "Acheron, Cocytus, Phlegethon, Lethe, the river Styx. Good Lord, girl." He leaned back in his chair and stared at me. "Do they teach children *nothing* useful in school these days? *The Underworld.*"

I felt as if someone had run over me.

I shouldn't have, of course. I should have known. It had been right there in front of me all along. Literally. It had been around my neck.

I don't know why I hadn't seen it. The psychiatrists had tried to tell me. My alleged dream had been full of things I'd seen on TV. Hadn't I studied the Greek myths in school?

Of course I had.

But I had never paid attention to things that didn't interest me, even before the accident. I had inherited that, too, from *both* my parents, though if I ever mentioned this, they would blame each other for it. Spoonbills, your fault. No, throwing stars, yours.

But who *did* pay attention to the myths, really? All those strange names and people being hit with arrows in the Achilles heel and girls being swept down into the Underworld. It was complicated and weird and had nothing to do with reality.

And yet at the same time . . . something didn't make sense.

"But." I blinked at him. "There weren't any rivers when I was there. Just a lake."

Now *he* was the one staring at *me*.

And no wonder, really. "When you were there?" Mr. Smith took his glasses off. "What do you mean, *when you were there?*"

Sometimes I just got so tired of all the pretending. It was exhausting, really, trying to fit in, trying to be "normal." Even if that word wasn't therapeutically beneficial.

"This necklace," I said, putting my hand over it. The stone felt warm and comforting under my palm, the way it always had.

But now that I knew a thousand people had been killed because of it — that a queen had, indirectly, lost her head because of it — I didn't feel quite as friendly towards it as I once had.

"It's supposed to protect its wearer from evil," I said.

"Well," Richard Smith said, blinking rapidly. For the first time, he didn't appear to be quite so sure of himself. "Yes. That's how the legend goes. That's supposedly why Hades had it made. And if anyone *not* a chosen consort of the death deity attempts to possess it —" He shrugged, then rubbed his eyes, then put his glasses back on. "Well, nothing good will happen to her, obviously. But all of that is just a story. What did you mean when you said —"

"He didn't tell me that part," I murmured, looking over my shoulder, back at the window. "He didn't tell me there would be evil spirits coming after me. He didn't tell me that's who he was. Or maybe he did. I was crying so much. . . ."

I got up out of my chair, feeling dazed, and moved towards the window. The view from the cemetery sexton's office was of the street but also of the corner of the cemetery where the poinciana tree stood, its dark and twisted branches spreading out across the Hayden crypt.

I don't know what I was hoping to see out there. *Him?* As if there was a chance he might be there, by the crypt where he'd thrown away the necklace he'd given me (because I'd given it back to him)? Or by the gate he'd kicked apart after telling me to go (because I'd called him a jerk)?

I wasn't sure if I wanted to see him, or feared seeing him.

I needn't have worried. The cemetery, like the street, was deserted. Everyone was trying to avoid the coming storm.

Just like he was trying to avoid me. Or didn't care.

"Miss Oliviera," the cemetery sexton said from behind me. "I don't understand any of this. Who is *he*? What did you mean when you said you were *there*?"

"It doesn't matter." I laughed. I couldn't believe any of this. "I threw a cup of tea in his face."

I heard the cemetery sexton's chair creak, like he was getting up.

"Wait," he said. "Are you telling me that you —"

"What do you want?" I swung around from the window. I don't know why I was taking it out on him. It wasn't *his* fault, poor man. I think it was going to the window and looking out and realizing he wasn't there and that he'd never be there again, and that even after everything I'd been through, everything I'd just heard, when I should have been *relieved* to see he wasn't there, what I felt was disappointment.

I didn't belong in New Pathways. I belonged back in kindergarten.

"What do you *want* from me, giving me mysterious notes and trying to intimidate me like this?" I demanded. "Is it money to repair the stupid gate? Fine. I'll get my dad to pay for it. Just don't tell anyone about it. My mom is trying to make a new start here."

I walked over to the desk and snatched up the necklace. As soon as I did, I felt better. Comforted.

This might have been the most disturbing thing of all.

"And I lied to you," I said. "This *is* mine. I'm taking it back. I don't care about any stupid curse. So." I looked him in the eye. "How much?"

He looked surprised. More than just surprised.

He looked horrified.

"Money?" he echoed. "I never wanted money from you, Miss Oliviera. Money never had anything to do with this."

I looked at him in confusion.

"But if you don't want money," I said, "what *do* you want from me?"

"Well, to begin with, the truth." He looked past me, towards the window I'd just been staring through. "How long have you known John?"

"Dost thou not hear the pity of his plaint?
Dost thou not see the death that combats him
Beside that flood, where ocean has no vaunt?"
DANTE ALIGHIERI, *Inferno*, Canto II

M e?" I stared at him. "You mean *you* know John?"

Then I realized what I'd done. I'd just admitted John's existence to him.

Except . . . hadn't *he* just admitted John's existence to *me*?

"Well, of course I do," Richard Smith said, looking at me as if I were a little slow-witted. "Not as well as you do, evidently. But then, when I passed, *I* didn't go to the Underworld."

Suddenly, my knees felt weak. I fumbled for the chair, then sank down into it, clutching my necklace to my chest.

"You mean you —"

"Yes, yes," he said, patting his chest impatiently. "Heart attack. Bypass surgery. But *I* just saw a light." He sat back down in his chair and gazed at me with a completely different expression than he'd worn before. Now he looked . . . well, a little impressed. As if I weren't the "idiotic teenager" he'd originally thought me.

Which, I had to admit, I'd been acting like, sort of. But there'd been mitigating circumstances.

"What about you, Miss Oliviera? How did you pass?" His gaze was gentle.

"I tripped and hit my head," I said. "And drowned. But I had hypothermia," I added, because I hated the way I died. It sounded so stupid. Especially when you factored in the bird.

He nodded. "Ah. Of course. That'll be why they were able to revive you." He fumbled with his glasses again, polishing the lenses with a cloth that had been lying on his desk, then putting them back on, and then eyeing me some more. "You said something about throwing . . . tea in his face?"

I looked down at the floor. "Yes. That's how . . . well, that's how I escaped."

"I see," he said in a completely nonjudgmental tone. "And this would have been about . . . a year and a half ago?"

I glanced up again, surprised. "How did you —?"

"Oh, just a guess," he said, his gaze suddenly far off. "It would explain a lot, that's all."

"About what?" I didn't understand.

"Never mind," he said, looking back at me. "So." He leaned forward in his chair, causing it to creak. "Tell me what happened with the necklace. If you don't mind, that is. I'd ask him myself, but . . . well, he hasn't been terribly communicative lately." He grinned suddenly, his eyes twinkling from behind the lenses of his eyeglasses. "Now of course I know why. Though I'm sure you'll agree, John *does* have his moments."

I shook my head, unable to believe what I was hearing. All this time, I'd been insisting to people that John was real, and no one had believed me.

And now, sitting across from me was someone who not only believed me but had seen him — spoken to him — himself.

And apparently didn't think he was a monster. He called him John. Just like that. Just . . . John. *John does have his moments.*

I wasn't crazy. I had never been crazy.

"I don't understand," I said. "You *talk* to him? You *talk* to him. You two have . . . *talks.*" I needed a soda, an espresso, my pills, a very, very fast ride down a hill on my bike, *something.* I could not process this information. The idea of John sitting in this office, in this chair, talking to this man, did not compute.

"Well," Richard Smith said, leaning back in his chair and looking thoughtful. "Not often, of course. But occasionally, yes, I run into him out there, and we chat. It hasn't always been easy. He can be a bit . . . what does your generation call it? Oh, yes. Moody."

Moody? Popping in and out of nowhere, attempting to murder everyone who touched me? That was putting it mildly.

"But I have the advantage of having experienced death before, which my predecessors in this position — who left numerous warnings about John's . . . moodiness — did not," the cemetery sexton explained. "So I am fearful of neither death nor the things that come with it, such as John."

My eyes widened. The fact that Richard Smith wasn't afraid of John, or the place he came from, struck me as foolhardy to the extreme.

"And some of the warnings, I will admit, have turned out to be warranted," he went on. "As he is, of course, quite a tormented young man. Who wouldn't be, in his position? But the stories about him — the things for which people tend to want to blame him around here — have grown completely out of proportion. The vandalism, for instance —"

"Are you kidding me?" I stared at him in shock. "Are you talking about the gate? Because that was him. I was there. And that was totally him."

Richard Smith's eyebrows rose.

"Well, he certainly isn't responsible for all the mysterious deaths for which my predecessors —"

I shook my head. "Let me ask you something. Were the people who died kind of scummy dirtbags who deserved to die anyway? Because if they were, he did it."

The cemetery sexton was shaking his head. "But —"

"What is wrong with you?" I burst out. "Can you not hear that thunder out there? That's all totally him!"

He broke off and stared at me. "He certainly cannot control the weather."

"All right," I said. This guy lived in a fantasy world. "Fine. He can't. How long has he been here? Was he around during that big hurricane you mentioned, the one where this necklace disappeared?"

The cemetery sexton's eyes widened. "He's a death deity, Miss Oliviera, not a murderer or a weatherman. You of all people should know that."

I didn't think this guy really knew John very well at all, but I didn't say anything to correct him.

"But from what I understand," he went on, "yes, the Great Hurricane of 1846 is when John originally appeared on this island . . . or at least when sightings of him first started being recorded." I must have looked surprised, for he said, "Oh, yes. Other people have seen him, too, not just us cemetery sextons . . . although most sightings have occurred around here. Why do you think we've never had to bother investing in security cameras? Because everyone on Isla Huesos knows to stay away from here after dark, as no one wants to run the risk of encountering him." His expression darkened. "Well, with the exception, of course, of teenagers who haven't learned their lesson yet, especially during the days leading up to Coffin Night —"

I shook my head. "What *is* that? Does that have something to do with John, too?"

"Of course it does," he said. By now the room had gotten so dark that I could barely see the sexton's face in the shadows. Outside, the wind had calmed. It seemed deadly still, the kind of still it only gets just before it starts to pour. "Except it all happened so long ago, no one remembers the story or, at least, remembers it correctly. They just remember that it's important to build a coffin, and then hide it. . . . Of course the hiding is symbolic. The hiding represents burying."

"But *why*?" I asked. "It makes no sense."

"It does, actually," he said. "Because no life — if it was led by a decent person — should go unremembered. So if, for instance, a soldier was betrayed by people he thought were friends, his body tossed from a ship and abandoned to the waves, his family left to wonder forever what had happened to him, never knowing if he was alive, if he was well . . . That is a certain kind of hell all its own."

I blinked at him, my mind going back, for some reason, to those moments at the bottom of the pool in our backyard in Connecticut, when I had lain there looking up at the tassels on my scarf. Abandoned. That's sort of how I'd felt. Even though, of course, no one had betrayed or murdered me, really. My death had been no one's fault but my own.

"Is that what happened to *him*?" I asked, a sudden throb in my voice. Even though of course I didn't care about John, I didn't like to think of that having happened to him. It must have been scary, being tossed around on all those ocean waves. It had been nice under the water of my pool. At least my mom had known where to find me.

Do you think I like this any more than you do? John had asked me that day in his room, his voice raw. *Don't you think* I'd *like to see* my *mother?*

I think my heart broke a little bit more right there, in the cemetery sexton's office.

I hadn't known. I hadn't had any idea what John was talking about.

I did now.

The cemetery sexton leaned back in his chair suddenly, causing it to creak noisily. The moment — whatever it had been — was broken. He wasn't going to tell me more about John's death, if that's even what he'd been talking about.

"Like anything," he said, all business again, "the tale's gotten twisted. And perhaps, in this case, that's a good thing. Because sometimes when people know the real story, they can't take it. It's too frightening. And so it turns into something like Coffin Night and has more to do with football and setting things on fire than it does with honoring the dead. But I'm still curious," he said, "about what happened to you, Miss Oliviera, after you died. Is that when John gave you the necklace?"

I felt myself blushing for some reason.

"When I died . . . what happened . . . it was . . ." I shook my head. It was amazing. Now that I'd finally found someone who'd actually believe me, the words wouldn't come. I could never tell this nice old man what it was really like in the Underworld, or what I'd been through there. "It wasn't like in books," I said finally. "I had to run. I *had* to."

Mr. Smith raised his eyebrows. "I see," he said. "But first, he gave you that?" He pointed to the necklace in my hands. "And somehow it came back with you?"

I was still too ashamed about what I had done back then to look him in the eye. I stared down at the stone. It seemed to wink back, white as Mr. Smith's shirt.

"Yes," I said. "I'd met him before, here, on the day of my grandfather's funeral, when I was seven. He was . . . nice, that day. Then I died when I was fifteen, and I saw him again. That day, he wasn't so nice. At least at first. I've only seen him a couple of times since then. Once was last night." Suddenly, I realized I'd ruined my back-to-school manicure by peeling off most of the polish as I'd talked to him. It was lying in flakes all over the wood floor beneath my chair. Great. "John . . . he scares me," I heard myself admit. "He can act a little bit . . . wild. I didn't know why before, but now, thanks to you, I think I have a better idea. I want to help him, but he won't let me —"

Mr. Smith made a slight hooting noise. "Oh, no. I would imagine your help is the last thing he wants."

I lifted my hands in a helpless gesture. "Then I don't know what to do. Doesn't he scare you?"

"Well . . . maybe a little, at the beginning. One hazard of working in a cemetery, I guess, is that you see scary things all the time. But —" Richard Smith shrugged. "You know why they call this place Island of Bones, don't you? You can't have a place that's routinely littered with the dead and not have it be an entrance to the Underworld —"

I looked up at him, my heart seeming to shrivel inside my chest. "Is that what Isla Huesos is?"

"Well, of course, Miss Oliviera," he said, grinning a little. "What did you think? And with that, of course, you have to have a keeper of the dead. And someone with a job like that is bound to be a bit scary."

"And is that who he is?" I asked, thinking of the name written above the door of the crypt beside which I'd met him twice now. I didn't want to ask it. But now that I knew about the necklace, I had to. "Is he . . . Hades?"

Outside, the first few drops of rain began to fall, pelting the tin roof. Slow at first. But hard. They sounded like bullets.

"Of course not." The old man looked surprised. "Hades was a god, and John Hayden's not that. He was born a man, and lived like a man, and died like one, and only *then* came to be what you and I know him as now . . . ruler of the Underworld."

"So, he took Hades' place when he . . . retired?" I asked, still not understanding.

Mr. Smith shook his head. "No, no," he said. "As close as I've been able to figure out — and please understand, you're the only person I've ever met besides John who's actually been there — John's isn't *the* Underworld. I personally don't believe there can be a single Underworld. That would be quite an honor for our little island, but there's been a bit of a population explosion since the days of Homer, don't you think?"

I stared at him. "I didn't understand a single thing you just said." Except that John wasn't Hades. Which was a relief, I supposed. But I still didn't get what he was, exactly. "Who's Homer?"

He sighed as if wondering how he'd been cursed with such an inept pupil, then turned back to his book about death deities, showing me a section of brightly colored illustrations, each depicting a different representation of what looked, to me, like hell. But I supposed to someone like him, they looked like super-fun playgrounds.

"Look," Richard Smith said, obviously trying to be patient with me. "It's quite simple, really. Every culture, every religion in the world, has had their own mythology relating to an Underworld through which the souls of the newly dead pass before heading to the afterlife, from the Aztecs to the Greeks to the Muslims to the

Christians. There may be dozens, even hundreds of Underworlds, for all we know. They act as . . . as sort of processing plants for the souls of the departed, sorting out the worthy from the unworthy, before they're sent off to their final destinations. And this little cemetery here just happens to be centered over one of them. Your grandfather — who shared my interest in this subject — and I studied the matter extensively —"

Shocked, I interrupted, "My *grandfather* knew John? I thought you said you only played bocce with him."

He looked slightly ashamed of himself. "Oh, you mean what I said back at the high school today? Well, yes, that was a small fabrication. And no, your grandfather never met John, though he knew *of* him, of course. The person who held this position before I did —" He cleared his throat. "Let's just say his views on the existence of an afterlife were somewhat narrow. You can't imagine how unreceptive some people can be to the idea of a young man who is able to walk both the earthly as well as the astral plane, and has been doing so quite comfortably for the past century and a half —"

Actually, I could very easily imagine how unreceptive "some people" might be to this idea. Like my dad, for instance. Which was why I'd never mentioned it to him.

"My grandfather," I said, trying to steer him back to the subject.

"Oh," he said. "Well, yes, as I was saying, we didn't see much of John in those days. It wasn't until my own tenure here as sexton that I got a chance to know him, and by that time your grandfather had unfortunately passed. As for the bocce, your grandfather never wanted your grandmother to know that he was a member of our little, er, society. As I mentioned, some people consider the study of death deities and the Underworld slightly . . . well, just morbid. And your grandmother is one of those people. I'm not saying she's not a lovely woman," he added hastily. "And an asset to the community. My partner knits, and buys all his yarn at her shop. She's just a very conservative lady, and I think she might have found the fact that your grandfather was involved in something so . . . esoteric a bit harder to understand than his being on a bocce team."

I shook my head. "That's weird."

The cemetery sexton eyed me over the rims of his glasses. "Why is it weird?"

I'd been about to say, *Because she's the one who introduced me to John.*

But she hadn't, I remembered. In her kitchen, she'd actually insisted I'd made the whole thing up.

It's not safe for you here.

Underworlds? Death deities? Furies? John hadn't been kidding: It wasn't safe for *anyone* in this cemetery. No way Grandma would have let me out of this office if she'd had a clue.

"It's weird," I said instead, "that Grandma didn't know. Because you said everyone knows. *Everyone* knows about John, and that Isla Huesos is just sitting over the top of this Underworld."

"There's knowing," Mr. Smith said, "and then there's believing. Your grandmother knows the stories about John. Everyone around here does. But whether or not she believes they're actually true . . . that's different. Your grandmother is well known for having her feet planted rather firmly on the ground."

He was right. Grandma didn't believe in anything she couldn't see with her own two eyes, except for what it said in the Bible. That's what she'd told Mom about the dispersant Dad's company had used.

"I haven't seen any sign of it," she'd said. "Or of any of that oil people were complaining about so much."

"That's the point, Mother," Mom had said. "Just because you can't see it doesn't mean it isn't there. No one knows what damage it could do to the ecosystem years from now."

"Oh, for God's sake, Deborah," Grandma had said. "I put in my claim for lost tourist income, and that company paid up pronto, every last cent. So I'm sorry, but why should I care about a bunch of dumb birds?"

"In any case," Richard Smith was saying, "your grandfather and I always espoused a theory that there must be as many John Haydens in the universe — souls who, for whatever reason, are destined to spend eternity sorting out the spirits of the dead and setting them on the path to their final destinations — as there are Underworlds."

"But then how did I get sent to *this* Underworld, in Isla Huesos, when I died in Connecticut?" I asked. "Wouldn't it have made more sense for me to go to one in, say, Bridgeport?" I'd been to Bridgeport. If there was an Underworld in the tri-state area, it definitely seemed to me it would be located under Bridgeport.

He looked thoughtful. "You said you met him before, when you were seven. Maybe that's why."

I shook my head. It wasn't that everything Mr. Smith was saying didn't make sense. . . . It was just that I couldn't believe I'd been so blind for so long. And I still had so many questions.

"And there's nothing anyone can *do*?" I asked the cemetery sexton. "About the Furies? To help John?"

He smiled at me a little sadly. "What do you propose we do about them, Miss Oliviera? You're talking about a region where people's souls go after they're departed. Are we to storm it with lighted torches and pitchforks? How are we even to get there without dying first?"

I wanted to cry. Furies seemed like an even worse disaster than the one Dad's company had helped cause.

"How did John get chosen for such a crummy job anyway?" I asked. "It doesn't seem fair. What did he do to deserve it?"

"*That*," Mr. Smith said firmly, closing the book, "is something you're just going to have to ask him yourself."

I flushed.

"I can't talk to him," I said flatly. "He hates me."

"Oh." Mr. Smith stood up. He was clearly preparing to leave. "I'm certain that's not true."

"No," I said. "You don't understand. I've *tried* talking to him. It's all I can do just to get him to listen. I tried apologizing to him for what happened — well, when we met. About the tea. And do you know what he did? He threw this necklace across the cemetery."

"Finally," Mr. Smith said, looking vaguely amused, "an explanation for why I found it next to the Wolkowsky family plot this morning."

"He's a nightmare," I said. It felt good finally to have someone to vent to about this stuff. Someone who would actually listen, who knew what I was talking about. It was just too bad it was an old man who clearly didn't know about anything except death deities. "I don't know what I'm supposed to do. If I'd known about any of this — that Isla Huesos was sitting on top of some kind of Underworld — do you think I'd have agreed to move here? And all I ever did was die. Then, just because I recognized John from meeting him in this cemetery when I was seven, I thought he might be able to help me, and I casually made a few suggestions as to how he could run the place a little better —"

The cemetery sexton, who'd started shuffling papers into his briefcase, winced. "Oh, dear. I'm sure he didn't like that."

"Yeah," I said. "I know, right? And then the next thing I knew, he had me in this room *with a bed*, saying we were going to be spending forever there or something because I missed the boat, which I happen to think he made me do on purpose, by the way, and what was I supposed to do? I was freaking out. You would have been, too."

"Well," Mr. Smith said. "Yes. I'm sure I would have been, er, freaking out."

Suddenly, I was up and pacing the little office again, clenching the necklace. Outside, the rain streamed down as hard as if all of the angels in heaven were weeping for me at the same time. Except, of course, they weren't, because I was pretty sure all of the angels in heaven had turned their backs on me, or none of this would be happening.

"Do you realize that ever since I've gotten back from that place, every time I turn around," I informed him, "he's either giving someone a heart attack, or pulverizing their hand, or smashing a gate right in front of me, and *I'm* the one who gets blamed for it? Every time!"

He looked troubled. "I hardly think you can hold John responsible for *all* of those —"

"I saw him do it!" I exclaimed. "I had to keep him from doing anything worse! And now you're saying I've got to *talk* to him? How can I talk to him? Every time I talk to him, something horrible happens. I came here with my mom to try to make a new start, to be normal. Even though the word *normal* isn't therapeutically beneficial. But how can I be normal when you tell me I have to talk to someone who's in charge of some Underworld, and who, by the way, gave me a necklace that Hades gave Persephone, and P.S., killed a thousand people?" I shook the diamond at him. "This whole thing is *crazy*."

"No," Mr. Smith said, closing his briefcase with a determined snap and turning towards me with a face that had suddenly gone as grimly gray as the stone I held in my hands. "It isn't. It all makes perfect sense to me now. When I first started working here, John was a challenge, it is true. But I was able to get through to him, probably because like you, I've seen death. . . . There's very little that scares me anymore. But exactly a year and a half ago, something happened that turned John into the, er, nightmare you describe. I never knew what it was until tonight because he wouldn't talk about it. But now I do. It was *you*."

I lowered my arm in surprise. The rain had started to slacken off.

But the tension in the sexton's voice didn't.

"Miss Oliviera, I just bury the dead. John sorts out where their souls go after they're departed. I don't know what role *you* play in all this . . . but I do know that you need to figure it out, and you need to do it quickly. Because it took me *months* after you came along the first time to get John settled down. And everything was fine until last night, when you got him all riled up again. Next thing I know, my gate is smashed, there's a dead queen's necklace lying in my cemetery, and now a hurricane has sprung out of nowhere and is apparently headed directly our way. So if I might make a suggestion for all our sakes, why don't you try" — his brown eyes were pleading — "just being a little sweeter to that boy?"

I opened my mouth. There were a lot of things I wanted to say to Richard Smith. One was that no matter how sweet I was to John, it wasn't going to make a difference. John was a wild thing and, like any wild thing, was going to do whatever he wanted, and no one could stop him.

And two, it didn't matter how sweet I was to John Hayden. He could go anywhere and do anything he wanted to with just a blink of his eye.

But then I realized saying all those things would be the wrong thing to do. It would be like dashing Richard Smith's romantic notions of the Underworld, with its five rivers of sorrow and lament and whatnot. Pointing out the hideous truth — about the tattooed guards and the boats and the lines and the freezing beach — to this old man wasn't going to make anything better.

What good would it do? It would just crush him, learning those things he loved didn't really exist.

The same way it would crush Mr. Smith to know that John had not, whatever he might think, fallen in love with me, for all he'd said he knew my nature because of what he'd seen in my eyes and the fact that I'd cared more for the poor people down there than I had for myself.

If he was so in love with me, as Mr. Smith seemed to be implying, why hadn't *he* been a little sweeter? All those months when I'd been suffering in my own coffin, instead of popping up and trying to kill people in front of me, why hadn't he just *told* me he loved me, if that was true?

Of course, there was always the possibility he'd grown so wild — being tortured night and day by Furies for letting me get away — he'd forgotten how important it is to people to hear the words *I love you.* Maybe he didn't know how to say the words *I love you.* He certainly seemed to have a problem with the words *I'm sorry.*

Oh, God, what was I doing? I couldn't believe I was even entertaining the idea of taking Mr. Smith's suggestion seriously. He was an Isla Huesos kook — no different, really, in his own way, than my grandmother. Who owns a knitting store in a place where the median temperature is eighty-seven degrees? And no wonder they'd appointed Richard Smith cemetery sexton: He was obsessed with death deities!

Coming to his office, I realized, had been a bad idea. What had I really accomplished, anyway? Nothing good. Except that I had gotten my necklace back.

My necklace that, I had learned, killed whoever touched it. Great.

"Look," I said to the cemetery sexton, dropping the chain back down over my head. When I felt the pendant's heavy weight thump against my heart, I felt a little calmer. Which in and of itself was depressing. "Never mind. It's fine. I understand."

He looked at me in the lamplight. "Do you, Miss Oliviera? Because I get the feeling I haven't been any more successful at getting through to you than I've ever been at getting through to John."

"Well," I said, "now you know why I wasn't so thrilled at the idea of spending all of eternity with him. Because he's impossible."

The cemetery sexton looked thoughtful.

"Impossible, yes," he admitted, after a few seconds. "But interesting. Like you. And eternity *is* a long time. So if you have to spend it with someone, I could see wanting to spend it with someone impossible . . . but interesting."

As turtle-doves, called onward by desire,
With open and steady wings to the sweet nest
Fly through the air by their volition borne.
DANTE ALIGHIERI, *Inferno*, Canto V

Honey, some boys stopped by to see you. They had wood."

That's the first thing Mom said to me when I got home. It took me a minute to figure out what she was talking about. Then I realized what must have happened.

"Sorry, Mom," I said, when my anger at Seth Rector had abated enough to allow me to speak. "I didn't tell them they could do that. I said I had to ask you if it was okay first."

"That's what they said." Mom was in our new kitchen — which I guess wasn't so new anymore — making pasta. "But they said they couldn't get through to you. Since your phone was in your book bag in the garage — as I found out when I tried to call you, too, and that's where I finally heard it ringing — I'm guessing that's probably why."

I winced. I couldn't believe I'd spaced this. Actually, I could. No wonder there was so much speculation over at Grandma's about me.

"Mom," I said. "I'm so sorry. But they shouldn't have just —"

"Honey, it's all right," she said, sliding a bowl in front of me as I sat down at the counter. "They explained that it was for Coffin Night, so I told them it was fine and let them come in. They seemed very nice. Even if they ma'amed me."

Mom mock scowled as she took a seat next to me in front of her own bowl of pasta. She hated being called ma'am. She said it made her feel old, and wondered when she'd gone from being a miss to a ma'am.

She didn't seem to hold it against Seth and his friends, though, nor did she give me her usual lecture about forgetting my cell phone.

I found out why after her gaze fell on the chain around my neck.

"Oh," she said. "You're wearing it. That's funny. Today in the New Pathways office, I could have sworn that horrible old man from the cemetery —" She made a face, then took a sip from the glass of wine she'd poured herself. "You know what? Never mind. Maybe I need bifocals. Anyway, I assumed it was all right to let them in. It was, wasn't it?"

What could I say? I'd been intending to tell Seth and his friends that, unfortunately, my mom had said no. Too bad, so sad.

How had they known this was what I'd been planning on doing? No wonder Alex hated them so much. The dirty sneaks.

I put a fake smile on my face and said, "No, Mom. It's great. Super, in fact. Exactly what I wanted."

Oh, well, I told myself. At least this way I could enact Phase One of my plan: Steal Serena's cell phone, find incriminating photos on it (she seemed like the type who'd have them), then blackmail her into leaving Kayla alone.

"Anyway, you'll never guess what happened," Mom said. "You know that guy Tim from your New Pathways program? Well, he asked me out." She winked. "That's why I don't really mind so much that those friends of yours ma'amed me. I guess your old mom's still got it."

"Mom," I said, lowering my spoon. "I'm actually eating right now."

"Don't worry," she said with a grin. "I knew you'd feel that way about it. That's why I told him I was too busy at the moment to date. But it was still very nice. He asked me to the boat show next weekend. You have to admit, Tim is very cute."

"Still eating," I said. "And I don't have to admit anything, except that between you and Dad, I don't know which one of you is going to kill me sooner. Permanently. I mean it."

I wanted to inform her that I had just found out her birthplace was parked over an Underworld — which shouldn't really have come as much of a surprise to her, all things considered.

But I didn't want to destroy her good mood, especially since she'd made dinner and been so nice about the wood, even if that wasn't exactly what I wanted.

Mom laughed and drank some of her wine. "So I take it we're the lucky home that's been selected for the building of the senior class coffin," she said, tactfully changing the subject. "How did you manage that on your first day? You're not even on a sports team."

"We live in a gated community," I said, sullenly stabbing a piece of broccoli I could see she'd hidden in the pasta so I'd get some vegetables. "No one can drive by and see what we're doing unless they live here."

"Oh," Mom said knowingly. "They've wised up. They used to just build them in someone's mausoleum in the cemetery for that reason."

"Yeah," I said, giving a little shiver. "Well, they can't use the cemetery anymore because the police are onto them about that."

Which would explain why, when I'd accepted Mr. Smith's offer of a ride home — the rain had let up by then, but not enough to make riding through it more tempting than a seat in his warm, dry minivan — we'd run into Jade, my counselor from New Pathways, cruising around the cemetery in bicycle shorts and a plastic rain poncho with IHPD written on it.

"What in heaven's name are you doing out here?" Mr. Smith had put down his window to ask as she'd ridden up. "Don't tell me they didn't cancel patrol on a night like this. Haven't they heard there's a hurricane coming?"

Jade put down her hood and grinned at us. "It's just a watch, not a warning," she said, referring to the hurricane. Then she pointed the beam from her bike light into the car. "Is that you, Pierce? What are you doing in there with Mr. Smith?"

"Um," I said, a little embarrassed that I'd chosen the minivan over my bike when Jade evidently didn't mind the rain at all. I was the one wearing a necklace that apparently warded off demons, and I was scared of some drizzle. Also, I had no idea how to answer her question about what I was doing in Richard Smith's minivan.

He answered for me.

"I saw her out riding in that last downpour," he said. "And had mercy on her. I'm taking her home. Are you sure I can't do the same for you? Her bicycle is still locked up over by the gate, so there's plenty of room to put yours in the back here, if you choose to. Which I highly recommend."

"Naw," Jade said, putting her hood back up as another car drove by, splashing water everywhere, its high beams flashing against the sides of the nearby crypts as they loomed behind the high, spiked black metal fence. "Are you kidding me? I'm having the time of my life out here patrolling with the IHPD. They gave me a walkie-talkie and everything." She pulled up the rain poncho to reveal the two-way radio on her hip. "We're gonna make sure no more baddies mess with your gate, Mr. S. And if they do, I'm going to pepper-spray them, don't you worry."

I leaned forward in my seat. This was ridiculous. Jade was riding her bike around the graveyard, at night, in a rainstorm, because of something *John* had done? She was going to get all wet for nothing.

Not to mention, John's words from the night before were still ringing in my ears:

It's not safe for you here.

"I really don't think —" I started to say, but Mr. Smith interrupted.

"That's fine, Jade," he said. "It's you and Officers Rodriguez and Poling tonight?"

"Till one in the morning," she said cheerfully. "They're going around in the squad car." She made a face at me. "Like little babies, all snug and warm."

I didn't laugh. "Really," I said again. "I think you should —"

"I don't think you're going to see any action tonight because of the rain," the cemetery sexton interrupted me again. "But the officers have the keys to get into my office if you need anything, and of course the chief of police has my home number. Have fun. And be safe."

She grinned and saluted, then rode off. I looked behind us as Mr. Smith hit the power window to close it.

"Why didn't you *make* her get in the car?" I demanded. "That's completely nuts, riding around on a bike in this weather —"

"Probably the safest night shift she could pull," he said, "with this silly program your school has. Pairing teachers up with the police. Makes no sense to me. Nothing they teach you kids in school today makes sense to me."

"She's not a teacher," I said, still looking back at her bike lights as she pedaled away. "She's a counselor. And she's really nice. This is so stupid."

"It doesn't matter. No one's going to be out on a night like this, anyway. And what did you mean, *make* her get in the car? You're a strange girl. How, precisely, do you *make* a woman like that do anything? You saw her; she's having fun. She'll be perfectly safe, just like you were, the many times *you* rode your bike through my cemetery. Nothing bad will happen to her. John will see to that."

"John told me the cemetery wasn't safe," I explained to him. "He told me that last night. He told me never to come back. He said if I did, I'd end up dead, forever this time. That's when he kicked the gate."

Mr. Smith chuckled. "That sounds like John. Was that before or after he threw the necklace?"

"It's not funny," I said with a scowl. "Why would he say it wasn't safe if he didn't mean it?"

"He meant it wasn't safe for *you*," the cemetery sexton said. "Because you were clearly aggravating him so much, he felt like killing you. But he didn't mean it literally. He was exaggerating to make a point. John's never killed a woman yet — that I know of — and if he were to start now, I assume he'd kill you, not your guidance counselor. Good Lord, do they teach you *nothing* in school these days? Have you ever heard of hyperbole? I highly suggest you look up the word, Miss Oliviera, if you intend to pursue a relationship with a death deity."

I'd given up after that. Especially later, after having cleared the dishes and made a halfhearted attempt at my homework — I had to at least *look* as if I were trying — I turned on the eleven o'clock forecast and saw that Isla Huesos was now dead center inside the three-day cone of uncertainty. Forecasters were still calling it a watch, so no evacuations were being announced, but officials were encouraging those living in "low-lying or flood-prone areas" to take necessary precautions. And since the bridges that attached

Isla Huesos to the mainland would close once winds reached seventy miles per hour, those who wished to relocate needed to do it soon, especially because they were opening up only one shelter, way up in Key Largo.

"Mom," I said nervously. "Are you seeing this? Should we evacuate or something?"

Mom was on her laptop.

"Oh, honey," she said distractedly. "It's only a watch. And it's going to hit Cuba first. These storms always die down over Cuba. And they haven't even canceled school tomorrow. If they haven't canceled school, it's nothing. Trust me on this. So I hope you really did do your homework" — she grinned at me — "because there's no chance you're getting out of it."

I turned off the TV, feeling dejected. Not that I'd been *hoping* for a hurricane to come and hit my school. Only a little kid would want something like that.

But when I'd flicked on the lights in the garage while getting my book bag earlier and seen the four-by-eights Seth had left there, leaning up against all the outdoor furniture Uncle Chris had left stacked so neatly, I wondered how was I going to break the news to Alex that I was on the Coffin Night committee with these people he hated so much.

And it had all kind of hit me. It was too much. All of it. I was going to have these people in my house, building a coffin that had something to do with a guy who was the ruler of this Underworld that none of them knew existed, right underneath the island on which they'd lived their whole lives. . . .

If a hurricane did come and wipe all of us out, at least I wouldn't have to deal.

But that was no way, I knew, to cope with my problems. Nor was calling my dad and telling him I'd decided to take him up on his offer of boarding school.

Because I couldn't help thinking Switzerland was sounding pretty tempting all of a sudden. It would break my mom's heart, but she'd get over it if I convinced her it was so I'd have a better chance of getting into a decent college.

Surely, this would be better than telling her the truth . . . that I needed to get away from this crazy place she'd brought me to, which also happened to be on top of the exact place I'd spent every day since I'd died trying to forget.

I even went so far as to dial Dad's number as I was sitting there in the garage — after carefully closing the door so Mom wouldn't overhear.

"What?" Dad yelled, picking up on the first ring, as he always did when I called.

I could tell he was at a business dinner. I could hear the buzz of conversation and clink of cutlery in the background. Dad never ate at home. Why should he, when there was always some client willing to take him out to eat at one of Manhattan's finest restaurants?

"Dad," I said. "Is this a bad time?"

"Never," he said. "I'm at that place we went, remember, with that glass wall of wine bottles that you said should spin around so you could just point to make your selection?" Suddenly, my dad was in a rage. "But they did not implement your suggestion! The racks still don't spin!"

"They're stupid," I said. "Dad, I need your help. I have to get out of here."

He sounded delighted, as I'd known he would be. I heard a snapping sound.

"Plane," he said to someone. "Isla Huesos. Tomorrow."

"It's just," I said, "there are some things going on. Mom's great, you know —"

"Is she going out with anyone?" Dad asked, too casually.

"Uh," I said. "What? No. Of course not. But —"

"What?" Dad was suddenly yelling. "No. I said the 2005 Chateau La Mission Haut Brion. Not the 2008. If I wanted the 2008, I'd have asked for the 2008. Are you people trying to kill me?"

I looked down at the diamond on the end of my gold chain. It was back to its usual color, pale gray on the edges and midnight blue inside.

What was I doing?

I couldn't leave, I realized. Not *now*. Leaving now would be no better than crawling back inside my glass coffin.

"Dad," I said, rubbing my forehead. "Never mind. I —"

Dad got back on the phone with me. "Now they're telling me there's some kind of hurricane coming your way. Did you know this? I *told* your mother not to go back to that godforsaken hellhole."

Hellhole. Dad, you have no idea.

"It's okay, Dad," I said. "I changed my mind. I want to stay."

"Pierce," Dad said. "It's fine. I can get the plane there. Just the commercial airport is closed. All the pilot has to do is land at the naval base, and then I can get this friend of mine to pick you and your mom up."

"Look, Dad," I said. "It's fine. I just had a weak moment. I have to go. Mom's calling me. Forget we had this conversation. I'll talk to you at our usual time on Sunday." I hung up.

Mom went to bed right after the news, which she always does. I took a shower and washed my hair, then threw on an ancient cami and pair of sleep shorts. By then the feeder band, or whatever it was, had died. The rain had stopped. Peeking out through the curtains of my bedroom window, I could see that the sky was completely clear and the stars were out. The lights Mom's environmentally conscious landscaper had strategically planted at the base of a few of the royal palms in our backyard had come on and shined up against the trunks, even though my mom had fretted about "light pollution" and worried the lights would cause confusion to migratory birds.

The landscaper had looked at her and said, "Ma'am, I think the birds will be fine. And these low-watt bulbs will make it so you can see if there are any prowlers in the backyard without having to use high-energy security lights."

I'd fixated on the word *prowlers*.

·"We'll take them," I'd said firmly.

Peering out into the yard, I saw that Mom had left the pool lights on. Now steam came off the turquoise-blue surface in the humidity left after the storm.

There was something small and black floating in the middle of the pool. A body. Not just floating. Struggling. Whatever it was — and it was tiny — it had legs.

And it was pumping them in a frantic effort to get to the stairs and save itself before it drowned.

But it couldn't save itself. Because even if it reached the stairs, it wouldn't be able to pull itself up onto the first step. It was too small. Anyone could see that.

I let the curtain fall back.

Why me? That was all I had to say. Just . . . *Why. Me.*

Sighing, I left my room, moving through the darkness of the second-floor hallway. I could hear Mom's gentle breathing through the open door to her room. She could fall asleep faster, and stay sleeping harder, than any human being I'd ever known.

When I reached the French doors to the backyard, I entered the code into the alarm, then opened them.

Stepping outside was like stepping into soup. That's how humid it was.

Frogs were croaking everywhere. A cicada screamed. Somewhere behind the twelve-foot Spanish wall crawling with bougainvillea, a cat — or possibly a tree rat — made rustling noises. I ignored them all, walking barefoot down the stone path towards the pool, intent on my mission. The brick path was still wet from the storm, and covered in snails. There was enough glow from the lights at the base of the royal palms for me to be able to see the snails and avoid stepping on them.

Mom had not only left the pool lights on, she'd left the water-fall running, too. The water cascaded from a blue and green tile wall at the far end of the pool. I walked over to the little cottage where we kept all the rafts and cleaning equipment and opened the door. I'd already seen that the creature struggling in the water was a bright green gecko. Now he was in danger of being sucked into the filter.

"Hold on," I said to him, pulling out one of the long-handled poles with a net on the end the pool guy used for scooping out debris. "I've got you."

Seconds later, I'd scooped the gecko up and dropped him from the net onto the leaf of a hibiscus bush. Stunned at first, he just sat there. Then, seeming to realize he wasn't going to die, he leaped away.

The applause seemed to come out of nowhere. I was so startled, I dropped the long silver pole into the pool. It splashed before sinking to the bottom.

"You didn't," John said, stepping from the shadows as he clapped for me, "even hit your head this time."

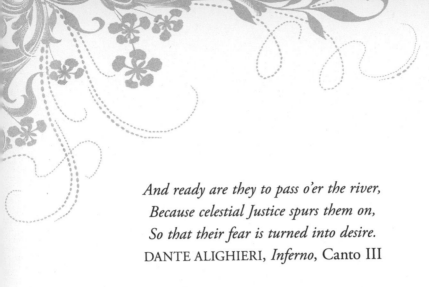

And ready are they to pass o'er the river,
Because celestial Justice spurs them on,
So that their fear is turned into desire.
DANTE ALIGHIERI, *Inferno*, Canto III

Seriously." I pressed a hand over my heart. It was pounding so hard, I thought I was going into cardiac arrest. "You *have* to stop doing that."

"I'm sorry," he said, lowering his hands to his sides.

He stood across the bright blue water, as tall and intimidating as ever, and still dressed all in black as usual, which was probably how I hadn't noticed him in the shadows.

But something about him was different. At first I thought it was his eyes. Maybe they were reflecting the blue light from the pool, because they seemed to be shining as brightly as it was.

But then I realized it was something else.

And when I did, I gasped.

"Wait," I said, taking a few hesitant steps around the edge of the pool towards him so I could get a better look at his expression. "Did you just say what I *think* you said?"

He stayed where he was. He looked wary, like the gecko had when it fell onto the hibiscus leaf . . . like *What just happened? Is this some kind of trap?*

"What?" he said defensively.

"You did," I said in disbelief. When I reached him — he never moved a muscle the whole time I padded, barefoot, around the edge of the pool towards him, until I was standing just a foot away from him — I could see it etched in his face, in the glow from the landscape lights, and the wavy reflection the water was casting up from the pool. "You just said you were sorry."

His weight shifted uncomfortably. So did his gaze. He looked at the pool instead of my face.

"I was only apologizing," he said stiffly, "for startling you. The applause was to compliment you on the improvement in your life-saving techniques since the last time you —"

"No," I said, holding up one hand, palm out. "Stop. Just stop. We need to talk. *Really* talk. I promise I won't call you names if you promise not to try to kill anyone."

His gaze shifted back to mine. I read a myriad of emotions in his eyes in that moment — anger, shame, confusion, pain among them — before it fell to my necklace.

"You're wearing it," he said in a voice I'd never heard him use before.

"Yes," I said. My heart still hadn't stopped its loud thumping. The way he was looking at me wasn't helping.

"I saw Richard find it this morning," he said. "I saw you go into his office tonight."

So he *had* been there. I should have known. No wonder the weather had been so awful.

That's when I realized what it was that had been in his voice . . . the thing I'd never heard before.

Fear. He was afraid. Afraid of what Richard Smith might have told me.

"Yes," I said again. "Look —" I glanced around. Though Uncle Chris had put all the outdoor furniture in the garage, there was a single spot where the uncompromising heat had already dried out a section of flagstone by the side of the pool.

"Come here," I said, reaching for one of his hands.

He took a step backwards — not exactly yanking his fingers away but not willing to let me touch him. Yet.

"It's all right," I said in what I hoped sounded like a soothing voice. He really *was* like that gecko — unsure what we humans might do to him. "I just want to sit down somewhere that's dry. It's what I like, remember? Being dry."

I don't think he got the joke. He continued to eye me suspiciously as I seized his hand and pulled him towards the spot where I wanted to sit down . . . and even after I let go of his hand and sat down at the edge of the pool, putting both my feet in the cool water, he just stood there for a moment, looking at me as if he couldn't figure out what, exactly, was going on.

I decided to ignore him. This is what you did with wild things, I'd learned from my volunteering with animal rescue groups. It worked. Let them figure out on their own that you aren't a threat, that you aren't even interested in them at all, really.

Then, eventually, if you were very lucky, *they* come to *you*.

Which, after a while, John did, sitting cross-legged beside me . . . but looking prepared to take off at the slightest sign of danger. Which was ironic, considering he was a death deity.

I didn't even think about suggesting he take the boots off. There'd probably be an apocalypse or something.

Somewhere in the yard, the cicada, which had taken a break, started up again. Fortunately, the sound of the falling water was strong enough to drown out it and the frogs.

"What did Richard say?" he asked finally, after we'd sat there for a minute in total silence. He seemed stunned, which I guess was understandable. I'd neither screamed, called him names, nor thrown anything at him, a first in our relationship. He had to be wondering what the cemetery sexton could possibly have said to produce this change in my attitude towards him.

"Well," I said slowly. I couldn't quite believe myself that any of this was happening. I wasn't quite sure *how* it was happening. If anyone had told me, even an hour earlier, that it was going to, I never would have believed them.

But now, somehow, it seemed natural.

Be sweet. That's what Richard had said.

Well, that was one man's opinion.

"He said this necklace had killed a thousand people," I said.

John immediately tensed up, as if he were going to get up and leave — or possibly throw me in the pool.

"Hey," I said in what I hoped was still a soothing voice, reaching out and laying a hand on his knee. "You asked what he said. I'm just telling you."

The hand seemed to work. He stayed where he was, the tension leaving his body.

"That wasn't the necklace," he said, scowling. "Do you think I'd give you something that kills people? Why would I do that? The Furies did that because they were angry that the stone wasn't being used by the person for whom it was intended."

"And who is that?" I asked.

John scowled some more. "You know perfectly well who. Richard said he told you. Are you *flirting* with me?"

"Of course not," I said, hoping he couldn't tell in the pool lights that I was blushing. "I'm just trying to keep the facts straight. Mr. Smith talked an awful lot about the Furies."

He frowned. "Richard's obsessed with the Furies."

"Well," I said, "they seem pretty awful. He said they're the spirits of the dead who are unhappy with where they ended up."

He scowled some more, but at the pool, not me. "That's more or less accurate."

"And you told me," I said, "they're the ones who do the punishing if people break the rules in your world. That's how you got these?" I traced a scar on one of his hands, which was resting near mine.

For once, he didn't jerk his hand away. Though his gaze did leave the water and focused on my fingers instead.

"Yes," he said quietly.

"And now there are Furies after me," I said.

Now that bright silver gaze finally turned full on my face.

"There aren't any Furies after you," he said. He looked genuinely puzzled. "Why should there be?"

"Well," I said. *Because you chose me*, I wanted to say. Like Hades chose Persephone. I opted to play it safe, however, in case he accused me of flirting again, and settled instead for saying, "Because you gave me the necklace."

"And you threw a cup of tea in my face," he reminded me drily. "Then you left. I'm fairly certain even the Furies got *that* message loud and clear. They're hardly likely to come after someone who hates me just as much as they do. In fact, the Furies probably consider you one of their closest allies."

I moved my hand away from his, stung . . . even if most of what he'd said was true. Well, the tea part, anyway.

"I told you, I only did that because I was scared," I said. "And I'm not a Fury. Although I don't think it would hurt if you checked yourself a little more often, before you went around wrecking yourself." When he just stared at me, uncomprehending, I explained, "You could be slightly more hospitable to guests when they arrive in your world, and you could also not go around trying to murder innocent people all the time, like that jeweler you almost killed."

He looked indignant. "He wasn't *innocent*. He was an ass. He should never have touched you. He deserved everything he got."

I lifted my gaze to the stars, which burned cold and clear above us, now that the clouds had parted. Because Isla Huesos was so small and so far from the mainland and any major city, I could see way more stars in my backyard here than I'd ever been able to see in my backyard in Westport. Sometimes I even caught glimpses of the Milky Way.

"John," I said, fighting for patience. "Mr. Smith told me Furies can possess any human they want to, if they have a weak enough character."

"They can," John said, sounding skeptical. "But they hardly ever do unless it's to punish me somehow. So I still don't understand why you think they would come after you, when you've made it so clear you want nothing to do with me."

I lowered my gaze from the stars to look at him. He was so frustrating.

"Why *else* do you think that old man was so interested in the necklace?" I demanded. "If he wasn't a Fury?"

"Maybe because he was a *jeweler*," he pointed out.

I buried my face in my hands. How was I ever going to get through to him?

"What about my teacher, Mr. Mueller?" I asked from between my fingers. "Are you trying to tell me *he's* not a Fury?"

"You just admitted to me last night that you put *yourself* in that danger," John said. I saw, when I lowered my hands, his expression darken. "You willingly walked into it in order to trap him. He didn't come after you."

I wanted to correct him. Mr. Mueller had very much come after me, by going after my best friend.

But he hadn't killed Hannah. She'd killed herself.

Still . . .

"What he did to Hannah was wrong," I said. "Someone needed to stop him."

"But you didn't *really* want him dead," he said. In the dancing blue light cast by the pool, his expression was half grave, half amused. "You know how you are, Pierce. You came out of the house at midnight to scoop a lizard out of the swimming pool to save it from dying."

"How do you know that?" I asked wonderingly. "Unless . . ." I broke off, staring at him, realization dawning at last. "Wait. You threw that lizard into the pool. You knew I'd see it and come out here to save it, and then you could talk to me. Didn't you?"

He didn't even bother denying it. Instead, he leaned forward until his face was just inches from mine to counter, "If Richard Smith told you so many terrible things about that necklace, like that it killed a thousand people, and that Furies would come after any girl I gave it to in order to hurt me through her — which you obviously believe or you wouldn't be asking me all these questions — why are you still wearing it? I thought you hated me because I'm such a jerk."

My pulse gave a violent leap. Was it because of the question — he'd seen right through me — or his sudden proximity?

"I do," I said, climbing to my feet in what I hoped looked like an indignant manner, though inwardly, I was shaking. "In fact, I'm going back inside. In the future, John, I would appreciate it if you would stay on your side of the island, and I will stay on mine. Also if you didn't try to kill people — or lizards — to get my attention. Good night."

But I hadn't gone more than a single step before my hand was seized. The next thing I knew, he was pulling me back — just as I'd taken him by the hand and pulled him earlier.

Only he hadn't even bothered to get up. He merely pulled me into his lap.

I was so surprised to find myself there, at first I could only stare up at his face in shock, trying to make sense of what had just happened.

"John," I started to say. "You really can't just —"

Then his lips came down over mine. And all of it — the sound of the waterfall, and the croaking frogs, and the whine of the cicada, and the lights at the base of the palm trees, and the wavy blue reflection of the pool water over everything — went away, and it was only about John and the hardness of his arms as they tightened around me, and the wood-smoke smell of him, and the softness of his hair beneath my fingers, and the way I could feel his heart drumming against mine, and the fact that I couldn't believe any of this was happening, couldn't believe it had never happened before, couldn't believe I'd never *allowed* it to happen before, never wanted it to stop. . . .

"Wait," I said breathlessly, pulling my mouth away from his. "John. Wait." I had to put a hand to his chest and physically push him back. *"Wait a minute."*

"What?" His arms hadn't loosened their hold on me one iota. "What's wrong?"

What was wrong? Everything. Nothing. I didn't know. I couldn't think. I felt as if the Milky Way, hovering above our heads like a celestial pitcher, had suddenly overturned, pouring suns and planets down my throat. Stars seemed to be shooting out of my fingers and toes, the ends of my hair.

"We can't do this," I said, even as he was kissing my throat.

"Yes," he said, a glow in his eyes I'd never seen there before. "We can."

"No," I said. "I mean, *I* can't." My pulse was racing so fast, I thought my heart was going to explode right out of my chest, the way it had seemed to when I'd run down those steps away from him. Only now it was definitely *not* from epinephrine. "I need to think about this."

He lifted his head to look down at me.

"I've given you long enough to think about it," he said. "Almost two years. You wore the necklace that whole time. You even took it back after I gave you a chance to be free, by throwing it away. Now you know what it is, and you're *still* wearing it. You know what that means, Pierce."

I realized now what the glow was in his eyes. It was triumph.

No wonder my heart was beating so fast. He was fire, and I was kindling.

I was doomed.

"All that means," I assured him, struggling to wiggle out of his arms, "is that it's possible you aren't as big a jerk as I may once have accused you of being."

To my relief, he let go of me. He didn't look happy about it, just like the time I'd made him let Mr. Mueller go. But he did.

"It means you care about me," he said.

"I care about everyone," I retorted. "You said so once yourself. I'm a very caring person."

"When can I see you again?" he demanded.

Of course he'd seen right through me. My sarcasm was just a defense mechanism to hide how truly unnerved I was at my body's reaction to his.

I'd known from the fact that I hadn't been able to keep away from the cemetery that I was drawn to him.

But I'd been telling myself it had just been because of the unfinished business between us. And the fact that he kept going around trying to kill people on my behalf. How could I ever have anticipated what I'd heard in Richard Smith's office? Or *this* . . . the immediate chemical reaction that seemed to occur when our lips met? My mouth was still tingling.

What did any of it mean? Where could it go? He was a death deity. I was a senior in high school.

This was never going to work.

He didn't share my pessimistic views.

"Tomorrow," he said, climbing to his feet. His gaze seemed to consume me. "I will see you here tomorrow. At dawn."

"John," I said, shaking my head. This was happening way too fast. "No. Not dawn. That's when normal people are still sleeping. Plus, I have school."

"Dusk, then." The silver eyes flashed. "Meet me here at dusk."

"John. We need to talk about this rationally. You warned me last night," I said, "not to go back to the cemetery. That it wasn't safe for me there. Was that just hyperbole?" I had looked up the word. It means an exaggerated statement not intended to be taken literally. "Or did you really mean it?"

He stepped forward, wrapped an arm around my waist, pulled me against him, then kissed me some more.

It was impossible to think about the cemetery or Furies or Coffin Night when he was kissing me. It was impossible to believe anything bad could happen, ever, when he was kissing me. All I could think about was him.

He let his mouth linger on mine, neither possessively nor sweetly . . . like his mouth just belonged there on mine.

And he was right. It did. It always had.

I couldn't believe I hadn't known this before. Maybe I had.

Maybe that had been the problem all along.

When he finally let go of me, I felt as if my skin might actually be giving off the same shimmery reflection as the pool water.

"You should very, very definitely stay out of the cemetery," he said in a slightly raspy voice. "That is not hyperbole. I'll meet you here tomorrow night at seven o'clock. I won't wait a minute longer. Wherever you are then, I'll come looking for you." He looked down at my pajamas and frowned a little. "Wear that dress you had on last night, the one with the buttons."

And then he was gone.

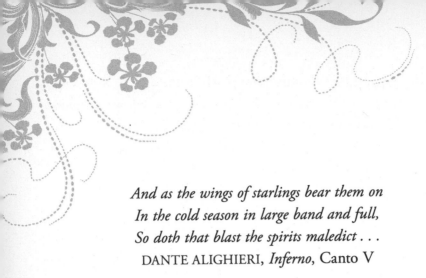

And as the wings of starlings bear them on
In the cold season in large band and full,
So doth that blast the spirits maledict . . .
DANTE ALIGHIERI, *Inferno*, Canto V

The next morning, I didn't get up so much as float up.

"You're in a good mood," Mom said as I poured milk on my cereal.

"What?" I asked her distractedly.

"You're humming," she said with a smile. "You seem like you're in a good mood."

"Mom," I said. "You know that guy Tim?"

She raised her eyebrows. "Yes?"

"You should totally go to the boat show with him. I think it would be good for you."

"Really?" she said, looking amused. "What caused this change of heart?"

"Oh," I said. "I don't know. You should be happy."

"Well," Mom said. "Thank you, Pierce. That is so generous of you to give me your permission to be happy." She looked thoughtful. "Maybe I will give him a call later, though. I was thinking the New Pathways kids might like a tour of the marine lab. You know we've made a lot of strides in —"

"You do that, Mom," I said, and patted her on the shoulder. I wasn't so blissed out that I wanted to hear about the strides the marine lab was making.

In the car to school, Alex wasn't so amused by my good mood.

"I'm still mad at you for yesterday," he said, honking at a chicken that wouldn't get out of the middle of the road. There were chickens and roosters all over Isla Huesos. They ran wild around the island. "It's just not cool. Seth and those guys — they're bad news. You just don't know."

"I do know," I said. Alex had no idea what I knew. But he'd reminded me of something. How was I going to see John if I had those stupid A-Wingers in my house, building that coffin?

And what about Uncle Chris? He was supposed to give me driving lessons after school.

Oh, well. I didn't care. Everything would all sort itself out somehow. It always did. What did it matter, anyway? For the first time in the longest time I could remember, I was happy. Didn't I deserve to be happy? I certainly thought so.

"Are you even listening to me?" Alex demanded. We were pulling into the parking lot at school.

"I'm sorry, what?" I asked him.

"Jesus," he said. "What is wrong with you this morning? Did you not take your pills?"

"I'm sorry, Alex," I said. "I'm listening. It's just . . . well, there's something I should probably tell you. But you're not going to like it."

He swung into a parking space and pulled on the brake. "I swear to God, Pierce," he said. "If you tell me you're going out with Seth Rector, I'm going to throw you out of this car."

"No," I said. "What? Don't be stupid. But those guys kind of invited themselves over to my house to build the senior coffin this year."

He stared at me for what had to be a full minute. For a few seconds, I actually got scared, thinking he might be having a stroke or something. His eyes looked as if they were starting to cross.

"Look, Alex," I said hurriedly. "Don't be mad. I only told them they could do it if Mom said yes, because you saw how happy she looked when everybody was talking about Coffin Night in the New Pathways office yesterday. And then they just showed up with the wood before I even got a chance to talk to her. She let them in. You know how much she wants me to fit in here. I can totally tell them to come pick up the wood if it really upsets you —"

But by then he was already shaking his head. "Pierce," he said. "Pierce, Pierce, Pierce."

"What?" I asked anxiously. "Please don't tell me anything about how they burned down the garage of the last guy whose house they built the coffin in, because I already know that, Alex. I know what I'm getting myself into, okay?" I reflexively touched my necklace. "It's going to be okay."

It was going to be *more* than okay. At least, I hoped so. But I couldn't tell him that, of course.

He was still shaking his head. But he was grinning, too.

"You know what?" he said finally. "You're right."

I stared at him, not sure I'd heard him correctly. "What did you say?"

"You're right." He shrugged. "It's going to be okay. It's going to be *great,* actually. It's kind of perfect." He reached out his right hand. "Put it here, cuz. You're my girl."

I looked at his hand warily. But I stuck mine into it and let him do some complicated things to my limp fingers.

"What are you talking about?" I asked him as we made our way into school along with the rest of the hordes. "How is it kind of perfect? I thought you'd be mad at me."

"It just is," Alex said. There was actually a bounce in his step. "Don't worry about it, all right? Forget you even told me. It's all good. Hey," he said to a guy who'd greeted him with a cry of "Yo, Cabrero."

"But . . ." My bubble of happiness wasn't entirely shattered. Though it was slightly tarnished. "I don't get it. I thought you hated those guys."

"Oh, I do," he said. "But here's the thing." He slung an arm around my neck. "If they're at your house, I'll always know where they are. Because you'll let me know when they're there. Right?"

"Of course," I said. "If you want me to. But why do you need to know where they are?"

"Don't you worry about it. Like I said." He grinned down at me. He really did look happy. "We're good."

"But you're not going to tell, right?" I still had a slightly bad feeling about all of this. "Where the you-know-what is? Because that would reflect badly on both of us, I think."

"Oh, you do not have to worry about that, cuz," he said, and gave me a wink. "See you at lunch? Don't screw it up this time. At the flagpole in the middle of the Quad. It really couldn't be simpler, Pierce. I don't know how even you could have messed it up yesterday."

Yeah. Neither did I. Except that I'd been scared of the cafeteria.

Today, I didn't think I'd have that problem. Today, I couldn't see myself feeling scared of anything.

My happiness restored, I floated through first, second, and third periods. I was sitting in fourth period — which happened to be econ, the class I shared with Kayla, who'd greeted me with a smile and a "Hey! How you doing? So you and Alex made up, huh? I just saw him in English. Why is he in such a good mood?" — when there was a knock on the classroom door.

That was what roused me from the little doodle I'd been making of a girl in a coffin rocket ship that shot flowers at people. That and the teacher saying my name.

"Pass for you." She handed me a pink slip of paper with my name written on it. "You're wanted in the office."

The New Pathways office. Everyone in the class began to hoot, knowing I'd probably accrued an ISS or OSS somehow. Though for the life of me, I couldn't think what I'd done. Unless . . .

"Stop it," the teacher — I hadn't been in there long enough to remember her name — chastised them. "Take your things, Pierce. It's close to the end of the period. You probably won't have time to come back for them before lunch."

I scooped up my books and bag. Kayla made a questioning face at me. I shrugged. I had no idea what it was about.

Except of course I did. I only hoped my fear didn't show in my face.

What had John done *now*? I'd thought things were finally better. Better? I thought things were good.

And okay, maybe I'd only been fooling myself. Maybe a girl — not even an NDE — can't have a normal relationship with a death deity.

But why does she have to be punished for trying?

Because as I approached the office, I saw through the windows around it that things were even worse than I'd imagined. Worse than those hoots back in the classroom had indicated.

Chief of Police Santos was there, along with some other police officers.

Oh, *God*.

I broke into a run.

"What," I said as I burst into the office. "What happened?"

"Whoa there," the police chief said. He lowered the cup of coffee he'd been sipping. "Who's this?"

"Pierce Oliviera, Chief." Tim was looking paler than usual. His button-down shirt looked rumpled and had come untucked in the back. "She's the one from the cemetery —"

"Oh, right." The police chief indicated an office. "Follow me, young lady."

What was happening? The chief of police wanted to see me? Was I being blamed for the cemetery gate after all?

"Do I need to call my mother?" I demanded, staying where I was.

"I don't know," Chief of Police Santos said, raising his gray, bushy eyebrows questioningly. "Do you?"

"No, Pierce," Tim said. He looked exhausted. "You don't. It's all right. The police just want to ask you some questions."

If it had been anybody else but the person to whom I had surrendered my cell phone the day before — I had forgotten to do it that morning. But then, I had forgotten to bring my cell phone to school, I'd discovered a little while earlier, I'd been so caught up in my happy little love cloud — I probably would have insisted, Zack Oliviera–style, that I needed a lawyer.

But since it was Tim, my mom's future maybe-boyfriend, I shrugged and followed Police Chief Santos into the office, which happened to be filled with cardboard boxes and pamphlets that said *New Pathways: A New Pathway to a New You!*

A female police officer was sitting at a conference table inside the office, writing something down in a notebook. She looked up when we came in. She didn't smile.

"What was your name again?" Police Chief Santos said to me as I followed him. "Pierce what?"

"Oliviera," Tim answered for me. He'd come in after us. He was holding, I saw, my file. Over the past year and a half, I'd become expert in reading my name upside down.

"Oh." The police chief pulled out a chair at the conference table. "Have a seat, Ms. Oliviera." He said it wrong. "This won't take long."

Bewildered — but knowing from experience that nothing good was about to happen — I took the seat he offered.

"If this is about the cemetery gate," I said, "I had nothing to do with it."

The chief of police regarded me with some surprise over the top of his coffee mug.

"The cemetery gate," he said, when he'd lowered it again. "And what do you know about the cemetery gate?"

"Nothing," I said. "That's what I'm telling you. I don't know anything about it. I don't know who did that to it."

"Did what to it?" I saw the chief of police exchange glances with the female officer, who'd stopped scribbling in her note-book and was looking at me as if I were a perp she was longing to tase.

"Kicked it like that," I said. "And broke the lock."

Police Chief Santos exhaled gustily enough to send some of the droplets of coffee left in his mustache hairs scattering into the air. The female police officer sighed and went back to her scribbling. Tim, who'd taken a seat at the end of the conference table, opened my file and pretended to be busy reading it. I couldn't be sure, but I thought I heard the female officer say *D-Wing* under her breath. She shook her head in disbelief.

"Ms. . . . whatever your name is," Police Chief Santos said. "The force that was applied to that gate the other night in order to inflict that kind of damage to it was equal to the amount of force it takes to launch a small grenade. Therefore, we have already determined that it was not caused by a mere *kick*."

I sat there and stared down at my fingernails, now shredded of all traces of polish.

"Oh," I said.

Who was I to tell the police they were wrong? *Again.*

"We aren't here to talk about the gate, anyway," he said grumpily. "Officer Hernandez?"

The female officer flipped a page in her notebook, then asked in a monotone, "Do you own a blue Sun Cruiser bicycle with a white flowered basket, large purple seat, red combination lock, and the serial number R-dash-one-hundred-dash-seven-fifty-one-eleven-seventy?"

I looked at them in a blind panic. My mind had gone blank. "I don't know," I said.

"Pierce," Tim said gently. "You do. You and your mom registered a bicycle under your name with the police department, in case it was stolen."

I blinked, my heart beginning to thump harder than ever.

"Oh," I said. "Well, I do have a blue bike with a purple seat and a flowered basket and a red lock and stuff. And I did register a bike with the police department, in case it got stolen. But I don't remember the *serial number* off the top of my head. Who goes around memorizing their bike's serial number? That's just — I mean, that's asking way more than anyone should be required to know —"

"When is the last time you saw this bicycle?" the police chief interrupted, taking a sip of his coffee.

"Last night," I said. "When I rode it down to see the —"

I stopped. All the blood seemed to have frozen in my veins.

My bike. I'd left it chained to the fence down by the cemetery.

When I'd gone to see Richard Smith.

"Oh, my God." I stood up, almost knocking over my chair. "What's happened to him?"

He was dead. I knew it. He was the last person to have touched my necklace.

And now he was dead.

I should have known. I should have known I would never be happy. I should have known I wouldn't be able to handle him. Why would *I* be able to handle a death deity? The freaking ruler of an Underworld? Who was I kidding? I hadn't been able to keep my best friend alive. I couldn't do long division. *I couldn't even drive.*

"Calm down, Pierce," Tim said, getting up and coming around the table to my side. I'd started to hyperventilate. "It's all right. It's going to be all right. That's what we're trying to figure out."

"But what *happened*?" I cried. I could feel hysteria beginning to sweep over me. "He was fine when I last saw him. He was fine when he dropped me off at home."

"Who was fine?" Tim glanced at the police chief, who seemed as confused as Tim did. "Who are you talking about, Pierce?"

"Mr. Smith," I said. Some of the panic began to ebb as I saw, from their expressions, that they didn't know what I was talking about. "The cemetery sexton. Why? Wait. Who are *you* talking about?"

"Jade," Tim said gently. "We're looking for any witnesses who might have been in or around the cemetery last night. She never made it home from her shift. This morning she was found inside the cemetery, dead."

Through me the way is to the city of woe;
Through me the way is to eternal pain;
Through me the way among the people lost.
DANTE ALIGHIERI, *Inferno, Canto III*

They made the announcement during lunch.

Not that Jade was dead. Why would they do *that*? Isla Huesos High School didn't want to "glamorize" a death any more than the Westport Academy for Girls had.

No, the announcement was that the hurricane watch had been upgraded to a warning by the National Hurricane Center. All after-school events were canceled, as were classes the next day. We were being dismissed at two o'clock instead of three fifteen.

"Why don't they just let us go now?" Kayla complained over her chef's salad. "I mean, what good is one hour more of class going to do, with everyone freaking out because a gigantic hurricane is coming? It's not like we're going to learn anything after this."

"Yeah," I said. "And it would give us less time to memorialize her death. Just cancel school now so we can't even talk about her."

"What?" Kayla asked.

"Nothing," I said, lowering my burrito. Who could eat at a time like this, anyway?

"Remember the time she didn't kill her teacher?" Alex explained to Kayla. "It was over something like this thing with Jade."

"No, it wasn't," I said. "Jade didn't hit *herself* over the head with a blunt instrument."

Tim had told me that as near as the police could figure out, since Jade's body hadn't been found for so long and no witnesses had come forward yet, she'd been the victim of what looked like a random mugging. As soon as the EMTs got to her — she was discovered behind a crypt by Richard Smith when he'd gone to the cemetery for work that morning — they had her airlifted to Ryder Trauma Center in Miami.

But even they hadn't been able to save her. The damage to her skull — though she'd had her bicycle helmet on — was too extensive.

"I'm sorry, Pierce," Tim had said to me, patting me on the back as I broke down in the conference room and cried. "I'm so sorry."

Not as sorry as I was.

Nothing bad will happen to her. John will see to that.

That's what Richard Smith had said to me in the car after Jade rode away into that rain.

But something bad *had* happened to her. The worst thing that could possibly happen to someone.

Because John hadn't been in the cemetery to take care of her.

He'd been with me.

That's what I'd said to him — Mr. Smith — when I stumbled out of the New Pathways office after they let me go. I'd called him in his office immediately from a pay phone.

"It's all my fault," I said, sobbing.

"I don't see how that's possible," he replied. "Unless you were the one who struck her from behind with the pipe or shovel or whatever it was that was used to kill her, and then took her wallet — and her bicycle. And her police radio. That's missing as well, which I find odd. You can hardly pawn a police radio —"

"You know what I mean. John was with me when she died," I hissed into the phone. The bell had rung by then, and people were filing by, throwing odd looks at me because not only was I on what had to be the last remaining pay phone on Isla Huesos, but I was *crying.*

"It wasn't John's fault, either, Miss Oliviera," he said with maddening calm. "Although he feels as badly as you do. Who do you think woke me and led me to her?"

"It wasn't safe," I wailed. "John said the cemetery wasn't safe!"

Why hadn't I told him last night that she was in there? I'd been too distracted by his kisses. . . .

"For you," Richard Smith reminded me. "He said it wasn't safe for *you.* No one could have predicted this, Miss Oliviera, not even a death deity. It was just her time. It's unfortunate, of course, and when they find the person responsible, I hope he's punished to the fullest extent of the law. But you can hardly blame this on John, much less yourself. Jade chose to be out there. She knew the risks of what she was doing. And you saw how much fun she was having. John said she's moved on to a better place —"

I'd hung up on him, I was so furious. *This* is what had come from Richard Smith's suggestion that I "be sweeter." Someone I'd liked — *really* liked — was dead.

Check yourself before you wreck yourself.

Yes, I suppose rationally I knew in the back of my mind that Jade's death wasn't my fault, or John's either. . . . But when something horrible happens, it's human nature to want to blame it on someone. We want someone to be held accountable, even though sometimes things just *happen*.

The problem, like my dad said, was that too often, we hold the wrong person accountable. Sometimes even the victim herself. We do this so we can reassure ourselves the bad thing will never happen to us. "Oh, this terrible thing happened to this person because she did such-and-such. All I have to do is never do such-and-such, and then the terrible thing will never happen to me."

I died trying to rescue a bird. My mom holds my dad accountable for this, since he didn't get the pool cover fixed, or notice I was drowning. When really it was my own fault for being so clumsy.

In Jade's case, as soon as the details of her death hit the caf — which they seemed to as soon as I walked into the Quad — everyone was saying, "Well, what was she doing riding her bike so late at night, and in the cemetery, of all places? She should never have been doing that. No wonder she died."

Like it was Jade's own fault.

There was just one small problem with this theory:

Jade had been killed by someone. The police wanted to find that person or at least a witness who could say they'd seen him.

By the time the first of the day's big gray storm clouds started to roll in, the pieces all began to come together. Later, I couldn't believe how long it took me to see them.

But it was all so horrible. Who could even begin to imagine something so horrible?

And the thing is, people die. Sometimes they trip and fall, then they hit their heads and roll into the pool and drown.

Other times they get seduced by their basketball coach and then dumped, and they go home and swallow a bottle of prescription pills.

Other times they get mugged while riding their bikes and don't get found in time and then they die.

It's just the way things are. It doesn't have anything to do with you, necessarily.

"Aunt Deb?" Alex said, answering his phone when it rang as we were dropping off our empty lunch trays. "I know. Pierce forgot her phone again, didn't she?"

But then again, other times, it *does* have something to do with you.

Alex's face drained of its normal color as my mother spoke. Evidently, she didn't want to talk to me.

Other people did, though.

"Hey, Pierce," Farah said, smiling and waving as she and Seth walked by, arms around each other's waists.

"Oh," I said to them. I couldn't quite summon a smile back. But I waved. "Hey."

The storm clouds overhead rumbled. It was so weird that they made everyone at this school eat lunch outside. What were we supposed to do, I wondered, when it rained? Like it was about to do right now, for instance?

"Pierce," Bryce yelled at me, as he walked by on his way to the trash cans with what looked like about twelve burrito wrappers. Cody was with him. "Pierce, Pierce, Pierce, Pierce!" They yelled it like it was a chant. Like it was the Mueller Shout-Out.

"God," Kayla said to me. "What did you have with them yesterday, ice cream or sex?"

I made a face at her. "Ew. Shut up."

Alex hung up his phone.

"Hey," I said to him. "What did my mom want?"

"She was calling from the police station. They just took my dad there for questioning," he said. He looked sick, as if someone had punched him in the gut. "For Jade's murder."

I felt the ground shift beneath my feet. At first I thought it was thunder.

But there hadn't been any thunder. Not then.

"What?" I said, my mind whirling. "But how is that even —"

"A witness phoned in an anonymous tip," Alex said. "They said they saw Dad driving around near the cemetery last night, in Grandma's car. They just came over and impounded it. They're testing it for trace evidence." He let out a laugh that sounded nothing like his normal one. "Grandma's car. They just took Grandma's car. I wonder what they'll find in it. A lot of yarn, that's for sure."

"Alex," I said uneasily.

This couldn't be happening. Not so many terrible things at once. How could they?

Something was wrong. Not just wrong but planets-out-of-alignment wrong.

Check yourself before you wreck yourself.

As soon as I thought it, a gust of wind swept through the courtyard, so strong everyone still sitting at the many lunch tables had to grab their food wrappers to keep them from blowing away. Farah and Nicole let out good-natured shrieks and clung to their skirts. Every guy in the Quad but Alex noticed.

"He didn't even go out last night," he was saying angrily about Uncle Chris. "You know him. He never goes out, except for his meetings with his parole officer. He just sits in front of that TV, watching the Weather Channel, drinking —"

"Mountain Dew," I finished for him. "I know."

I looked around. Lightning was beginning to flash out at sea.

No. This could *not* be happening.

But at the same time, the sinking feeling I'd been experiencing since I'd seen the police in the New Pathways office told me that it most definitely *was* happening.

No. Not ever since I'd seen the police in the New Pathways office. Ever since I'd come back from the dead.

If I really wanted to be honest with myself, though, I had to admit it had all started long before that:

"Did you like him?" Grandma had asked.

"I don't know," I'd replied.

Grandma had smiled.

"You will," she'd said.

And tucked a scarf around my neck. A scarf she'd knitted herself, just for me.

A red one. With tassels.

Wait. That wasn't how it had happened. What was I thinking? Grandma was right: I really did have an overactive imagination.

"Is this just a case of rounding up the usual suspects?" Kayla asked. "I saw that in a movie once. Maybe just because your dad went to jail once, they're questioning everyone who —"

"No," Alex said bitterly, looking as if he wanted to punch something. But there was nothing nearby soft enough to hit without injuring himself, except possibly some A-Wingers who were scattering because it was about to pour and the warning bell had just rung for class. "I told you. Someone says they saw him. A witness. Some witness, if he managed to see my dad somewhere he wasn't, driving a car he was never in."

"Oh, Alex," Kayla said, and put her hand on his shoulder. Her expression was softer than I'd ever seen it. "I'm so, so sorry."

My mind flashed back to Uncle Chris from the day before, when he'd urged me never to let anyone tell me I couldn't do something I'd set my mind to.

That wasn't going to be a problem anymore, I didn't think.

"Give me your phone, Alex," I said, holding out my hand.

"Why?" he asked, instantly suspicious even in his despair.

"Because," I said, "I'm going to call my dad."

Alex shook his head at me. "Pierce. Your dad *hates* my dad. Remember?"

"No, he doesn't," I lied. "Just hand it over."

"Pierce," Alex said. "It's nice of you to offer. Really, it is. But you do not want to get involved in this. It's not something you can really handle."

I had to laugh. Although the truth was, I didn't feel like it.

"Oh, Alex," I said to him. "Trust me. What I handle on a daily basis makes this look like cake."

This statement was followed by a crack of thunder so loud, it sent the rest of the few students who were still standing beneath the breezeway with us scrambling for the safety of the various wings where they had classes.

"Look," Alex said, raising his voice to be heard above the wind. "I appreciate it, Pierce. But I think your dad's done enough damage around here. Don't you?"

Kayla inhaled sharply. I felt my eyes sting, then realized it was because they were tearing . . . although it wasn't anything I hadn't heard before, and from my own mother.

"We're late to class," Alex said, and pushed past us both. "I'll meet you at the car at two o'clock if you want a lift home."

He hurried down the breezeway towards D-Wing, his head ducked, his shoulders hunched in on themselves. He looked smaller than I'd ever seen him. And Alex had grown two whole inches over the summer. Uncle Chris had proudly shown me the marks on the kitchen doorway.

"He didn't mean it," Kayla turned to me to say.

"Yeah," I said, shaking my head. "He did."

"Well," Kayla said. "Maybe he did. But you know. He's upset. Hey." She was staring at something over my shoulder. "Isn't your grandma the lady from Knuts for Knitting?"

"Yeah," I said. "Why?"

"Because she's here."

I spun around. Kayla was right. My grandmother was coming

down the breezeway towards us, wearing one of her usual artsy outfits of beige gauchos, white peasant blouse, and laceless white Keds.

Around her neck was one of the many colorful scarves she always wore, all knitted by her own hand. At each end of the scarf dangled a set of tassels.

Grandma was semi-famous around the island for these. Some people used them as pulls for their ceiling fans.

"Pierce!" Grandma lifted a hand to wave. Even as far off as she was — two whole locker banks away — I could hear her loud breathing. Grandma wasn't very athletic. She didn't like to walk places, preferring to take her car. "Thank God I found you. Did you hear the news about Christopher? It's just awful."

"She must be here to sign you guys out of school," Kayla whispered to me. "Except for lunch, they won't let you go off-campus unless it's a family emergency and someone over eighteen signs you out."

"Oh," I said. "Except didn't Alex just say her car got impounded?"

Kayla shrugged. "She must have driven your mom's car."

"Then why didn't my mom tell Alex she was on her way over?"

Kayla looked at me. "Chickie," she said. "What are you saying? You think your grandma's here to kidnap you or something?"

Did you like him?

I don't know.

You will.

284

I put my book bag down on the ground, still staring at Grandma, who had almost made it to the end of the last bank of lockers. The tassels at the end of her scarf swayed.

Just like the ones at the end of the scarf I'd worn the day I died had swayed in the water above my head.

It had been there all along, right in front of me, and it had taken this long for me to figure it out.

I'd been such a fool.

"Just how dysfunctional *is* your family, anyway?" Kayla was going on.

"Kayla," I said, rolling up my sleeves. "Do me a favor, okay? Go to class."

"Uh," Kayla said with a little laugh, "okay. So I guess I won't be seeing you at Alex's car at two?"

"If I'm not there," I said, "call the cops."

Kayla laughed some more. She obviously thought this whole thing was a hilarious joke.

"Don't worry, chickie," she said, and headed off to D-Wing. "I will. The cops and I go way back."

What Kayla didn't know — and I did — was that the diamond tucked inside my shirt, which had been the cheerful purple it usually turned whenever Kayla was around, had gone onyx the minute my grandmother showed up.

It always turned this color when my grandmother was around. I'd figured this was because her disapproval of me made me nervous.

Now I knew the real reason why.

"Why," Grandma panted, when she finally got up to me, "didn't you come over when you saw me? I'm dying here."

"It might help," I muttered, "if you ditched the scarf."

"What was that?" Grandma had blue eyes. She was the only one in our family who did. Because she wasn't an Oliviera. Or a Cabrero. What she was instead, I was only just beginning to figure out.

"Why are you here, Grandma?" I asked.

"Oh," she said, fanning herself with the ends of her scarf. "I'm here to get you. Your mom wants you home. Something terrible has happened. Your uncle Chris —"

"I already know," I said flatly. "They took him in for questioning."

"Oh," she said again, looking surprised. "Well, if you already know, why are you just standing there? Let's go." She took my arm, and then, when I didn't move, tugged on it.

"Pierce," she said, annoyed. "What's wrong with you? We don't have time for games. It's about to pour, can't you tell? There's a storm coming. I don't want to get wet. Let's go."

"What about Alex?" I asked.

"He left already," Grandma said without skipping a beat.

"Really?" I said. "He did? Did you call him?"

"Yes," she said. "I did. He said he couldn't find you. Now come on, I don't have all day. I have to get back to the shop. Let's go."

"No," I said, shaking my head. "Not with you."

"What are you talking about?" Grandma was a little bit shorter than me, but she was wider and therefore had a lower center of gravity. When she pulled, she pulled hard.

But I could be stubborn, too.

"Pierce! What is the matter with you?" she demanded. Her grip was so strong, it felt as if it was cutting off my circulation. "I've told your mother again and again to keep you away from all that caffeine —"

"Oh, you'd like that, wouldn't you?" The courtyard. The breezeway. Her tassels. Everything was starting to turn red. But I didn't care. "Anything you can do so I won't remember. But guess what? I *do* remember, even more than you've guessed. You sent me into the cemetery the day of Grandpa's funeral on purpose. You did it so I'd meet John."

Grandma blinked at me uncomprehendingly. "What?" she said. "I don't know what you're —"

"Grandpa didn't know anything about your little plan, did he?" I went on, ignoring her. "Richard Smith told me you told Grandpa you didn't believe in death deities. But you *do* believe in them, don't you? You not only believe in death deities, you like torturing them, don't you? Because that's what Furies do."

Now Grandma had gone the color of her gauchos. Outside the breezeway, the wind had picked up. It was stirring her short gray curls. But she kept holding on to my arm.

"I don't know where you're getting this stuff," she said. "But if you've been talking to Richard Smith, I can only imagine what you've heard. That man's a lunatic, obsessed with the idea that death is a natural part of life, or some such nonsense, when you should know better than anyone, Pierce, what really happens when we die. So you just take everything he says with a grain of salt. I only came here to pick you up and take you to your mother —"

"Using whose car?" I demanded. "Not Mom's, because she just called Alex from wherever they're questioning Uncle Chris, and yours got impounded. So big mistake, Grandma. You know what the other mistake you made was? Killing me."

That's when I saw a flicker of something in those blue eyes. Not fear. It was too reptilian to be fear.

It was more like . . .

Hatred.

"Oh, I know you thought I'd never figure it out," I said, still trying to rip my arm from her grip. But she hung on, her expression changing. Now *she* looked like the wild thing I'd once been so convinced John was.

Except his eyes, even at their most hopeless, had never looked at me with such hatred. Never once. His eyes might once have looked dead, but I had never doubted that there was life in there somewhere. With Grandma, I suddenly wasn't so sure.

"You sent me into that cemetery when I was seven so I'd be certain to meet John, didn't you? Then that way when I died, I'd be sure to go to the Underworld here in Isla Huesos, and I wouldn't be afraid of him, and then maybe he'd notice me and choose me to be his consort, the way Hades chose Persephone. Right?"

It had started to rain, fat, hard drops that made rattling noises against the metal roof of the breezeway.

I ignored them. All my attention was focused on the woman in front of me. If that's what she even was. I got the sense she hadn't been my actual grandmother for a long time.

"*That's* why you asked if I liked him that day, and why when I told you I didn't know, you said I would. Admit it." I shook my head. I had put it all together at last. But I was still having trouble believing it. Because it was just so awful. "*You're* the one who knitted me that scarf, the one with the red tassels. You sent it to me for Christmas. *I remember it all now.* What did you do to it to make sure it tangled up around my legs and tripped me? How did you know for sure I'd wear it outside by the pool, and fall in and drown? Did you hurt the birds, too? The one on the pool cover in Westport, and the one on the path, here in Isla Huesos? *What kind of person are you? Who would murder her own grand-daughter?*"

That's when she finally let me go. And stood in front of me, panting.

But not because she was old and weak. She was far from that.

Because she was a Fury. And she was finally showing her true face.

And it was more hideous and frightening than anything I could ever have imagined.

"*You're* the one," she said, her eyes blazing. "You're the one who ruined it. You were supposed to *stay* dead. But you're so stupid, you couldn't even do *that* right, could you?"

I blinked at her, horrified. It had taken me forever to put it all together. Now I couldn't believe I'd been right.

"I tried to tell them," Grandma went on, breathing hard. Her tongue darted out like a snake's as she licked her dry pink lips. "I tried to warn them about you. When Deborah was born, and she was so beautiful, and smart, and perfect, it seemed like fate. I was sure our family would be the ones to finally destroy him. I was positive he'd fall in love with her the minute he saw her.

But he didn't. I tried everything. I must have spent a thousand hours in that cemetery with her, roaming up and down between those crypts, trying to get his attention. But did he ever give her so much as a glance?" Grandma gave a snort, her gaze flicking back towards me.

"But you?" She sneered. "I leave you alone in the cemetery for five minutes, and what happens? I could hardly believe it." Her face crinkled into something that, had she any bit of humanity left in her, might have been a smile. "If I'd known he liked them stupid and ugly, I wouldn't have wasted so much time making sure your mother did all her homework and got those weekly manicures."

Tears stung my eyes. I knew intellectually of course that she wasn't really my grandmother anymore.

But being called stupid and ugly by her hurt more than it should have.

"Killing you was the easy part," she went on. "The problem is that you won't *stay* dead. You have far more of your father in you than any of us ever anticipated."

"You know what?" I said, raising my chin. "I'm going to take that as a compliment." Although I knew she didn't mean it as one.

"I told them because of that, it was never going to work," she hissed, as if I hadn't even spoken. "But would they listen? Of course not. And now look what's happened. If you're not dead and at John Hayden's side, he'll never know true happiness. And if John Hayden isn't happy, then we can't take that happiness away from him, can we? But that's a situation I can easily rectify—"

That's when she lunged . . . directly into the fist I'd thrust in front of me, exactly the way Dad's driver had taught me to, in case I were ever in a situation where I had to defend myself.

She staggered and fell back, letting out a scream like nothing I'd ever heard before in my life. It was so shrill, it shattered the red haze that had fallen over my eyes.

That's when John showed up.

Just appeared out of nowhere, in his black jeans and T-shirt, like materializing in the Quad of Isla Huesos High School in the middle of a downpour and a fistfight between his girlfriend and her Fury grandma was something he did on a daily basis.

"Let's go," he said to me in a calm voice, wrapping an arm around my waist and lifting me off the ground to cart me away.

No *Hello.*

No *Hi, Pierce. Nice right hook you have there.*

No *It's lovely to see you. Sorry about your counselor being killed last night. Yes, I see your grandmother is a Fury even though I told you none was after you. I guess I was wrong about that.*

Just *Let's go.*

"I'll be back for you," I tossed over my shoulder at the thing that used to be my grandma. I think I was slightly hysterical. John carried me around the corner towards the entrance to B-Wing.

"No," John said to me in the same voice he'd used that day in the jewelry shop. Like he was refusing beverage cart service. "You will not be back for her."

"What do you mean?" I lifted the hair that had fallen into my face so I could see where we were going. "John, do you know what she is? She's a Fury. You said there weren't any Furies after me, but guess what. There are! My own grandmother is one. And she killed me! She knitted me the scarf I tripped over when I died. John, she's been trying to hurt you since before I was even born —"

But he wouldn't put me down, even when I squirmed, until we reached a portion of the breezeway that he seemed to feel was a safe enough distance from my still-screaming grandmother that I'd be out of danger — or she would. Even then, when he stopped and set me back down on my own feet, he kept me pressed up against a locker with his hands on my shoulders so I couldn't get away.

"I know" was all he said, his expression grave.

I gazed up at him, shocked. "You know? About my grand-mother? *How?*"

"Not about your grandmother," he said, shaking his head. "Although it makes sense. I should have guessed. You were right about Furies being after you."

"I knew it!" I burst out. "My necklace turns black when they're around." I lifted the pendant to show him. The diamond was still as dark as tar. "It did this with the jeweler *and* Mr. Mueller. I don't care what you say, John, I think they were both Furies, too. This thing has not been wrong once. I just didn't know how to read it. It's too bad it didn't come with a user's manual or any-thing. Because knowing what all the different colors mean would be really bene —"

"Pierce," he said. His expression was grimmer than I'd ever seen it. "The Furies killed Jade."

My eyes instantly filled with tears. I dropped the necklace. The heavy diamond struck my chest with a thump. "Oh, John, no. My *grandmother* —" I was too upset to finish the sentence.

"No, not her. But if what you're saying is true, they were probably friends of hers. It was three men who killed Jade. She said she didn't recognize them. They were wearing masks."

"Why Jade?" I asked. "Jade never did anything to anyone."

Except offer them good advice and red licorice.

"Don't you see?" His gray eyes looked haunted. "Jade died because they mistook her for *you*, Pierce. You're always tearing through that cemetery on your bicycle —"

I lifted my anguished gaze towards his. "John. If Mr. Mueller was a Fury, then this isn't even the first time they've hurt someone else because of me. Because . . . Hannah. What about Hannah?"

He stared back at me, speechless. The rain had picked up. Now it was starting to pour.

"I should," I said in a small voice, "have let you kill him."

"No," he said, tightening his grip on my shoulders. "You were right to stop me. With the jeweler, too. It's not *them* doing the killing, Pierce. It's the Furies possessing them. I forget sometimes."

"There must be some way we can stop them before they hurt someone else, John," I said. "There *must* be a way."

"They're unstoppable," he said. "You can break their bones, you can even kill the bodies they're in. It doesn't do anything."

"But when I hit my grandmother just now —"

"If hitting them was any use, do you think there'd be any of them left?" he demanded. He kept looking around the corner, as if he expected my grandmother to show up there any minute. "Believe me, I've hit enough of them enough times, they ought to be extinct by now. But they always come back. They just find some new body to inhabit, some new weak-minded soul to corrupt."

"Then what are we going to do?" I asked, reaching up to put my arms around his neck, desperate for some kind of comfort.

He buried his head in the place where my neck met my shoulder, clinging to me as tightly as if he were out there in the waves again, abandoned to the storm, and I was the one solid thing he'd found to hold on to. Instead of my finding comfort in him, he was looking for it in me, I realized. This frightened me almost more than anything else that had occurred so far.

"I don't know why I ever thought just because you chose not to be with me," he said, his voice muffled in my hair, "you would be safe from them, when all this time, you weren't even safe from your own fami —"

"Shhh," I said, unable to bear letting him finish that sentence. What could he possibly have done to make my *grandmother* hate him so much? "It'll be okay. We'll find a way —"

"No." Suddenly, he straightened. But still he didn't release me. He held on to my shoulders. "It won't be okay, Pierce. They're Furies. They're on earth. And they're after *you*."

"But the necklace," I said, gesturing to it. I wanted to let him know that I could protect myself. I *had* protected myself. I just hadn't managed to protect anyone else. "With a little more practice, now that I understand what's going on, I'm sure I —"

He shook his head.

"Pierce," he said. "I've been thinking about this ever since I found Jade. And there is *one* thing I can do to protect you from the Furies."

I looked up at him, hardly daring to let myself hope. "Really? What?"

"I'm afraid you're not going to like it," he said.

"Why? What is it?"

He kissed me gently on my forehead, letting his lips linger there.

"Close your eyes," he said.

"Why?" I asked in confusion.

"Just do it. I promise it won't hurt," he said.

When realization of what he was about to do dawned, I lunged. When he caught me, I kicked him. I pried at his rock-hard grip and pleaded with him. I struggled to escape.

"John," I cried. "No. Don't do this. Not *this* way. It's what they want, my grandmother told me. Please, I'm begging you —"

But it was too late. He was too strong. I couldn't get away.

And of course, eventually, I blinked.

One.

Two.

Three.

"Before me there were no created things,
Only eternal, and I eternal last.
All hope abandon, ye who enter in!"
DANTE ALIGHIERI, *Inferno*, Canto III

None of it had changed. The gauzy white curtains in the elegant archways, blowing in the gentle breeze. The tapestries hanging from the smooth marble walls. The fire in the hearth. The fruit in the gleaming silver bowls on the long banquet table. Even the sky was the same. It was still pink, a perpetual twilit evening.

And the bed. The bed was still there, of course. It was still white-sheeted, canopied, and built for two.

I broke from his arms as soon as he released me — which happened the second we got there.

"No!" I gasped as soon as I opened my eyes.

I couldn't believe it. I couldn't believe I was back there, the place from so many of my nightmares.

"Pierce," he said in that infuriatingly unruffled voice. "Don't get upset. You know this is for the best."

Don't get upset? This is for the best?

I was even in the same dress.

Well, maybe not quite the same. But looking down at myself, I saw that I was wearing something remarkably similar to the gown he'd put me in — with his *mind* — the last time he'd flung me to this place. It was long and white and flowy. When I lifted a hand defensively to my hair, I felt something prickly in it.

"Flowers?" I pulled them from my head and hurled them to the floor in disgust. "Are you crazy? And stop dressing me! I can dress myself."

"I thought you'd like it," he said, seeming hurt. "You look very pretty."

There was no response I could make to this except to burst out, "I'm going to kill you!"

He considered this. "You're too late," he informed me.

Then he crossed the room to one of his shelves, pulled a book down from it, went to the couch, sat down, opened the book, and began to read.

Just like that. Conversation over. Wonder what we'll have for dinner later?

Well, if he thought this was the end of it, he was very, very mistaken.

I stormed past him on shaking legs, straight through the archway I'd taken to the hall to freedom the last time I escaped.

He didn't try to stop me. He didn't utter a sound.

I should have suspected something then. But of course, I didn't. I had hope. Then.

They were still there . . . the staircases, exactly the way I remembered them. Looking back over my shoulder, I waited for him to say something. *Stop. Wait. Let's talk about this. The Furies. What do you plan on doing about them if you get out?*

But he didn't say a word.

Lifting the hem of my idiotically long skirt, I plunged down the stairs, exactly as I had last time.

The door was locked. Of course.

I should have known he'd have thought of this. He wouldn't be tricked a second time.

Still, I threw my weight against the door. I kicked and shoved at it.

When it became obvious it wasn't going to budge, I took the second staircase, the one that curled upward. The door at the top of that one was locked as well.

Even then, I didn't give up. I was all over the rest of the hallway like a sniffer dog at customs, my hands pressed to the walls for secret passageways.

I found nothing but an elaborate bathroom — complete with a sunken tub and a view over a pretty garden, where the flowers he'd put in my hair grew.

I scrambled out the bathroom window and raced across the garden, then attempted to throw myself over the wall. When I got to the top, I saw . . .

The lake. The same lake beside which, a year and a half ago, I'd stood and shivered with the rest of the dead.

There were no boats, of course. Except *the* boats.

And those were picking up passengers only on the other side of the lake, not on the one where I was.

When I returned — defeated, my dress torn and dirty from climbing the garden wall — to the room with the bed, he was sitting exactly where he'd been when I left, reading the exact same book.

"I hope you're not planning on kicking me," he said, not even bothering to look up from his book, "as hard as you did those doors."

"I will," I said, "if the next words out of your mouth are *Pierce, you just need to relax.* How long have you been planning this?"

"You know it's the only way," he said, turning the page. The fact that he'd ignored my question did not slip past me. "If you want, we can visit the stables later. I'm sure Alastor has gotten over his animosity towards you by now."

I sat down on the couch beside him. I was starting to understand why, every time I'd seen him over the past year and a half, he'd looked so wild. I felt the same way, as if the castle walls were already starting to close in on me.

"John," I said, reaching out and laying a hand on his arm. "Am I dead?"

He lowered the book and looked me in the eye. His expression was guarded. "No, Pierce," he said. "Of course you're not dead. The whole reason I brought you here was to protect you from the Furies, who are trying kill you. I thought you understood that."

I was speechless. "Then back on Isla Huesos, I just . . . disappeared?"

"I suppose so," he said, after giving it some thought. "I don't really know. I've never rescued a girl I love from the Furies before." He looked alarmed as he noticed my eyes were filling with tears. *"Don't cry."*

"How can I not?" I asked him. "You just said you love me."

"Well, why else did you think all of this was happening?" He set the book aside to wrap his arms around me. "The Furies wouldn't be trying to kill you if I didn't love you."

"I didn't know," I said. Tears were trickling down my cheeks, but I did nothing to try to stop them. His shirt was absorbing most of them. "You never said anything about it. Every time I saw you, you just acted so . . . wild."

"How was I supposed to act?" he asked. "You kept doing things like throw tea in my face."

I glared up at him through my tears.

"This isn't funny," I said. "Do you know that if I don't show up at my cousin Alex's car at two o'clock today, my friend Kayla is supposed to call the police? She'll do it, too. Who knows what kind of lies my grandmother is going to tell them when they ask? She'll probably say you killed me and dumped my body in the ocean somewhere. My mother will never get over it." I began to sob against his chest, just thinking about my mom. "She has no idea who you are."

"Shhh," he said, smoothing my hair with a rough hand. "It doesn't have to be like that. Richard knows who I am. I can tell

Richard. I can have him tell your mother, if you want, that he knows me, and we ran away together and got married. I can even give him letters from you, if you want, to give to her —"

"John," I said, lifting my head to look at him. "What century do you live in? Nobody writes *letters* anymore, let alone runs off to get married at seventeen. And if you give letters from me to Richard Smith to give to my mom, not only will my dad make sure Richard gets arrested for colluding in my disappearance, he'll probably have him taken to some secret location to be waterboarded. Do you even know who my father *is*?"

Now John was kissing my hair. "I don't care who your father is."

"Well, you should care, John," I said, "because I have news for you. I'm not the kind of girl who can just vanish into thin air and not have my disappearance get noticed. As you yourself once pointed out, there are people who care about me. Maybe not as many as I used to think, considering my grandmother is a Fury, but enough. I just can't believe *you* would do this. Especially as someone who gets to have a whole *night* dedicated to him because his body never got a decent burial. Am I right? Coffin Night is about you, isn't it?" He neither confirmed nor denied it, just went on kissing me. "You have to admit, it's not very fair that you're not allowing me the same basic courtesy."

"Pierce." He finally lifted his head and looked down into my soft, wet eyes. His own gaze was far from soft. It was as steel-flecked and determined as I'd ever seen it. His voice was even harder. "I know what you're trying to do. And the answer is no. You can be upset with me. That's fine. You've been upset with me before, and I survived. You're usually upset with me, so I'm actually used to it. I'm prepared to sit here and have you be upset with me for months, if necessary. For *years*, if that's what it takes. Just so long as I know you're somewhere I can protect you."

His arms tightened around me. They were as hard as his voice and gaze. "You don't know what they're capable of. What they did to Jade — that was nothing. They must have realized she wasn't you. If it *had* been you, what they would have done . . . I can't even tell you. Because it would have been unspeakably evil."

I'd stopped crying. Not just because I'd realized it wasn't going to do any good — he was onto me — but because something in his voice had made me forget my own sorrow for a moment, and recognize someone else's.

His.

"When I first saw her lying there this morning," he went on, "I did think she was you for a second or two. If it *had* been you . . . well, I don't know what I would have done."

I thought I saw something — a flicker of pain — in his eyes. It was there, and then it was gone, like the fish that sometimes flashed beneath the surface of the water when I rode my bike across the bridge above the highway.

Whatever John had been through — whatever they had put him through, whatever *I* had put him through — had left a scar. On the inside this time, where I couldn't touch it.

This was something else for which I was accountable.

"So you can't try to leave here again," he said in a hard voice. "Do you understand? No matter what. *You can't leave this time.* It won't be easy, but I at least have a chance of protecting you here. Out there, I have none."

I don't know what made me do it.

But I reached up and ran a hand along his face. I should have been angry with him.

And I was.

But I was also sure that despite how tightly he'd sealed those doors, there had to be another way out.

I knew I was going to find it. I had to. Not to get away from John, but to get back to *my* world to let my mother know I was all right. And to help prove Uncle Chris was innocent. And to make sure my grandmother and all the rest of the people being possessed by Furies were brought to justice, or at least didn't hurt anyone else, including John, ever again.

Because in spite of what John and Richard Smith said, I was sure there had to be some way to stop the Furies. There just had to be.

In the meantime, I wanted to let him know how sorry I was . . . truly sorry for any pain I'd caused him and for the way I'd hurt him the last time I was in this room. I'd said I was sorry before, back in the cemetery.

But this time, when I reached up to stroke the face I'd burned with tea a year and a half earlier, and whispered "I'm sorry" to him, I really meant it.

He took my hand and pressed his lips to my palm.

"Why don't you give it more of a chance this time?" he said with another one of those smiles that tugged on my heartstrings. "Who knows? You might even start to like it here."

I smiled back at him . . . then glanced, involuntarily, at the bed looming behind him.

And I realized, with a sinking feeling, that he was right. There *was* a chance I might start to like it here.

And maybe that — not him — was what I'd always feared most of all.

AUTHOR'S NOTE

What really happens to us after we die? That's a question every culture in the world has attempted to answer, from the ancient Aztecs to the Christians and Muslims of today. Each has developed their own mythology relating to an afterworld through which the souls of the newly dead must pass. It was while studying those afterworlds (when I was in high school) that I first became interested in death deities, in particular the myth of Hades and Persephone, and the roots of the story that would become *Abandon* began to dig in.

Although *Abandon* is fiction, many aspects of the story are based in fact. In general, of people who report a close encounter with death, 20 percent also report having had a near-death experience, which can encompass any of a number of sensations. Often merely having come so close to dying is reported as being much more distressing for people than the near-death experience itself. Obviously, this is not the case for the main character of *Abandon*, Pierce Oliviera.

During the French Revolution, Louis XVI and Marie Antoinette were stripped of possession of the crown jewels, which then became property of the nation, and were promptly stolen from the royal storehouse. Many of the jewels were recovered, but not all.

The setting of *Abandon* is partially based on the island of Key West, the original Spanish name for which was *Cayo Hueso* (*cayo*, in Spanish, means "small island" and *hueso* is "bone"). Key West is thought to be an English mispronunciation of the words *Cayo Hueso*.

The island was given this name by Ponce de Leon, who is rumored to have been searching for the Fountain of Youth when he discovered human bones littering Key West's beaches while he and his crew were charting the area around 1515. Most likely, the bones belonged to the island's original inhabitants, the Calusa Indians. It was a poisoned arrow shot by Calusa Indians that killed Ponce de Leon in 1521.

In 1846, a Category 5 hurricane known as the Great Havana Hurricane destroyed nearly every building on the island of Key West (which had by then grown to be the largest town in Florida, as it was ideally located for trade with the Bahamas, Cuba, and New Orleans), although reports of the exact number of deaths are still in dispute.

That the hurricane destroyed the Key West lighthouse and naval hospital, then washed most of the coffins from its cemetery out to sea, are known facts. It was because of this hurricane that the Key West cemetery was moved to its current location on Passover Lane, and why aboveground stone crypts are now mandatory there.

It is rumored that this is also how Coffin Week — during which the Key West High School's senior class builds and hides a coffin somewhere on the island for the junior class to find — became a yearly (though much frowned-upon) ritual.

Each chapter of *Abandon* begins with a quote from Dante Alighieri's *Divine Comedy*, or *Dante's Inferno* (in which Dante describes his journey into the Underworld, guided by the Roman poet Virgil), because many of the characters in *Abandon* have been abandoned in some way. Some may have even abandoned all hope.

If you are interested in reading more about the Greek Underworld, I recommend Edith Hamilton's *Mythology: Timeless Tales of Gods and Heroes*. Is John Hayden's Underworld and the Underworld of the Greek gods the same place? That's a question to be answered in further books.

I am very excited about this series, and I hope you are, too. I can't wait to share the next installment, *Underworld*, with you.

MEG CABOT

THE ABANDON TRILOGY
The Myth of Persephone, Darkly Reimagined
— BOOK TWO: UNDERWORLD —

 *scape from the realm of the dead is impossible when someone there wants you back.*

Seventeen-year-old Pierce Oliviera isn't dead.

Not this time.

But she is being held against her will in the dim, twilit world between heaven and hell, where the spirits of the deceased wait before embarking upon their final journey.

Her captor, John Hayden, claims it's for her own safety. Because not all the departed are dear. Some are so unhappy with where they ended up after leaving the Underworld, they've come back as Furies, intent on vengeance . . . on the one who sent them there and on the one whom he loves.

But while Pierce might be safe from the Furies in the Underworld, far worse dangers could be lurking for her there . . . and they might have more to do with its ruler than with his enemies.

And unless Pierce is careful, this time there'll be no escape.